CLASS DISMISSED

Class Dismissed

MIKE CONKLIN

Write Stuff Publishing

Contents

Foreword

This is a work of fiction inspired by experiences and observations of the author, whose career as a journalist and college instructor provided much material. *Class Dismissed* is his second novel in a Town & Gown series highlighting the flinty co-existence between the college community and the small, rural town where it is located. The first in the series was *Transfer U.*

Prologue

50 Years Ago

The weather turned unusually warm and sunny for late March. Two straight days of sunshine, enough to bring Burt Kohl out of hibernation to inspect his southern Indiana farmland.

He was debating whether to commit more of his 350 acres to livestock and less to corn. The crappy springs, with late snow and rain, shortened the growing season. It was getting harder and harder to get plowing and planting done on time.

This also meant he could better utilize an unused 15-acre patch---covered with boulders, deep-rooted trees and thick shrubs. It was too coarse for crops, but, with a little pruning, cattle could wander through and nibble away.

Farming, he liked to tell anyone who'd listen, is all about maximizing land-use. Getting something out of these lost 15 acres definitely could improve his revenue stream.

On this day, Burt decided to take a closer inspection of that patch. Why not?

He parked his pickup truck on the graveled, country road, and unleashed the family dog, Scout, a beautiful Black Labrador. The dog bounded from his pickup truck and took off down the rutted, muddy and impassable lane that bordered the land in question.

The trees, Burt observed, would be tough to remove from the rough patch. They were big, strong Oaks that, over the years, steadfastly withstood some mighty windstorms. But he could remove boulders and smaller rocks, making it more agreeable for grazing animals. This could be done with little effort.

Burt walked back to his Chevrolet, half-ton pickup truck, propped one leg on the running board, and whistled to get Scout's attention. The dog came bounding around a faraway corner of the rough patch.

From a distance, it appeared Scout had something in his mouth as he trotted happily down the lane with tail wagging. When he got closer, Burt still was not sure of the object's identity.

Then, the dog plopped it down at the feet of his master, who let out a yelp.

The object was a human hand.

Part I: The Launch

Chapter 1

Hoop Dreams

Funny how these things work. Two years ago, and late in the summer, the good fortune for Phillip J. Doyle, me, was to get hired to teach in a small college in downstate Indiana.

Since it was August and classes started in two weeks, there was one, obvious conclusion to draw. The school, Harrison College, was desperate. Later, I learned this was precisely the case.

The vacancy opened when one of its revered, still-on-the-job English professors, 79 years old, dropped dead in the library preparing for the new academic year. He was found at closing time in a reading carrel nose down in an "Anthology of Beowulf Criticism."

This became my first, full-time, benefits-and-all teaching position in the U.S. and, as I soon discovered, I was in the first class of hires by Harrison's ambitious, new and unconventional president. His name was Jonathan Casey. He was a lawyer, not an academic.

My resume was even thinner, no question. After graduating from the University of Iowa with an MFA degree in writing, I taught a year in China when nothing materialized in America.

At the time of this new opportunity, things were getting bleak. I was headed for a second year tending bar in Iowa City, writing freelance pieces, and conducting clinics for the Iowa Writers Workshop.

While my freelance work landed in several popular magazines as well as USA Today, these were not publications that typically impressed college hiring committees. They were partial to writing that came with footnotes, not exactly a strong suit of mine.

My new college home was named for William H. Harrison, a war hero in Indiana in the early 1800s and, as you may recall from an American History class, a former U.S. President.

On the other hand, you may not recall this at all. He remains the most forgettable and obscure chief executive to get elected to the nation's highest office in the land. His term lasted 31 days.

Harrison died after contracting pneumonia during an outdoor inauguration speech longer than the Potomac River. He did this without a topcoat in cold, damp spring weather in Washington D.C.

Bad karma for his namesake school?

Like many small, liberal arts' schools in the Upper Midwest, when I arrived Harrison's enrollment was slipping, the endowment was stagnant, and curriculum was held hostage by hidebound, tenured faculty---now minus one, dead English professor.

In my first year, adrenalin got pumped into the scene with me in the middle. Thanks to a boost from my Chinese connection, the college forged an association with the university where I had taught.

This led to a modest exchange program, which brought a handful of students from China to Harrison. As improbable as it may seem, some were excellent basketball players and led Harrison into the NCAA small division championship game.

In Indiana, basketball success is as good as it gets. But could this be parlayed into meaningful growth for a small, liberal arts college? Was it a one-time shot?

Or could there be some sort of encore now going into my third year? Something that raises the school's reputation above and beyond the latest college basketball rankings?

President Casey thought so. He had a plan. He wanted me to join the local Rotary Club. Me, a Rotarian?

Chapter 2

Town & Gown

The relationship between a city and its college is not always harmonious. It's two communities under one roof, often with conflicting priorities, cultures and biases.

Take Harrison, for example.

The students were middle-class, predominantly white dormitory residents, and from outside the immediate area. Maybe 10-15 per cent were African American, Hispanic, and Asian. With few exceptions, they tended to be oblivious about off-campus surroundings.

The faculty? They could be just as oblivious. There was a definite pecking order and cliquishness among professors, and definite unanimity about this: They took a condescending view of local townsfolk. *Noblesse oblige* and all that.

Harrison the town, in southern Indiana? An isolated, Upper Midwest community of approximately 12,000 and the seat of government for Harrison County. Townsfolk generally were proud to be home to a college, though rarely ventured onto the campus. Some wrote if off as infested by "a bunch of weirdos" and snobs.

No question the college was the No. 1 economic engine for the community. From maintenance crews and administrative assistants to teachers and kitchen help, it was the city's largest employer. It also kept three taverns busy, with two--- Washington Wine Bar, The South Side---patronized almost exclusively by a college crowd.

President Casey wanted the school to do a better job bonding with Harrison's grassroots, play a stronger role in local affairs. Show their faces. Put some school expertise to work on local fronts and not simply be an employer.

"Call it the Town and Gown initiative, unofficially of course," Jonathan said.

With few exceptions, the president pointed out, the campus might just as well be surrounded by a moat. In addition to the taverns, the only regular intersections were a Wal-Mart out on the highway, two grocery stores, a restaurant called the Monarch Café, several gas stations, and a popular bakery on the courthouse square.

The local newspaper, the *Hoosier-Record,* was a barometer of sorts for this bi-polar environment. While it reported college news, it never was on the front page and typically amounted to spoon-fed PR releases from the school.

President Casey took everything personal. "We need to be a better partner. We've got plenty of Harrison townspeople who work at the school, and trustees who live here, but it's a one-way street. The faculty and administrators might as well be living in Fiji when it comes to getting active locally."

And, just for good measure, the president suspected this: A more harmonious, progressive atmosphere could help the school's stature as well as strengthen our blossoming China link, a hot commodity in higher ed. Ka-ching.

But me? Barely 30 years old and become a Rotarian? How was that going to help? Weren't these the good, old boys who wore those Fez caps with tassels? Secret handshakes, oaths of allegiance, and all that? Or was that some other group?

The president just smiled when he made the pitch to me in his office.

To President Casey's knowledge and research, no faculty member ever belonged to a local civic group like Rotary. Furthermore, no one from the college ever showed interest in running for Harrison's school board or city council.

A few faculty spouses get involved in the local arts scene and some of their kids were active in extracurricular high school activities. For the most part, faculty sent their offspring to boarding schools, ignored mixing with "townies." On more than one occasion, I heard colleagues refer to locals as "VI's"---village idiots. Ouch.

"I'm asking you and several more of your colleagues to consider joining and getting active in something ... city council committees, civic groups, school board, Friends of the Library, League of Women Voters, historical society...that sort of thing," he said.

"Rotary just seemed like a nice fit for you. I was a guest speaker at one of their luncheons right after I got hired by the college. Seemed like a pretty convivial group to me.

"Give it a year, that's all. We'll figure out an exit strategy if it doesn't work. Who knows? You might actually enjoy yourself. Only a few monthly meetings, and you seem to relate well with the public. Maybe it's those bartending days of yours in Iowa City."

He got me with that reminder of my previous work life. No question President Casey, who gave me a great break with this job, considered me part of a personal swat squad to help in his campaign.

How could I say no? And, as things developed, glad I didn't.

My role in Town & Gown produced an adventure that gave my students---and me--- insights they'd never get in a classroom.

Chapter 3

Final Papers

The meeting with President Casey behind me, it was off to my Durham Hall office to prepare for class. Long-awaited, warming spring breezes had arrived in the Upper Midwest. They were an antidote for anything.

I'd discuss Rotary tonight with Mary Jagger. As rookie faculty members together nearly three years ago---and also part of President Casey's new wave of instructors, we'd been locked at the hip since our first semester. (Not just metaphorically, too, if you get my drift.)

For now, I needed to get ready for class and, frankly, I really looked forward to the agenda. This was my favorite course, Writing & Storytelling II.

We were in the stretch run. There would be three final, student presentations per class until term's end. I could coast.

The format for these presentations was simple: 750-1,000 words, a reading of this work to the class by the presenter, and subsequent student-generated discussion and critiques.

They could produce short stories (difficult within the word count), essays, short memoirs, or creative nonfiction features. The general subject area had to be approved by me in advance. Sometimes their finished products matched what I OKed.

All the above would count for 75 per cent of the grade. "The heat's on," as one student remarked when informed of my specs. More than she knew.

Purposely, I liked to load the lineup. Most of my best students---those I knew would set high standards---were assigned to lead off in the opening week of presentations. This raised the bar immediately and gave others additional incentive---and time---not to look lame.

And I could do no better than have the leadoff spots go to Jingfei (Jing) Zhang and Peter Gray followed by Kate McDonald. Intimidating for the others? I hoped so.

Jing, in the first wave of Chinese transfers to Harrison several years ago---and one who stayed to work for a degree here with a scholarship---did a hilarious kickoff. Her personal essay on her cultural transition to the U.S. and, more specifically, rural Indiana. The title: "Pass the egg roll."

Pete, a townie who graduated from Harrison High School---and certainly no "Village Idiot," complemented this beautifully with an account of what it was like to attend college in your hometown. His title: "Somewhere *Under* the Rainbow."

Both got nice rounds of applause from classmates. Then Kate blew everyone away.

Her title, "A Day with Big Daddy," gave no hint of what that meant to anyone in the room except me. I knew her dad, Nate Stine. He just happened to be "Preacher," head man of southern Indiana's biggest, badass motorcycle gang, the Holy Rollers.

I met Preacher in a local bar on my first weekend in town. Nothing but leather, of course. He was an interesting guy after you got past his appearance: 6-foot-5, 280 pounds of finely sculpted muscle, long, red hair, braided beard, multiple earrings, wallet connected to his belt with a long chain, and tattoos that had tattoos.

Nate was an Indiana University dropout 25 years or so ago. He was there to play football, but lost his scholarship when, against the coach's wishes, he refused to quit riding his Harley.

Though no scholar, he was a voracious reader (loved Scandinavian mysteries), huge movie buff, couldn't get enough of Public TV's *Call The Midwives*, and liked to add a touch of wit to his otherwise menacing appearance and station in life.

"Call it *savior faire*, teach," he joked, with a wink. "Yeah, that's what I got. *Savior faire*. My brother Rollers all notice it, too."

We bonded immediately, especially when he learned his pride and joy, Kate---a quiet, self-conscious freshman at the time, was enrolled in my class the first semester of her freshman year. Her father thought she could be a writer. I came to the same conclusion, too.

Nate adored his daughter, his only child, who, thankfully for her, resembled her petite, pretty mother. Kate's parents never married. Her mother, after she split with Nate, moved in with a boyfriend whose potential for abuse was closely monitored by a scowling Nate.

"A first-class turd," was his description.

The Preacher lived 50 miles from campus, but found any excuse to be in the neighborhood on his chopper—"Hog 1." I sent him occasional updates on Kate's progress, which he appreciated. Hey, nothing like having the head of the area's most feared motorcycle gang as a friend. I did draw the line at letting him give me a tour of the campus on his motorcycle.

The truth, however, was that Kate was blossoming into a very mature, take charge student. Dad's leadership genes? She was among the school's first wave to go abroad in the China exchange and clearly benefitted from the experience.

She and Jing were roommates. If I had anything to do with it, Kate was headed for some prestigious university's MFA writing program. On a scholarship. Maybe the one at Iowa, or NYU.

I don't think anyone in my classroom would disagree after hearing her final paper, "A Day with Big Daddy," read to them. Mouths dropped, eyes widened as the identity of "Dad" grew obvious to them.

And that day she spent with Dear Old Dad?

It was on a motorcycle, riding her own Harley---pink---with the Holy Rollers on a weekend trek. The occasion was to show their colors in a St. Patrick's Day parade in Indianapolis.

Kate's paper was perfect, fully capturing the color and humor (absurdity?) of Beauty and the Beast imagery. Just the right words, timing of punch lines, and still leaving it to the reader to connect dots, too.

She had access to a unique opportunity, realized this, and seized it---though later I would hear Nate was not that thrilled over her idea. It really was a compliment to him and a "coming out party" for Kate, considering only me---and Jing---knew Preacher was her father.

Without a doubt, this was the most noteworthy final paper until the last week of presentations.

Then, Craig Conley threw a wrench into the mix. His paper would prove a summer annoyance for a handful of Harrison staffers and a headache for me. His paper was titled "It's Academic?"

Admittedly, I should have screened it closer.

Chapter 4

Crossfire

This was only my third year on the Harrison College faculty, but already I learned certain truths. When you near the end of the spring term, you sense student pulses quickening over final grades.

This was especially true for those who needed to hit a certain Grade Point Average (GPA) to (1) avoid flunking out, (2) keep a scholarship, or (3) graduate and participate in commencement exercises.

Never mind that, in some cases, students did little to earn what they thought was deserved. Like attend class and turn in work on time.

Parents often were the last to know. Nothing could be more embarrassing than to have them show up for graduation, after shelling out thousands, only to learn their kids would not be participating. They'd been left totally in the dark.

Already there were two cases in which I could've prevented a senior from graduating, but, hey, what was a little grade inflation at that point? Obviously, I could not have been the only magnanimous professor who helped a graduate. How else did they get this far?

Most problems occurred in my upper-level literature course, which was the second of my classes I taught each term. The course was not enjoyable. It was foisted on me by the department chair---at the meddling of his immediate boss, the school's No. 2 in command, Dean D. Nelson Brunk.

There was no question I, and several other new hires, were in the middle of a crossfire between President Casey and Dean Brunk, passed over for the school presidency in favor of Jonathan---an outsider in the Dean's mind---with few bona fide academic credentials.

Preserving the curriculum at all costs was Brunk's last stand. He was out to protect it against innovative, young faculty---especially Casey's handpicked appointments like me---with their new and inventive ways.

Under Casey, the school was on the brink of a glorious future if the China connection materialized. Technology, STEM, American Studies, Human Development, Global Environments, Urban Planning, Sociology, Film Production......?

Not exactly favorites of Brunk, whose idea of higher ed was Classics, Classics II, and Classics III. Chinese over Latin? Preposterous. J.D. Salinger over Jonathan Swift? Ridiculous.

For me, that meant a literature course with dry novels---and obvious favorites from Brunk forwarded through my department chair. Chaucer, Melville, Hawthorne, and The Gang. Maybe not authors I'd invite to dinner, but such is the life of a college teacher without tenure. They were not in my background.

I muddled through this course, staying one chapter ahead of my students, and occasionally snuck a few light-reads for them in the mix for a pace change.

My other class, Writing & Storytelling II?

This was my third year with it, and I massaged the description a bit each time, upgrading assignments in the process. This made it possible for my best students---notably Kate and

Jing---to keep writing with me since you could not take the same course twice.

Call it a comfort zone, but these kids had futures.

Chapter 5

Stop the Presses

My first Rotary luncheon was different than expected. No Fez caps, no secret handshakes, etc.

The weekly gatherings are held in a local restaurant, Gwen's, on the square. The food was good, too. Gil Munson, a Harrison trustee and my host for the day, and I met outside a few minutes before.

"Now, you know you don't have to make up your mind today about joining," he said. "Just give it a try. See what you think. For whatever it's worth, most of the town's movers and shakers are members.

"This organization does good things. It's also a way to get up to speed on local gossip. Believe me. A lot of non-Rotary connections get made here, too."

Who was I to argue?

Gil, a stylish, lean and distinguished looking, late 60-something, was a quiet sort who took in everything around him. He seldom offered an opinion, but everyone listened when he chose to speak.

A former Harrison board chair and generous donor, he opted to remain an active trustee rather than spiral off into emeritus status. He was a Purdue engineering alum, who started a small construction company, saw it grow, and now was a very wealthy, philanthropic man.

He lived on a farm on the outskirts of town, where he and his wife, Barbara, held numerous receptions and parties on the spacious, beautifully manicured grounds. It was a big deal to get invited to one of their events. You were as likely to run into the Indiana governor as you were his wife's beautician, Maxine.

Being in Gil's company at the luncheon obviously meant something. He introduced me to at least a dozen Rotarians--- insurance salesmen, bankers, high school principal, mayor, county sheriff, town librarian, two pastors, etc.

While they tended to blend, most seemed genuinely curious to be meeting a professor from the college.

"Can't remember that happening before," said Lester "Bernie" Birnbaum, the Harrison County sheriff. "Got familiar with lots of students cited for underage drinking over the years, but that's been about it between my office and the school."

The business portion of the Rotary gathering was quick, noisy and jovial ... committee reports, talk of scholarships, jokes, and a guest speaker from the county Department of Transportation. Apparently, a U.S. 231 highway bypass around Harrison was being considered, a hot topic among merchants.

The meeting adjourned at 1:15 p.m., cutting off the speaker in the process, with most members hustling out the door to return to work.

Sitting next to me at Gil's table was Newt Ames, publisher of the local newspaper *The Hoosier-Record*. Ames spent much of the gathering taking notes, adding: "This'll be in the next issue, if I have time and space."

Meeting him would prove fortuitous. The newspaper, like most small, print-centric weeklies, struggled. The economy, plus info-age technology, reduced his staff to himself and

Hazel, his wife, plus a handful of underpaid, part-time contributors ranging in age from 15 (high school sports) to 87 (church news).

The Ames's, with three kids in the Harrison public school district, spent most of their time chasing advertising to keep the paper afloat. If it weren't for mandated legal advertising published as the county's "official paper of record," plus paid obituaries and ads for the local supermarket, Wal-Mart, realtors and automobile dealers, the paper likely would go out of business.

There always was the possibility of becoming web site-only, like many other newspapers were doing on the local scene, but Newt was a holdout. For him, print and print only. "For one thing, just not sure that many of my readers know Instagram from a telegram," he told me.

No argument there. I'd slowly learned half the Harrison faculty and administrators hadn't advanced beyond e-mail. So, there was something the college and local general public had in common!

You could see it in Newt's tired eyes: He was a journalist at heart, having worked as a reporter on the Louisville *Courier-Journal*, with great intentions of turning the *Hoosier-Record* into a prize-winning publication. A decade or so of shrinking circulation and advertising, combined with overseeing the bulk of editorial content himself, had worn him down.

There was little enterprise writing. If a good story materialized, he almost never could give it the full reportorial attention it deserved. The pages got filled with PR handouts, short items off police blotters, school menus, church news, glorified minutes of meetings, and high school sports.

The Harrison College news was pictorial-only coverage of special events and occasional high-profile speakers. More evidence of the wall between the town and school that President Casey wished to level.

Our brief exchanges told me Newt loved the business, but his slumping body language indicated he likely would sell the newspaper in a heartbeat if there was an offer.

Gil, Newt and I parted the meeting with handshakes.

"Hope you enjoyed yourself," Gil said. "This was pretty typical today. I do think we have some initiatives that might interest you. They didn't come up. Probably at the next luncheon."

That night, Mary brought me up to speed on the big picture.

"My Dad is a Rotarian," she said. "I don't want to sound like an advertisement for them, but they're big on scholarships and international initiatives. Real boots-on-the-ground stuff. I know his chapter raised money for water wells in a remote part of Tanzania, then he and some others took a trip there to see things put in place. Our local chapter gave me a grant once, too, for a project in Mexico while I was working on my doctorate. Not that much money, but it helped."

I could always count on this kind of information from Mary, the most "global" person I knew.

Mary grew up in rural Kansas---Garden City---and got her BA at the University of Colorado and PhD in sociology at Arizona State University. These were universities overrun with foreign students and international programs. Her work specifically focused on U.S.-Mexico border issues (she spoke fluent Spanish).

Together with a handful of other ASU students and alums, she was a volunteer in several immigration initiatives.

One---are you sitting?---was collecting and identifying human remains of individuals and families who perished in the desert attempting illegal crossings. The identities provided closure for their families.

"Don't be shy," Mary added. "I think joining Rotary could be good for you. My Dad loved it. Just don't commit to too much at first."

"I don't know," was my answer. "I had to be 20 years younger---at least---than the next youngest guy."

"Get over it. Just do what you say to me all the time. Lay back and enjoy it."

Well, I couldn't argue with that. She had me there. The next morning, I called Gil to say OK. I was in.

He responded, "You'll enjoy it."

Chapter 6

Hit the Road

The finish to the school year? Now you see them, now you don't.

At Harrison College, like most institutions of higher learning I'm sure, it was the start of one. big. disappearing. act. Most faculty rushed off to grant-financed vacations masquerading as academic exercises. Others simply left town to parts unknown. Many did not bother giving final exams, they were in such haste. Who wanted to be grading papers and answering student complaints until Memorial Day?

Instead, it was becoming more and more common to simply assign a project to be turned in a week or so before the last day of classes. Also, few colleagues stuck around to don gowns and caps and participate in commencement exercises.

My summer was set in stone, of course. Mary had plans for me. I would be headed for the Phoenix area, where I would join her at Pima School...later, as in July and early August. That's when temperatures started to creep over 110 degrees in the Valley of the Sun. All the better to fry me, I guess.

Pima was a public charter school for kids whose parents depended on food stamps and lived in public housing projects. It was an experimental format, operating 12 months with a full slate of summer programming.

Bottom line: Arizona heat or no, the goal was to keep students, most of whom lived in high crime neighborhoods, off the streets and out of harm's way.

Mary headed a crew---Arizona State pals---that substitute taught Pima classes in the summer, giving regular teachers relief. My course would be a month-long writing session with high school students. I would "report for duty" in mid-July, according to her. Furthermore, I was expected to donate my salary to the school. Yes, ma'am.

Mary told me to pay special attention to one exceptional student, Maria Lopez. She had finished her third year at Pima and was in summer school to get enough credits to graduate a semester early before the holiday season.

I was told she definitely was college material, but in need of a scholarship. Her folks could not afford even the local Maricopa County Community College tuition, which was dirt cheap for residents.

And, of course, *that* was the rub: Residency. The Lopez family, parents and three daughters, did not exactly come to America on the Mayflower.

"Pretty rough story," said Mary. "A national park ranger friend of mine stumbled on the Lopez's near a town called Ajo, just north of the border in the Sonoran Desert. Five of them living in two tents. They were from El Salvador.

"The dad, a schoolteacher, supposedly had paperwork that qualified him for a visa, but it looked pretty iffy. His family was in these tents for a month or so. He'd walk into Ajo---about five miles---and did some off-the-books' work to buy groceries and a few other necessities.

"The ranger, Amy, tipped me off. A bunch of my ASU crew collected the family, brought them to Phoenix and put them in a sort of underground pipeline for migrants. The kids are enrolled in schools, with Maria at Pima.

"Doing well, too. I just hope paperwork doesn't become an issue down the road. It's tricky. Pretty sure the INS has him on some kind of list."

Chapter 7

Fake News

I was content to spend the first weeks of summer vacation hanging around the Harrison campus, going on runs for exercise, bicycling, playing pickup basketball games in Miller Fieldhouse, reading and pounding beers at Whitey's, a rural bar on the nearby Tippecanoe River.

The saloon's sage proprietor, Whitey, was a great source for local color. "There ain't a whole lot happening in Harrison," he'd tell anyone, "but it all gets discussed here."

Occasionally at Whitey's, I bumped into Nate "The Preacher" Stine, head man of the Holy Rollers motorcycle gang. Those nights could get long. Nate always wanted updates from me on his daughter, Kate. He knew she was one of my star pupils, no question, and he loved hearing this---again and again and again.

Neither Whitey or Nate could help me put out one brush-fire, however. Remember those papers done by my Advanced Writing & Storytelling class? And Craig Conley's entry, "It's Academic?"

Craig was last to make a presentation and, as my resident "tekkie" student, I was not expecting anything especially colorful. He definitely leaned on technology for this effort, but in a way I did not foresee.

In effect: He out-ed a Harrison professor. In the worst way. He poked fun at his academic resume, or Curriculum Vitae.

In higher education, many professors guard---and pad--- their CVs as if they were precious crown jewels. They list arcane accomplishments that no one understands. Typically, it's the ambitious, younger ones trying to impress.

I've seen young professors with five-page CVs pages crammed with so many published papers, lectures, and awards that it made them sound like Nobel nominees. All sorts of puffery. On the other hand, I've seen distinguished, accomplished profs at prestigious universities highlight work on a single page.

Craig picked apart entries in this Harrison professor's CV. His digging of data, while not exactly fraudulent, found "accomplishments" that were borderline bogus and definitely laughable.

The victim, a tenured prof named David Krugendorff, was generally regarded by some younger colleagues as a pompous gas bag. He was a Dean Brunk favorite. His area of specialty was loosely described as Inter Disciplinary Studies, which pretty much gave him carte blanche.

A recipient of an honorific, school-wide award for scholarship at his undergraduate alma mater, a small college not unlike Harrison? Turns out the annual honor is underwritten by his father's company and went to an older sibling three years earlier.

The article Krugendorff wrote that got published in the New York Times? It was a letter-to-the editor and only three paragraphs at that.

That fellowship at a major university? It was title-only for participating in a weekend conference.

And those officious-sounding journals that publicized his studies? Blogs, which anyone could contribute to.

To his credit, Craig made "It's Academic" a humorous piece, sprinkling derision and satire throughout the writing. His final punchline was a quote from a British communications scholar:

> *"In academia, it seems that when we have nothing much to say we attempt to distract attention from that sad fact by saying it as pretentiously and at as much length as possible."*

Ouch.

Why Krugendorff? Craig and I had a brief chat following his reading. Best I could gather was that in one of his classes, he got turned off over some point, and exacted cathartic revenge with this paper. He assured me there was no illegal hacking, which was a relief.

I could see where Craig, who could be precise to the point of annoyance, might object thusly to a final grade. Furthermore, Krugendorff was known as one of the faculty's more outspoken anti-technology campers.

If it ended here, no problem. As far as I knew, the aggrieved party didn't know he'd been aggrieved. But somehow the paper landed on President Casey's desk, which meant I was summoned.

"So, what do you think about this?" he asked. "Where did your student get all the background? Please don't tell me there was illegal hacking involved."

I assured the president nothing was obtained illegally. Everything Craig researched and accumulated came via Google or Yahoo. It was available to anyone by simply going beyond the first click. No passwords necessary.

"Well, let's put a muffler on this," said Casey. "I'm not going to bring this to Professor Krugendorff's attention and I'm sure you won't either. This was entirely an in-class exercise. Right?

"If he sees it and objects, I'm sure he'll come to you first, or Dean Brunk, but I don't think it's in his best interests. Especially after reading what I read. Pretty embarrassing."

He added, "We're on the cusp of a lot of good things here at Harrison with the Chinese. The last thing I want is a negative story about our hiring practices popping up in *Chronicle of Higher Education* or *Insidehighered.com*."

So, we agreed to let things ride over the summer, though I promised to give Craig a call. I'd make sure his paper went no farther.

As I walked out the door, President Casey had this comment:

"It was funny stuff, I have to admit," the president said. "That student is a good writer. He has a good grasp of technology. He's got a bright future."

Little did we know.

Chapter 8

Shaping Up

Jogging, it was the only answer. Well, it was one answer.

After whiling away most of June in Harrison, eating, sleeping, and hanging out at Whitey's, it was time to get in shape. Soon I would have to head for Phoenix for my volunteer teaching stint at Pima School. My goal was to lose at least five pounds, though there was the possibility the hot desert sun would melt some pounds.

I was in touch with Mary almost daily. She was teaching at Pima all three summer terms and making weekend Mexico border humanitarian runs with a volunteer organization that worked with migrants. Oh, and just for good measure, she attended spinning classes twice per week.

"I always feel energized when I'm here," she said in one telephone call. "The really hot weather hasn't arrived yet. Of course, when you get here there'll be more fun ways to use my energy. I'll give up some spinning for that."

So, there it was.

We'd been apart for four weeks, the longest stretch since meeting, and she made it pretty clear: If we were going to resume doing the Horizontal Mom-bo with any regularity, I'd better drop my new pot gut and get in shape. Otherwise I'd never keep up with her.

Time to hit the streets. On this day, my jog was seven miles. I'd been averaging 4-5 miles per day for several weeks. Over the years I'd done a lot of running, plus doing 5K and 10Ks. I'd gotten away from it in the last few semesters. Snow and cold weather will do that.

My routes took me through Harrison neighborhoods, occasionally in the countryside, and a lap around the high school football field before heading to my apartment and a shower.

Like many small, rural Upper Midwest communities, Harrison was losing a younger generation that left town never to return. Homes were mostly well-kept with tidy lawns along the Maple and Oak tree-enveloped streets. But there were plenty for-sale signs.

Unlike most small, fading towns, however, Harrison had a solid economic engine with the college in the mix. Whether or not town and gown mixed socially or culturally, the school was a big employer for a variety of non-teaching jobs as well as a general source of pride with outsiders.

I found my jogs both therapeutic and informative, a solitary way of getting some course planning and thinking done without distractions---as long as I did not get hit by vehicles by drivers distracted by their cell phones. Joggers in Harrison didn't really get noticed. They blended into the background.

There were occasional dogs that liked to bark at me and a few potholes to navigate. At the corner of Morningside and Beverly streets, there was a lemonade stand operated by some enterprising junior high kids. I always stopped and made a purchase.

This day my grand, stretch run included circling the courthouse in the middle of the downtown square. It was especially humid, so I plopped down on a bench near a water fountain on the square---and, by chance, in front of the *Hoosier-Record* newspaper office.

Seeing the editor Newt Ames, my new Rotarian brother through a window (badly in need of washing), I stepped inside to say hello. After introducing me to Hazel, his wife, we quickly retreated to his office.

It was like stepping into another century. Newspapers, directories, books, and atlases were stacked everywhere, including the carpeted floor. His desk was a big, wooden and messy affair with---and I am not kidding---a roll-top crown. "It came with the business," he said. "I can't bring myself to part with it."

A typewriter would not have been out of place in this setting. His PC was on a rolling stand. There was no room for it on the desk with the clutter. If Newt wore a darkened eyeshade, suspenders, and a shirt with garters hitching rolled-up sleeves, it would not have seemed out of place.

"Home, sweet home," said Newt. "I spend more time here than our house. I ought to have a shower installed. I do have a cot in the closet. Slept on it more than a few times."

His weeks were crazy.

There was periodic updating of the *Hoosier-Record* web site with daily bits and pieces that, augmented with some rewriting and additional new content, got recycled into the once-per-week print edition.

Using the old-fashioned, cheaper offset method as opposed to straight-up digital techniques, the actual printing was done by a production company 90 minutes away in Evansville.

The newspaper's official, weekly print version became public Fridays when it was distributed and mailed. This meant Newt's deadline for copy was Wednesday by midnight. His printer needed preliminary layouts early Thursday.

The routine meant he was up until midnight---at least---on Wednesday writing to finish supplying the content before rushing everything to Evansville on Thursday morning. At best, he got four hours of sleep.

Then, he would hang around until his 2,500 copies were printed and rush them back to Harrison. There, on Friday morning he handed them off to Clyde Downey, a retired farmer hired to take them to the stores and other distribution points in Harrison, U.S. Post Offices in the area, and a handful of retail businesses in surrounding, smaller towns for over-the-counter sales.

Whew. His explanation made me tired just listening. He was doing it the hard way. There couldn't be more than a handful of newspapers in the Midwest using his model. It was a case of adapt to the new ways or die---and most were dying.

"Want to buy a newspaper?" he joked (I think), in finishing the description of his weekly routine.

He was surprised to learn I had newspaper writing in my background. While living in Iowa City and working on my MFA degree in creative writing at the University of Iowa, I stumbled into occasional freelance features for the local, daily *Sentinel*. I also did book reviewing, which entailed interviewing visiting authors.

My brush with journalism seemed to impress Newt. His big regret, he said, was that he was getting farther and farther away from what he set out to do in Harrison: Own a paper that printed important news and information as well as entertained readers with features.

"When I left the (Louisville) *Courier-Journal* to buy the *Hoosier-Record*, I had all these dreams of prize-winning work," he confided. "We got off to a good start, then the economy tanked. I lost my entire staff. Couldn't afford them and stay above water.

"Now I'm lucky to have time by myself to cover school board and city council meetings. Too bad, too. There are really good stories around here to be written, both in the community and the college. I keep a list. I'd love to get to them all someday, but not at this rate. I'd love to hire a good writer and just turn him or her loose."

Newt ticked off a few on his list:

The area's growing Hispanic population, especially in Liberty, the county's second largest town with about 5,000 residents a little less than 10 miles away. Their community-building energies were breathing new life into the place. The Catholic church in Harrison, only one in the county, now had a Spanish-language service to accommodate the new residents.

A public, in-depth look at the college's new link to China and what it would mean for the local scene, both on campus and off. A big enrollment spike? Construction of new dorms? New classroom buildings? More jobs for locals?

A feature on a local Harrison High alum starting to make a name for herself in the entertainment industry as a writer and producer. She'd been attached to two successful Netflix series, and the trades had been hinting she was part of a blockbuster film headed for the big screen.

Newt added, "A lot of people remember her---Jenny St. Clair---being in a lot of our local community theatre productions as a little tyke. By the time she was a senior in high school, she'd written several one-act plays that got presented. Good, too."

The area also had seen a dip in recent years in the number of small, family farms. The corporate operators had made a big dent, though they did create jobs, and, if nothing else, Newt thought a definitive story quantifying this impact was long overdue.

There were several college faculty members with interesting backgrounds worth reporting. One was a Vietnamese native, who taught art and whose parents were among the "boat people" refugees.

"We're also coming up on the 50th anniversary of a great cold case never solved," he added. "A local, 19-year old girl's dismembered body was found by a farmer on his property. She was a local beauty. Saving her money to go to Hollywood and try to get into the movies.

"The case ran hot and cold. There were three prime and separate suspects, but never enough evidence to nail anyone. The law enforcement skills then were, according to what I hear, right out of Mayberry."

He was right. There were some good stories to be written.

"That's the best way to get readers," he said. "I'd love to have time to work them. I approached the college once about integrating an internship program, but that Dean of yours---Brunk---wouldn't have it."

This gave me something new to think about while I finished my jog.

Part II: Summertime Blues

Chapter 9

An Oasis

OK, it was June 30 and Mary greeted me at Gate A in Phoenix's SkyHarbor Airport. "C'mon," she said. "I've got a surprise for you." This immediately triggered many lecherous thoughts. After all, we'd been apart four weeks.

But the surprise involved a detour from our destination to Tempe, which was only a mile East. Instead, we headed a mile west and into a gigantic, sunbaked industrial park filled with warehouses, manufacturing plants, semi-trucks backed into loading docks, oil-stained parking lots, and no trees. Well, eventually I would see trees.

In the middle of all this 105-degree heat (remember, it was Phoenix) and urban density was an oasis, both figuratively and literally. It was the Vincentian Center, a huge, multi-faceted shelter for Phoenix's fast-growing homeless population. This was operated by a Catholic order, but ecumenical in its approach. There were dorm rooms, three-squares-a-day, counseling, tutoring and medical attention. Impressive.

Soon I was introduced to Father Tony, a rumpled, friendly guy clearly on his last assignment before retiring to wherever priests go when they ride off into the sunset. He lit up like a Christmas tree when he spotted Mary.

Ostensibly the good Father was the center's main man, but he made it clear: "My job is to not screw it up. This place was humming long before I got here. That's the way I want to leave it."

Father Tony had spent several decades working missionaries in East Africa. There, he told us, poverty levels in countries like Uganda, Zambia and Tanzania made the Vincentian Center seem like The Ritz.

Then, after introductions and some cordial chit-chat, he excused himself and limped off to participate in a counseling session.

"C'mon," said Mary, tugging at my arm. "The outside in the back is what I want you to see."

She led me out of the air conditioning and through a rear entrance into the outdoor oven to gaze at a 21-acre plot of land. This former parking lot had been plowed up, chunks of asphalt carted away, and the remaining dirt base turned into a garden.

There were rows and rows of peppers, tomatoes, melons, strawberries, beans, potatoes, and radishes. There were rows of lemon and apple trees. At one corner was a large water-filled, metal tank filled with fish---a fish farm, for God sakes, in the middle of Phoenix and probably the driest major metropolis in the U.S. This section was in shade provided by a rooftop canvas.

This was an industrial park? In the shadow of a busy U.S. Interstate 10-highway. In all the otherwise shade-less heat.

I was told everything growing in the acreage was continually recycled year-round, contributing upwards of 20% of what was served in the shelter's kitchen. There was no off-season for raising food. Everything was 24/7.

"Maybe we can get assigned to working with the fish," said Mary. "It might be a little cooler in the shade."

Err, assigned? Working here?

I thought I came to Arizona in July---the hottest month in a hot climate, I might add---to work at Pima school. You know. Teach in air-conditioned classrooms, donate my paycheck to the institution. Oh, and return to Harrison College to get ready for the new school year---and live happily ever after.

"I signed us up to be here as volunteers on Saturdays," she said. "It's actually hard to get a volunteer slot here. The Vincentians have a lot of groups wanting to supply helpers. Big companies give employees time off to be here. I had to pull strings, but I thought it would be a break from the classroom.

"Besides, it's only for four or five Saturdays."

A nice summer break, yeah.

Chapter 10

Home Sweet Home

Our summer residence was just off Mill Avenue in Tempe,
easy walking distance from the Arizona State University campus. The sprawling university grounds were huge and butt
ugly. Every building looked to be designed by a separate committee, none of which communicated with each other.

On the other hand, ASU was growing so big that new, large
high-rise buildings were being acquired or constructed several
miles away in downtown Phoenix.

The university's total enrollment is approximately 80,000,
ranking No. 12 in size among U.S. schools.

The central Mill Avenue area in Tempe remained ASU's
heart, soul, and breeding grounds. No self-respecting, big time
university is without a district like this. Bars, book shops,
clothing and sporting goods stores proliferated on Mill and ar-
terial streets. The eight-block long avenue was closed periodi-
cally to host art shows and festivals.

The Sun Devil athletic facilities were a few blocks away. On
Saturday when ASU had a home football game? Forget it.
Traffic was a crawl in every direction for miles.

We were above all this---literally. Our apartment was on the
14th floor of a new, mixed-use high rise a block off Mill's din.

One of Mary's ASU grad school buddies, now a young assistant professor there, gave her use of his place for the summer while he was in Europe on a subsidized junket with his wife. Nice for him, and us.

Tempe, adjacent to Phoenix, was booming in every direction---including vertically. Apple, Intel, Microsoft, Amazon and other brainy companies now had large footprints here. Land of opportunity, and all that.

We had a commanding view. Also, an indoor swimming pool and enclosed parking. If we looked to the northwest on a clear day, we could make out some of the landmarks near Pima School in central Phoenix. We also could see heat vapors rising from the ground.

Mary had been making the commute to the school for nearly six weeks before I arrived. She said it was a snap. Public transportation sucked, but it was easy to get anywhere by car. She drove a 165,000-mile plus, gasping and wheezing Hyundai from Harrison to get here. Hopefully, it would hold up. I'd ride back to Harrison at the end of the summer with her provided the car did not expire by then.

Whatever misgivings I had about my stint in Arizona's blazing sun, they were mitigated by our new---but temporary---living quarters. I would get used to them in a hurry, especially the indoor pool.

We were living large, but with a teaching experience ahead of me that would be more than expected.

Chapter 11

Meeting Maria

Pima School sat on a slab of concrete facing a busy 24th Street. On one side, there was wall-to-wall commerce. Behind us, there were small, very modest single-family homes on plots of brown grass.

The businesses on 24th were mostly independent, small, and places you'd never find local glitterati perusing. Resale shops, bars, currency exchanges, franchise eateries, tattoo parlors, siren-chasing law offices, bakeries, nail salons, filling stations with mini markets, and panhandlers shuffling up and down checking for change in newspaper boxes.

Not exactly skid row, but no more than a hop, skip and jump from desperation.

One bright spot: The Phoenix Public Library system, a good one, had an extension just a few blocks down the street. This would be an oasis I quickly adopted for classes at least twice per week. It had AC, and our school did not---something Mary left out in her descriptions.

The school building itself was a re-purposed, two-story cinder block structure that formerly was a mega storage facility. It was surrounded by a chain link fence with a touch-tone lock. The code, changed monthly, during my stint was J-U-L-Y. Take a guess what it would be in August?

Because there was lots of space to work with, I was told the transition from storage facility to a school was not difficult. A shower and laundromat were added, but not for athletic teams. There were none. It was for kids from homes in which personal hygiene was not a top priority. A monitor picked out "candidates" as students filed through the main entrance each day. There also was a "clothing store" the Salvation Army kept stocked for us with second-hand duds.

The students lived mostly in public housing projects. Families relied heavily on food stamps for meals, thus our cafeteria was popular. For most students, these free lunches were the best---and only, in some cases---meal of the day. It was not unusual to see students sneak food to take home, something that always prompted teachers and monitors to look the other way.

When the start of the regular school year would begin in late August, I was told a breakfast program was being added. I was also informed parents often accompanied their kids through the line---and not just to provide guidance.

Mary said meals were key. They kept attendance up and were a big reason why summer school was popular. "It's the only real food many of our kids get," said Mary. "The smart Mom's and Dad's realize this."

OK, enough with the infrastructure. My writing course I was to teach? Fun, especially since several students were quite promising. They could've easily handled themselves well in my Harrison classes---though tuition made college an almost impossible stretch without scholarships. Culturally, it would have been even more difficult.

Everyone in my class was in Pima's upper two grades of high school. Their English skills were more than sufficient, though a few grappled with idioms and punctuation.

The course makeup was like a mini-United Nations. A dozen students representing four countries beside the U.S.--- Mexico, El Salvador, Honduras, and Bulgaria (don't ask on the last one; I didn't). Maria, Annabelle, Tessa, Roberto, Tomas, Omar, Dominique, Sarah, Shaylyn, Britney, Kelli Ann and Ivan.

I had them for a full morning five days per week. No problem with using laptops we provided and cell phones, as long as it had to do with their writing and not for socializing. We spent entire class sessions writing. My goal was for each pupil to produce a polished, 1,000-word product by the end of the four-week term. They discovered this was not as daunting as it first sounded. Like the Nike commercial says, "Just do it."

They'd take breaks, chat with each other, and, as it turned out, give each other ideas and suggestions. It was loosey-goosey. I'd give a few tips, help them as they cranked away, and work on my own writing projects. We would break for lunch, and then they moved on to another class in the afternoon.

Mary had tipped me about Maria Lopez, and it was not difficult to recognize her ability. Though a bit shy at first, by the end of the first week it was obvious she "got it." Not every student---even the good ones---"gets it."

For starters, she looked you in the eye when we conversed. This always is a good sign. "I've never been in a class like this," she confided to me in the second week. "We're free to create. Is this how it is in college?"

Her writing was insightful and colorfully expressive. She was economical with words, but they were more than adequate to trigger images conveying themes. Hard to believe English was a second language for her.

Nobody turned in a weak final project, but Maria's was terrific. Playing on O. Henry's "Gift of the Magi" theme, her touching narrative substituted a Mexican-American daughter and father for the young couple in the author's original work.

She put them in an urban, Hispanic barrio in the United States.

"I like to write," she told me after one class, "but I like to read, too. I like it there is a library nearby. Books are my inspiration, kind of an escape. Writing makes everything more personal, but I need to read to learn things to write about. I've seen so little."

I never pushed, but I suspected---and knew from Mary's descriptions---she had seen many things in her background that would be good material. Did she get inspiration for her final essay from her family's torturous trek to the United States?

While never completely sure of the facts, the understanding among faculty was that her family crossed the border illegally. Her father's paperwork passed scrutiny, but---possibly costing his life savings---was obtained illegally and contained several falsehoods.

As far as we knew, they walked, rode buses and hitchhiked all the way from Santa Ana in El Salvador to get to the U.S. border in central Arizona. The trek covered approximately 2,500 miles, or the distance between Buffalo and San Francisco.

A good share would've been covered with the family sitting atop train car roofs (and ducking when they passed through tunnels). When they found them, nights could be spent in Mexican refugee shelters maintained by the Catholic church. In the deserts, secret water stations maintained by social service agencies like Humane Borders kept them hydrated.

Amazingly, her father was able to keep his daughters safe. No matter the age, women and girls were a magnet for sexual predators and cartels lying in wait on the clandestine, remote trails used by refugees.

"There are some very, shall we say, interesting backgrounds among our students," Jose Perez, Pima's music teacher, confirmed for me one afternoon over coffee. "Some of them tell me about them in confidence, maybe because they see we have some things in common. I should become a counselor," he joked. His hearty laughs were infectious.

Jose, from Cuba, was one of the school's most popular teachers. He was a talented jazz trumpeter and played with a locally famous band that deserved better on weekends, but mostly in Phoenix's low-rent venues.

He, too, was a Maria fan. We agreed: If she ever decided to tell her complete story, we'd gladly stand in a long line to buy the book. Clearly, she had wisdom beyond teenage years. Talent, too. You could see that in those brown, alert eyes.

Chapter 12

Wakeup Calls

The last day of Pima classes for me was the last day---Friday---of the summer term. Now get ready to return to southern Indiana and Harrison College.

There was a celebration party at the school. Teachers chipped in to buy small gifts for students, and there were awards, some formal and some not so formal. Jose brought several members of his jazz band to provide music.

Mary and I heard everyone had a good time. We never made it to the festivities, thanks to two early-morning telephone calls.

The first, from President Casey's office, was REALLY early. His secretary forgot Arizona does not recognize Daylight Savings Time and that meant a three-hour difference on our clocks between us and Indiana. We're talking 5 a.m.

"Sorry, Flip, but we may have a problem here, and we may not. At the very least I think we could use your presence at a meeting," the president said.

When?

"Monday," he said. "I don't know if you can make it. I understand you're involved in some summer teaching at a school in Phoenix. Maybe that's over now and you're on your return.

Or back, for all I know. I suppose, if we had to, you could phone into the proceedings. Make it a conference call."

The issue? Remember that outing of a professor and his resume? In a paper by one of my students?

Apparently, the prof, David Krugendorff, got wind of the essay (by Craig Conley). He found a copy, was livid and demanded a meeting with the president. He indicated his family lawyer would accompany him. He hinted at a possible libel suit.

Shit. Just what I feared.

I did not know how a copy landed on Krugendorff's desk or in his computer after my warnings to Craig. If it was found online, someone must have discovered it for him. At least half the faculty---the older half---were technology illiterate. I'm sure he, the aggrieved party, was in this group.

So, the lion was at my door. This could get tricky, considering I was only entering my fourth year at the college and Old Cranky Krugey, as students called him, was a showcase favorite of Dean Brunk.

I was not sure where President Casey would stand on this, but I knew one thing: He did not want publicity that could scare off Chinese interest in our school.

The second call that morning not much later demanded even quicker attention and, in the end, was a helluva lot more pressing than puffed-up academic ego. This call was for Mary, showering at the time. I picked it up only to hear a nearly hysterical voice at the other end.

It was Maria Lopez. "They're gone! They're gone!" she sobbed, in between pauses to catch her breath. "What am I going to do? Where do I go? Where are they?"

Mary, who'd become like a big sister to Maria, calmed her down somewhat. Since their frenzied conversation continued in Spanish, it wasn't until they hung up that I was told the crisis.

"Maria's by herself," said Mary. "Since school was ending, her parents let her stay overnight with a friend. When she got home this morning to finish getting ready for school, her parents and sisters were gone."

"Gone? What do you mean gone?"

"Maria says they got picked up by immigration officials, I.C.E. Apparently, there was a big sweep in their building. Someone must've tipped off the Feds. They got people spying all over the place. The government pays people to tip them off on neighbors, for God's sake. Tax dollars at work. Maria was lucky not to be there or she'd be sitting in some holding cell, and most likely separated from her parents."

"Jesus. Sounds like Germany under the Nazis. So, what now?"

"Well, she's on her own. Her Dad thought something like this could happen. He wanted Maria not to turn herself in. She's a big girl, he figured. She'll be 18 next month.

"He even stashed a few bucks away in their home; told his family it was for an emergency. I hope I.C.E. didn't find it. His Dad's got a cousin Reynaldo in Phoenix who's legal. The plan was for her to find a way to his home, but she doesn't want to do that."

"Why not?"

"Because Maria's pretty sure Reynaldo tipped off I.C.E."

Chapter 13

Divide & Conquer

We split up.

I packed my bags, headed for the airport and booked the earliest airplane to Chicago, where my car was in storage. Then, it was head back to Harrison College to do battle, or whatever they call it in higher ed.

Mary, like me, did not go to Pima school for the final day. The timing was horrible. There would be opportunities to explain things later to our summer colleagues. I wanted to stay and help with Maria. But as Mary said: "Go back. You get fired and you're no help to anyone." Comforting.

Mary went straight to Maria's home a mile from school. She had been in their residence several times during the school year. She instructed Maria to gather the necessities she needed. Then, they would meet in a Safeway grocery store coffee nook, just around the corner from the family's public housing apartment. There, they'd sort out the crisis.

I was confident Mary could find a solution for Maria. As a result of graduate schoolwork and networking at ASU, she was totally wired within the local, immigrant scene. Her contacts included organizations and people who worked with migrants, legal or not, and the pipelines and off-radar housing that existed for them.

"Think of the underground railroad for black slaves in the Civil War days," she told me. "It's a little bit like that."

We're talking real boots-on-the-ground stuff here. It was obvious to me that I simply would be a spectator in solving this crisis. Maybe I knew a dozen words in Spanish.

My flight landed in Chicago close to midnight. Once I recovered my car I decided to drive straight through to Harrison, losing an hour to a time zone in the process. My adrenalin was pumping, so the trip---with the help of at least a gallon of coffee---was an opportunity to sort out any responses I might need in my Monday meeting in the president's office.

A call to Craig was in order, too. Reached at his home in suburban Detroit, he was incredulous to learn his final paper had caused a stir. He had no idea how it got in Kruggendorf's hands. "All my information was there on the Internet, public record for anyone to find, or at least I did nothing illegal to obtain that information," he assured me. "It was just a simple matter of cross-referencing facts."

Craig offered to drive to Harrison to attend the meeting. It was not necessary, especially after his nearly 30-minute technology tutorial that left me feeling like I was Bill Gates.

He explained, step-by-step, how he went about his research. There was no hacking, no stealing of passwords, or any other Internet violations. He could justify every detail he used as something freely accessible to any schnook with a computer.

He also gave me information he left out that, if needed, might be helpful if the session became acrimonious. Sweet.

Craig pointed out any perceived disparagement of Kruggendorf did not come from the author (him). It was the conclusion of the reader. Debatable.

"If I present two and two, and a reader adds them up to come out with five, well, that's not my fault," he concluded. "Besides, my paper itself was never meant for public consumption. It's not like it got published in the *New York Times*. He's the one drawing attention to it. Duuuh."

No doubt, this kid was a genius. You wanted him on your side. It would be fun to follow his career path. For now, I was simply happy to have him in my classes.

I was in President Casey's office at 8 on Monday morning, a full hour before it was scheduled. I went over the whole project---and Craig's paper---word-for-word with background explanations.

"Well, I have to admit," said the president, "that this is terribly embarrassing for Professor Kruggendorf. You have to sympathize on that. Nothing is illegal, but it could be construed as a serious breach of professional ethics---a whistle-blowing work on a colleague.

"However, in my backgrounding efforts, I have to say Harrison's code of conduct pertains to students, not faculty. There is that technicality as a fallback position for you."

Well, possibly, except I had no idea the college had a code of conduct. Nor was I responsible for any dissemination of the paper outside the classroom. I had no idea how it landed in an outsider's hands (though I could imagine a revenge-minded student passing it around).

The president was in a tough spot. He had to play it down the middle, recognizing academic freedom on one hand and a possible libel suit on the other that could tarnish the school's reputation---especially at an important crossroads in school history.

Chapter 14

Showdown

He came through the door with a tight grip on Craig's paper. Professor Krugendorff had fire in his eyes. It was obvious he was humiliated at his outing by a student, no less,

He came to the meeting alone, however. There was no lawyer at his side. I spotted a twitch of relief in President Casey's face. Was that a sign there would be no lawsuit? This would be good for everyone concerned.

"What is the meaning of this paper, MISTER Doyle," he asked, as he took a seat. "I'm not quite sure how printing falsehoods about a faculty member fits into your pedagogy!"

His emphasis on the word "mister" was a tactic popular in academia, of course. In his mind, it put me on defense since I had neither a doctorate nor tenure, which meant I would not be called Professor Doyle by hidebound academicians. Especially important to him, I guess. Transparent, too.

Determined to stay cool, I explained the free hand I gave students to write a final paper in any direction they wished. While I apologized for distress it may have caused him, I added that every project was to stay within the class and not be made available without my permission.

In short: I had no idea how this was breached. Neither did my student. Unless someone hacked into Craig's computer.

"And the lies, please? How do you explain them? I would think you flunked this student, this Craig Conley. How does someone get away with lying like that in your course? Doesn't anyone fact check?"

Well, glad that he asked. Now we could get down to the nitty gritty, the part I welcomed. I came prepared. One-by-one, I ticked off how every fact was substantiated. I clicked my way through the entire paper. This was not fake news.

My technology vocabulary was slightly better than my Spanish, but I knew it was light years better than his. Quickly it became obvious he, like many of our esteemed faculty, was computer illiterate. He didn't know Instagram from a Telegram.

Each of my revelations was met with silence and an occasional sigh.

That school-wide award for a scholarship at his undergraduate alma mater, a small college not unlike Harrison? All one had to do was Google the name of the company that sponsored the award to learn the CEO was Krugendorff's father, whose company bio included names of his children including David.

"You didn't need to hock or hack, or whatever they call it?" he wondered out loud.

Answer: "Nope. It's the same as if it were in a public library. It's on file. Just dial it up."

The article Krugendorff wrote that got published in the *New York Times*? The newspaper's online archives open to readers had what he wrote: A letter-to-the-editor. This was the only time his name ever appeared in the paper's pages.

Those officious-sounding journals that ran his studies? Blogs that welcomed any contribution, no screening necessary of submissions. It was all right there in the web site's disclaimer that greeted readers.

And on and on.

I even tossed in a freebie, dialing up the public "*ratemyprofessor.com*" site that allows students to vent autonomously on the Internet about instructors. His overall rating was a 3 on a scale that had 10 as tops. The words "pompous," "gas bag," "archaic," and "opinionated" were most prominent under his name.

He had no idea how easy---and perfectly legal---it was to access internet content.

Rarely did I have to go beyond Google---or Goggle as Krugendorff called it the first few times---to unmask his portfolio. He sagged lower and lower in his seat, defeated.

His last stand: Why, in heaven's name, would a student target him? "I have no idea," was my reply. "Maybe you should take it up with the student?" This was something I knew would not happen.

President Casey tossed him a bone. "I can see that no rules were broken, but this is a very gray area," he said. "In fairness, Mr. Doyle could have steered his student into a different narrative. Also, I do not see any untruthfulness in Dr. Krugendorff's credentials. It's more a question of semantics. The basic facts were there on the Internet for anyone to see.

"Nothing leaves this office," he quickly added, a final comment that coaxed a tight smile from the professor.

There were several minutes of harmless chit-chat among the three of us and Krugey leaving before I placed a manila envelope on the president's desk.

"What's this?" he asked.

"An insurance policy," I responded.

He tore open the envelope, pulled a 9 x 11 photograph from it, and---slapping one hand against his forehead, said, "Oh, my God, where did you get this?"

Some deeper, but legal, snooping on my part turned up the yearbook from Krugendorff's senior year at his undergrad alma mater. There, in a page dedicated to his fraternity, was Krugey with several classmates in black face performing a tap dance in a skit while holding up slices of watermelon.

"He would be dead meat if this picture ever got out into any higher ed chronicles," I said. "The Political Correctness crowd would be all over him and, for that matter, Harrison too for not doing its due diligence."

The room grew silent. A full minute of quiet. Then, President Casey said he had a solution to make sure the photo never saw the light of day. With that, he took out a key from his pocket, opened a desk drawer, and carefully tucked away the yearbook picture.

His gesture was purely symbolic, of course. The picture likely could be Googled in an archive somewhere and reproduced, but I had no intention of doing this. I just wanted the new school year to get underway.

My summer vacation was coming to a skidding halt.

Chapter 15

The Plan

Mary and Maria, like Lewis & Clark, sat at the Safeway grocery store coffee shop in Phoenix for nearly two hours mapping courses. Later, I learned they consumed four Grande cups of coffee between them, sandwiches and soup from the deli with cupcakes from the store bakery for dessert.

A sugar "high" was not a bad thing. "We got it worked out," Mary told me in a phone call later that day. "It took a while for Maria to get past that she might not see her family for an extended period. I think she's going to be OK. She has to be."

The plan, in retrospect, was brilliant.

Maria would take up residence (hide?) at the Vincentian Center, which was considered a hands-off refuge by I.C.E. and assorted other alphabet-soup government agencies. A call to Father Tony found him very receptive to the idea.

"Giddy, actually," Mary said. "Father Tony likes the challenge, hates I.C.E., has room in the dorm for her, will find ways to get her to Pima school to finish the term and get a diploma.

A diploma with her name on it already could be a door opener, an extra layer of documentation that could come in handy. Maria needed only one more semester to graduate from Pima in mid-year.

It got better for her, according to Mary: "Father Tony said he'll put her to work tutoring the pre-school kids staying at the Vincentian Center, make her earn her keep. He said the center could use some 'fresh faces.' This way it would be an actual job, and make her look even better in a future application for U.S. residency."

She turned 18 in September, which helped. With a simple, fake ID, diploma and her fluency in English, she easily could integrate herself into Phoenix---or wherever---in the States. A job would not be a problem, possibly even college with the help of her Pima paperwork and---best case scenario---a scholarship.

For now, keeping a low profile would be paramount for her. No extra-curricular activities, or anything else that would draw attention. For all the Feds knew or cared, there were four---not five---in the Lopez family.

Meanwhile, Mary would monitor the status of her father (Ricardo), mother (Isabella), and her two younger sisters (Daniela, Sara) as best she could without drawing attention. Undoubtedly, they were in a detention camp, but where? Worst case scenario: They were deported and were scrambling in their native El Salvador.

Her father's plan---as discussed with Maria for such an occurrence---called for him to apply for asylum. This meant at least a three-to-four month delay while Feds did background checks, a period in which temporary housing was to be provided.

This was the hitch: The government had no housing available due to the influx of migrants seeking asylum. Mostly, they got bussed and dropped at doorsteps of Phoenix area churches and welfare agencies. The record-keeping was sketchy.

The migrants needed to stay accountable. If they wandered off and ever were discovered, they could forget asylum. It was straight back to Honduras, Mexico, Guatemala, or wherever. There'd be no second chance.

Mary, who had to get to Harrison in less than a week, would continue to track down the Lopez family. If she couldn't find them before returning to teaching duties, she had at least a dozen ASU pals lined up to help the cause. They were a tight group, unofficially calling themselves "Palomas."

"So, there's nothing planned yet for Maria after Pima," I asked (foolishly).

"We'll talk," she said. "I've got some ideas about that, too. They involve you."

Chapter 16

On the Move

With Maria safely tucked away (for now) in the Vincentian Center and Pima's final term nearly underway, Mary and I geared up for our first classes of the new academic year at Harrison College. Her well-traveled Hyundai, now nearing its expiration, wheezed its way to the campus with luggage, files, and a floor littered with empty, cardboard coffee cups.

The start of a new year on campus is always an energetic, optimistic time. There are freshmen feeling their new independence, energized returning upper classmen vowing to improve GPAs, and hormones again flowing faster than whitewater.

Mary and I, who live apart in the same building, had a happy reunion. Twice. She drove almost nonstop from Phoenix to Harrison, came straight to my unit in the middle of the night to say hello, disrobe, and jump into bed---even though her bedroom was the next floor up.

Well, hello there. Sleep? It's overrated.

This year it helped that weather for these opening Autumn days was drop dead gorgeous, a perfect Midwestern 65-70 degrees (compared to 100-plus degrees in the Arizona we just

left), trees showing a slight hint of Fall colors, and soft
breezes.

My course preparation was complete. I was scheduled for
another literature class in deference to Dean Brunk. There was
this consolation: The focus would be 20th Century writers, a
first for our plodding English Department.

My real joy figured to be another advanced writing class.
Happily, my favorite---and best--- writers enrolled: Jing, Kate,
Craig, and Peter. Maybe some new stars would emerge, too. I
was determined to break a few more barriers.

Also, I was back to Rotary meetings, where I was entering a
comfort zone of sorts. I was starting to successfully put
names together with faces. No longer did I need to stay next
to Gil Munson, who knew everyone.

President Casey's plan to get the school more integrated
into the community was obvious on several other fronts. Two
Harrison coaches---Marcy Burke (women's tennis), Pariti Khan
(women's soccer)---joined the Harrison volunteer fire department over the summer, making them the first females to become members. And in Pariti's case, I am sure she was the
first Muslim.

There were more developments for the new academic year
with the president's fingerprints all over them.

In a move no one could recall happening on the campus, a
formal, faculty workshop took place. It included a financial report by the college treasurer, panel discussion by trustees discussing the future, and a mandatory technology clinic.

There also were formal introductions of new faculty members, including those teaching ground-breaking courses to
start our infant international business major. This was to
show commitment to our new-found China connection (or the
China Syndrome, as some of us liked to joke when Casey was
out of earshot).

One new, visiting professor was from Xiamen University in the Fujian Province, where I taught for a year before getting hired at Harrison. This was part of the modest, formal exchange between the schools.

Another new professor would be teaching---exclusively---computer related courses. This was new for us, too. As an add-on, he would continue to hold workshops for faculty throughout the year on how to integrate technology with their pedagogy and, in some cases, simple Computer Use 101.

Fallout from the Krugendorff dustup?

Maybe the most revolutionary move was this: The hire of an e-sport coach, or someone to organize Harrison teams to compete against other schools in video gaming. I was told this will be a big attraction in recruiting students.

Meanwhile, there was talk of launching a capital campaign to build a new science center.

Could the 21st Century be far behind?

Chapter 17

Breaking News

Now that I was back in Harrison, I began to detect a certain rhythm to my Rotary gatherings at Gwen's. They started with 10 minutes of gossip and good-natured, and sometimes witty, jabs at each other that didn't generally end when salads got served.

"The bull-shitting part," as Gil labeled it.

Definitely a good way to learn about a community. Just for good measure, some programming could become useful to me. For instance, I continued to learn the Rotary organization, truly international, took on worthwhile humanitarian projects, like building wells in Tanzania, providing medical supplies for refugees washing up on Mediterranean shores, and that sort of thing. This could be good fodder for my students to explore with writing projects.

The Rotary programs also included generous scholarships and student exchange programs. This also went into my notebook. Naturally, the club lost little time in naming me---fresh meat---chair of the chapter's scholarship committee.

"You're at the college," said Fred Jackson, our president, supreme leader, and in charge of committee assignments. "Seemed like a natural to me."

Well, maybe this would come in handy at some point. At the very least, it was another brick in President Casey's plan to build better Town & Gown relations. I was holding up my end.

Typically, during the meetings, I sat by Newt Ames. We were the only attendees who knew anything about the inner-workings of the news media, which gave us plenty to share. When I popped an idea that had been growing in my mind over the summer, he jumped on it with both feet. Hard.

"Let's do it," he said. "I love it."

First, I needed to run it past President Casey. The proposal was too good for Dean Brunk to muck up.

Turned out the president loved it, too.

Chapter 18

Start the Presses

When my first writing class broke up, I said: "Jing, Kate, Pete, and Craig. Stay a few minutes, will you?"

Few heads turned as the remaining students exited. Hey, the others had places to go and important things to do. They thought.

There were new and other familiar faces in the course, but these four I knew from past classes and would be well-suited for my latest writing adventure. Along the way I felt we had reached a certain level of professor-student trust and frankness.

This would be delicate. As a teacher, how well did you really know your students? Did you *want* to know them? How far could you go without anything being misunderstood? Or someone being disappointed?

You really did not have that much contact time with students in college. In fact, I went out of my way to mostly avoid them outside the classroom in restaurants, bars, receptions, and the like. Political correctness ruled campuses. The most innocent comment or reference could be career-ending even at remote Harrison.

Many still were teen-agers and few were 21 (though fake IDs frequently said different). For them, inspiration was a lot easier than perspiration. On the other hand, you never knew. Today's mope could become tomorrow's Bill Gates.

I had no doubt Craig was headed in "Gates-ian" direction. His work in outing Krugendorff was a clue. He might need to do something about his wardrobe, however.

On this first day of class, when students typically were fresh, clean, and wearing their newest "Joe College" threads, he was in his customary unkempt Jeans, sandals, socks that did not match, and raggedy, plain white t-shirt that put to rest any doubts about his nerd-ness. "No. 1 Geek" was its inscription.

In addition to having done good work in previous courses of mine, these four students impressed me that they enjoyed writing and storytelling---though Craig had the annoying (to me) habit of calling his offerings "content."

Furthermore, they all seemed to have the correct skillset for what I had in mind. Pete especially so, being a "townie."

I told my "Gang of Four" that, if they were agreeable, they'd take the lead on this: Writing stories that would appear in the local Harrison *Hoosier-Record*.

If everything went well, we'd split them up to lead classmates in the final half of the semester. Implicit, of course, was these four were guaranteed A's.

I had worked out a plan with Newt Ames that he'd give us space to fill in his newspaper on a weekly basis with feature stories my class produced. We had carte blanche on the subjects, though Newt would give it a final read before publication. Also, he'd make a few story idea suggestions.

"Who'll read them?" was the first response I got.

This was not encouraging since it came from Pete Gray, the only townie in my Gang of Four. "My Dad advertises in the paper for his grocery store, but I sure don't think people run to buy it when it comes out."

At best, Kate and Craig seemed cautiously receptive. Only Jing, my Chinese student dating to my year teaching at Xiamen University in China, was excited. I expected that. She got enthusiastic over any opportunity to learn more about life in the U.S.

Grand opening of a downtown business? She was there. A Harrison College football game? Wouldn't miss it. Student recital? She led the applause. A senior thesis presentation? Front row.

My immediate plan split these four into two-person units---Craig & Kate and Pete & Jing. Craig, a tekkie all the way, could benefit from Kate, the most stylish writer I'd encountered at Harrison.

I had saved her paper on participating with her father, Nate Stine, and his Holy Roller motorcycle gang in the Indianapolis parade. Newt was blown away by that piece when I showed it to him.

Secretly, I got kind of a charge thinking about Kate introducing Craig someday to her Dad, known as The Preacher in his role as leader of the notorious Holy Rollers motorcycle gang.

Pete, with his knowledge of Harrison, would be good for helping Jing to plumb deeper into local American culture. At the same time, he could benefit from her outsider's perspective.

Let the games begin? Kind of. I'd give them two weeks to start ahead of everyone else to sort ideas, do research, and explore the community for stories. They would set a high bar for others in the class. Maybe some of the faces new to me would excel, too.

Rule one: The stories had to be local, or micro. Nothing big picture or national unless there was an actual, factual connection to Harrison, the community or college. And we would be telling feature stories, not handling real news.

Rule two: Facts mattered. The Society of Professional Journalists' ethics code would apply. This meant objectivity, full attribution, etc. I handed them SPJ materials to use as a guideline.

Rule three: No op-ed or first person. Readers don't care what the writer thinks or opines, especially if it's someone with so few experiences as a high school or college student. We're not approaching work as critics.

This generally came as a shock to those writing for the first time for a public audience. This would mean no reviews of movies, music, books, etc. "Think of it this way," I said. "A total stranger is in the room and will read what you write."

Rule four: Prepare to be edited by Newt or me. This happens to the best authors. Nobody's writing is golden.

Harrison College did not have a student newspaper. Dean Brunk saw it as a unnecessary, value-less headache. OK. But to have student work appear in a real paper (no matter what the college community thought of it) and read by the public, one with a paid circulation, was more significant.

Furthermore, space in the *Hoosier-Record* was a perfect entry in President Casey's "Town & Gown" push (which it proved to be).

"Trust me," I told my class. "It doesn't have to be a big newspaper either. Just a weekly like the *Hoosier-Record* is fine. People pay for the paper, and that adds credibility when you put this on your resume."

Of course, this drew a question I anticipated right from the start.

"Do we get paid?"

I did not anticipate it would come from Jing, which it did. She was catching on fast to capitalism in her new country. Maybe too fast.

"Well, no, but it could lead to something bigger and better. Your work gets seen, whether it's in print or online. And if the reader likes a story, it draws attention."

I explained that how, as a part-time contributor for a newspaper in Iowa City, my work got noticed by the parent Gannett Publications organization and occasionally the stories ran throughout its massive chain of over 100 newspapers including USA Today.

"Not saying this will happen here," I said. "Newt's independent and owns the Harrison paper himself. But it gets read, at least by the bigger papers around here like Indianapolis and Louisville. Who knows? There are lots of ways you can take this experience outside traditional journalism."

By now, I could see some fire growing in their eyes.

"The deal is this, guys," I concluded. "We're giving *Hoosier-Record* readers stories and information they wouldn't otherwise read anywhere else. Do that enough and you build anticipation among them, create followers. You guys have the chops for this."

We agreed to this: In a week, they'd get back to me with story ideas.

Chapter 19

Shadow Girl

Not long into the semester at Pima School in Arizona, Maria began to feel guilty.

Her new routine---early to rise at the Vincentian Center, prayers in the chapel, breakfast with staff, and a ride to Pima School for a full day of classes---was feeling comfortable. Too comfortable. Her own room. Clean bedding. Nice mattress. Air Conditioning. Showers. Laundry. Tasty meals. Library. Companionship. Spirituality.

After school, she taught English classes for the Center's Spanish-only-speaking residents. She worked in the kitchen, where she made friends with staffers and hid snacks to pass on in the evening. Enjoyable people. Occasionally, she subbed as a babysitter in the nursery.

She was not the least bit homesick for El Salvador.

But in confessions heard by Father Tony, she expressed much guilt. Through sheer luck, she eluded I.C.E. and now had a comfort zone with routines that were more fulfilling than those in her previous life. Certainly, they were better than those faced on the dangerous trek across Central America and Mexico.

All this, while her parents and two sisters were incarcerated in some distant, dirty migrant encampment. Maybe even shipped back to El Salvador, for all she knew. Their year-long odyssey through Central America and Mexico, at times sleeping outside with no shelter and exposed to the elements, built bonds among them that few outside their circle could fully comprehend.

"Why me?" she wondered. "Why do I get to feel so secure and productive in the Vincentian Center. My family assuredly is not, wherever they are? I should be with my family. I don't deserve this."

This was something a dozen "Hail Mary's" couldn't handle in the confession booth. The priest, realizing her torment, carefully explained she was experiencing a simple test of faith. Everyone faced them, in all shapes and sizes, at some point in life.

"It probably does not make you feel better when I say God moves in mysterious ways, but you must do exactly what you are doing now. Keep moving forward," he said.

"You represent your family. Collect experiences that can be helpful in the future. Do what is before you. You will be united again someday. Keep believing. I would say this to any other member of your family, if they were in your position."

Maria found some measure of solace in Father Tony's comments. Nevertheless, she was shaken several days later when there was a knock at the door of her bedroom. She was studying for a test at Pima and could get no hints from the person sent by Father Tony to bring her to his office.

This could not be good, she thought, as they walked quietly through the Vincentian Center hallways. Maria quietly prayed to herself all the way, "Please, God, let my family be OK."

They were. She could tell the second she walked into his office and made eye contact with the priest. He was smiling.

He handed a letter to Maria. It was written by her father. She recognized the handwriting.

It simply read:

> *"We have a good situation. We are together and treated well. I am hopeful for the future and confident the United States government will grant us asylum. This is a wonderful nation. We look forward to uniting some day with relatives and friends."*
>
> *---Ricardo Lopez*

Maria was relieved. Then, after reading it a second and third time, there was a growing look of puzzlement on her face. Ricardo Lopez? As if my father needs to use his formal name in a note to his daughter.

"I dearly love my father, but this note is so, so bare, so impersonal," she said. "There are so many details he did not tell me. This almost does not sound like him. He is a very talkative person. He loves to communicate. That is why he was such a good teacher at the university in El Salvador.

"Did he truly write this message? This does look like his handwriting."

Father Tony leaned back in his squeaky, unoiled-in-years desk chair, took off his glasses, rubbed the bridge of his nose between thumb and forefinger, and smiled. Then he got up, walked across his small office, closed the door, and plopped back in his chair.

"Yes, you can be assured he wrote this. I watched him do it."

Father Tony told her that he, personally, met with her parents and siblings.

Maria gasped. It had been over a month since she last saw them.

It took some effort, but he located her family. The Vincentian Center, he went on, had contacts throughout the immigrant network. This included Humane Borders, numerous churches, involved Arizona State University faculty, graduate school students and administrators, plus social work agencies.

Then, the priest proceeded to tell Maria the note was "intentionally void" of details, including mentioning her name. Federal agents were closely monitoring detainees, checking incoming and outgoing mail for evidence of more illegals, and monitoring calls with systems on loan from the FBI.

"You may feel guilt over your situation," he added, "but don't. I can assure you that your family is thrilled for you."

The priest said her family was ensconced in a facility used as a Japanese internment camp in Arizona during World War II, over 75 years ago. Not that knowledgeable about United States history and the ugly Executive Order 9066 establishment of camps to segregate Japanese-Americans during World War II, the priest gave Maria a Cliff Notes explanation.

Arizona was considered a good place to incarcerate the internees, he said. The space to build this camp during the war was leased on Pima-Maricopa Indian lands in east central Pinal County, many miles south of Phoenix.

There was no place to escape since the state was mostly a barren desert. And, just for good measure, there was this---intentional?---bonus: No air conditioning to make life even more miserable.

The update: Following dispersal of over 13,000 internees following the war, the Federal government continued to lease the property over subsequent decades.

Upgrades got made and the facilities were used for clandestine, off-the-chart projects. There were unsubstantiated rumors of lingering radioactivity from these activities.

"I will make more trips there," said Father Tony. "When I saw your family, I was there to conduct Masses for several days. The diocese rotates us in and out. I knew it was them when we met. Maria, you look very much like your mother. Very beautiful.

"But I can never draw too much attention going out of my way to meet families. The government is watching everything. Especially priests like me they consider do-gooder nuisances. Subversive, actually. That is why your father did not even use your name in his note.

"You must not try to reach them. Never. You can be a future asset to them on the outside. You must put your personal interests aside. You must go about your business as if they---I know this will be difficult---do not exist. You must remain in the shadows and do nothing to draw attention to yourself or your identity.

"Keep the faith."

Chapter 20

Off and Running

Amazingly, the idea of writing for the local *Hoosier-Record* weekly got a---grudging---thumbs-up from Dean Brunk. President Casey probably whispered something in his ear. Or the dean had an ulterior motive of some sort.

Newt was thrilled, but I cautioned him. Inspiration is easy, perspiration's hard---especially when dealing with college students. (I'm guessing this was something I was told by a coach somewhere in my athletic past.)

If Dean Brunk's enthusiasm for the project was lukewarm, my students made up for it. They liked the idea of contributing their work for the public no matter how small the *Hoosier-Record*. Of course, Pete, a townie, was the only student who had read the local paper. There also was the possibility that other students never held an actual newspaper in their hands, but I didn't go there. That was one for the don't ask/don't tell file.

We would be doing borderline journalism, but I rationalized it thus: Journalism is storytelling, and writing is one way to tell stories for audiences whether it's fiction, nonfiction, or creative nonfiction.

The plan had dual tracks: While my Gang of Four worked on specific assignments, their remaining classmates chose from a list of ideas I'd generate through their suggestions.

Also, there would be storytelling options with minimal writing. One would be photo-only features told through captions. I figured these could be especially attractive to readers, given the popularity of Facebook and other social media venues that stressed few words and many graphics.

A picture worth 10,000 words? I emphasized to them that well-written captions remained important. Pictures ate space and could be used when we ran short of stories, or "content" as Craig insisted on calling it. We could also plug work into the web site, which Newt liked to update with occasional posts between printed issues.

The other staple was a weekly "this date in local history" feature. I knew these would get read by the public and, in a sense, they introduced newer residents to the community. We'd be doing sort of a public service thingie here. The key would be to locate interesting occurrences and events of the past in the *Hoosier-Record* files, which were, sadly not digitized before the year 2000.

I broadened the range to include all of Harrison County and not just the city of Harrison. About 30 per cent of Newt's readers lived outside the county seat. For the history majors in my course, this gave them a good opportunity to work on research skills. Little did I know the impact one "date in history" item would have for readers and the community.

Chapter 21

Story Time

The story ideas for the *Hoosier-Record*, and from, my students rolled in hot and heavy. A sampling:

Sure-fire:

- An ode to Veterans Day later in the semester. In addition to printing a roll call of county vets, it would feature short pieces on individuals who saw combat in the Korean, Viet Nam, Desert Storm conflicts and aftermath. Sadly, the county's sole World War II resident died two years ago.

- Mildred Briggs and Dorothy (Dot) Dotsauer, two widows, who lived above a successful, independent bakery they owned and managed on Harrison's commercial square. Its name was "The Dough Girls." I could personally vouch for their cinnamon scones.

  There was some thought about calling it Milly & Dot's or Dot & Milly's, but they could not decide whose name should be first. Interestingly, each wanted the other to come first.

· Profile of Amy White, director (part-time) of the Harrison community theatre, which does three well-done productions per year. Amy wrote plays that she occasionally produced as well as directed.

· Harrison College's new e-sports initiative, where students take courses in video gaming and participate in competitive intercollegiate leagues sprouting on campuses.

Apparently, these new offerings at our school made us cutting edge among smaller, liberal arts colleges. Only three other schools in Indiana were into e-sports gaming: Purdue, Rose-Hulman Institute of Technology, and Ball State.

This initiative was new ground to me and, considering the tekkie ineptness I'd discovered among faculty, made me laugh when I first learned of it. Our sleepy school, deep in Indiana on the Tippecanoe River, was breaking new ground?

Naturally, this story idea was Craig's. There was no surprise to me also that he already was regularly in touch with the person hired to lead the e-sport program. Nerds united, apparently.

· Bicycling across America. A college faculty member in the Economics Dept., Randy Young, was doing the ride in two-to-four-day increments whenever he found time. He'd fly or drive to where he last stopped and parked his bike, add to his total, and then return to Harrison. At his current rate of mileage consumption, he figured to complete the 2,500-mile trek in slightly less than six months.

The cool part of the adventure was this: He switched directions with each increment. He started East-to-West in Jacksonville, Fla., then followed up with a West-to-East leg starting in Long Beach, Calif. Then, he kept alternating with the same pattern, calculating he would meet himself in South Lead Hill, Ark., in late Winter.

A celebration was planned at the finish. Plans called for him to cross a finish line in one direction, turn around, and cross it again in the opposite direction. "Anyone could go one way," he told me, following a faculty meeting. "But who does it in both directions on the same ride?" Difficult to argue with that. Furthermore, the media, including *Bicycle Times* and *AARP The Magazine*, expressed interest in his first-person account. He kept a diary.

· Attempts by the local Harrison Historical Society to get the old Baltimore & Ohio Railroad station, dating to the 1870s, landmarked. Trains still pass through town on a regular basis, but there is no passenger service anymore. The station is used for storage.

· The county's Hollywood film history. This included the birthplace for Alice Sylvester, who appeared in 41 films stretching from the silent movie era in 1916 to talkies in 1934. Alice was buried in the local Mt. Greenwood Cemetery.

Also, several locations in the county were used for sites in two successful Hollywood productions, "Hoosiers" with Gene Hackman in 1986 and "Friendly Persuasion" with Gary Cooper in 1956. The challenge (or hook?) here: The location in "Friendly Persuasion" was now the home for one of Indiana's largest hog farms.

Possibilities:

- History behind the oldest gravestone in the Harrison city cemetery. Who was Elijah Stone, anyway, and why is he buried there?

- A close look at Hispanics energizing the county's second largest community, Liberty. It became a popular Midwestern magnet for Mexican-American migrants four or five decades ago. At the time, they were lured by jobs in a local turkey processing plant. This was Newt's idea planted in the mix.

- A replay of the victorious barnstorming appearance at the county fairgrounds racetrack in 1904 by Dan Patch, the world's fastest and most famous trotter in racehorse history.

- History of the Harrison County Horticultural Society. Nothing exciting, except the current president is Luella Brunk, wife of Dean Brunk. This effort could come in handy for future schmoozing.

- The Humboldt Inn, a bar in rural Harrison County, that displays what owner Zeke Zahorik labels "the world's largest Cheeto." Who knew? I planned to check this out before assigning it.

- Profile of Bernard "Buns" McCready, who played two years with the old St. Louis Browns and, as far as anyone knew, was the lone, local baseball player from the county to play in the big leagues. The challenge: Buns was a crabby recluse living alone in a rented farmhouse with a Pit Bull, Spike, known to be equally angry at anything that moved.

- Local postmaster Rick Schmelzer and his beer bottle collection, which included over 3,500 brands from nations such as The Netherlands, Japan, Norway, South Africa, China, Monaco, Mongolia, Belize, Lichtenstein, and Iceland.

Delete-able (or circular file):

- Profile of the Holy Rollers motorcycle gang. My new students had no idea that, when this was suggested, the daughter of the gang's leader---Nate "The Preacher" Stine---was their classmate Kate McDonald. She opposed the idea. End of story.

- The (alleged) spread of illegal methamphetamine (meth) labs in the county. No way likely we'd tackle this land-mine-laden story. Even if true, it was too complex for my students to handle. My theory: We learn to walk before we run. Maybe next year.

- Legal dispute over planned construction of state's largest cattle farm capable of accommodating a 200,000 inventory. Construction was opposed by a coalition of animal rights' advocates and neighbors within smelling distance. Too hot for us, and besides there already was coverage of this issue in the newspaper.

We'd probably stick in a review of a play scheduled for late October in the community theatre, possibly packaging it with the

Amy White profile. That was as close as I wanted students to get to being critics.

We had a good semester's supply of stories to write, bolstered by Newt's suggestions. Outside my hand-picked Gang of Four, I figured to pair together students with complementary abilities that emerged after a few weeks of prep work.

Newt was ecstatic. He hoped to count on contributions in future semesters, either through similar class projects. One possibility would be establishing a scholarship or internship.

"This fills a huge hole for me," he said. "I'll be interested in what it does for circulation."

Chapter 22

Just Desserts

To say my advanced writing class got off to a fast start would be an understatement.

Our first *Hoosier-Record* contribution was a winner, and it was a simple narrative. I almost wrote the story idea off as too soft even for a small-town weekly. The piece was done by two upper class students, Jennifer Schanz and Ron Thomas, both new to my course. They showed promise.

Their effort proved that good material can be right under our noses. In this case, it was about "The Dough Girls Bakery." Here was how the piece started:

By Jennifer Schulz and Ron Thomas
Hoosier-Record correspondents

Six mornings a week, Jeannie Lane awakens to the aroma of freshly baked rolls, doughnuts, tarts, pies, cakes and other goodies wafting into her apartment above The Dough Girls Bakery. "Can't beat it," she said.

Occasionally, when co-owners below Mildred (Milly) Briggs and Dorothy (Dot) Dotsauer get swamped filling

80

special orders or hosting an event, Jeannie goes down-stairs to pitch in and help her pals. "I just love the place," said Lane, who used to live in an apartment on town's edge. "It's why I moved closer."

Everyone likes a good bakery, but in this Tippecanoe River town, where homey, local businesses appeared to have drifted downstream, the busy Dough Girls is more than a friendly gathering spot to drink coffee and sample region-famous cranberry scones.

Vance Dennis, executive director of the Harrison Chamber of Commerce, is not alone when he says the bakery is important to a community comeback. In its 10 years, the business has been cited by the Indiana Commerce & Industry Association for its success and won a Woman Entrepreneur Achievement Award for Briggs and Dotsauer from a small-business organization.

"That Dough Girls is a cornerstone for our downtown," said Dennis. "It's got to be the best-known place to eat in south central Indiana and parts of Kentucky. I know several businesses close by benefit from people who come there to eat or put in orders."

Presidential candidates Mitt Romney, Joe Biden, and Pete Buttigieg, plus U.S. Vice-President Mike Pence, have made campaign stops in the bakery. A Time magazine reporter, wandering through town in 2000, called The Dough Girls "sinfully addictive" in a story on life along the campaign trail. "Pastry to die for," was another description.

The Dough Girls gets orders for graduation parties, club gatherings and assorted receptions, but on any morning it's obvious that its main ingredient for success is the informal stream of townspeople -- business persons and retirees -- stopping in for coffee, pastry and comment on the news of the day.

"You've basically got your 7 o'clock shift, 8 o'clock shift and 9 o'clock shift," said Dennis, describing the way the local ritual of American life unfolds in Harrison at the bakery. "I'm there at 8, and I know everyone tells me what I should be doing."

Interestingly, the bakery does a brisk business with Amish settlers living in the area. Never mind followers of this religion reject just about any modern convenience---electricity, automobiles, etc.---introduced after the late 1800s and pride themselves on their own cooking.

Every Saturday, like clockwork, a horse and buggy shows up outside the business with the driver and a helper inside purchasing 10 dozen doughnuts to be served after their Sunday church services.

The city with its population of a little over 10,000 has seen a steady loss of jobs with the closing of plants and other small manufacturing concerns, a depressing dynamic taking place in many Midwestern U.S. communities.

But The Dough Girls' co-owners see great future benefits in Harrison College's new connection to China and partnership with Xiamen University. "You can bet we'll be doing some research, see what kind of baked goods would appeal to those visitors," said Briggs. "Be kind of fun to see our Amish customers lining up with any new Chinese customers."

****

The story by Jennifer and Ron had another 300 or so words. There were interesting, personal details the students extracted from Milly (an Army nurse in Vietnam during the war) and Dorothy (a Bridge player with Master ranking).

The students were thrilled to see their names in print. They bought a dozen or so newspapers between them to send to relatives and friends. As a bonus, their infectious excitement ramped up enthusiasm among classmates working on their articles.

Even more clever: Jennifer and Ron got the Dough Girls to rank their baked goods' popularity with customers: 1, doughnuts; 2, cinnamon rolls; 3, (tie) cookies; 3, (tie) pies; 5, tarts; 6, cupcakes; 7, cakes; 8, brownies; 9, scones; 10, croissants.

It was not exactly Bernstein & Woodward, but a simple, informative and well-crafted tale about a local subject taken for granted. Even if you did not patronize the bakery, most readers were aware of the business and the two owners. Now they knew more about the operation.

This, I told my students, never would've happened if you had not reached a public audience with your writing and storytelling. We also made Newt happy. He said, "This is exactly the sort of piece we need in the paper, and I surely don't have time to write."

Little did anyone know the story would grow. After it was posted on the *Hoosier-Record*'s web site, some bright bulbs working for the public television station in nearby Evansville called for copies of the newspaper.

"They're thinking of building a local, dessert-only cooking show around The Dough Girls," Newt told me. "It'd be low-budget, produced, shot and shown from their studio. There'd be a chance, if it looks good, it could get picked up on other PBS stations.

"I didn't say anything to the ladies because the station manager said, for now, nothing's certain. It's on his list of ideas for the new season. What a nice boost it could be for them and Harrison."

And my writing program.

Chapter 23

Give Them Liberty

After they saw the response to the Dough Girls effort, my students began to understand how connections can be made with readers. Nothing like seeing your name in print over a story. And somebody paid to read it! What a rush.

Maybe this idea of a printed newspaper was OK with them. "I sent a copy of the story to my parents," said co-author Ron. "My mom got all excited. She wants to subscribe to the paper. I told her she could find it on the web site."

And?

"She said that wasn't the same as seeing it in print."

Thus, my class began churning out work with added enthusiasm. Some students struggled, but, with some editing by me and suggestions from classmates, things began to fall in place.

Apparently there still was a market for local news, something that got overlooked in the journalism landscape. Newt reported a slight uptick in sales. The Dough Girls now made the paper available in their bakery.

Ideally, each class pairing---like my Gang of Four---needed one of the two to write and the other to be a decent researcher, or at least be able to effectively navigate the web for background and facts.

In the end, no story they wrote in that semester had an impact to match the piece suggested by Mary.

By Craig Conley and Kate McDonald
Hoosier-Record correspondents

Twice each workweek for almost 20 years Ben Stevens made a round trip in his truck between Harrison and Evansville, where he owns furniture stores. Maybe 10 or 12 years ago, he said, he noticed a very subtle change in the landscape.

"I'd pass through little towns and I started spotting these fields with goal nets, or whatever they're called, at the schools and parks," he said. "I didn't give it much thought.

"Heck, I'd never seen fields like that before. I wasn't even sure what was played on them, lacrosse or baseball batting cages. I knew they weren't for football."

What Stevens did come to realize was this: The fields were tangible evidence of a significant shift in the demographics of his native southern Indiana.

As farms, small towns, and schools became new homes for migrants from south of the U.S. border, they brought with them their favorite---and foreign to Indiana---sport, soccer. The fields he saw was where the games, or matches, were played.

"It was a big learning process for us to integrate this sport," acknowledged Ned Pachel, superintendent of

schools at one of those small towns, Downey, Ben traveled.

"Some older coaches and parents were not ready to accept it. But, as I look back, it made perfect sense. The sport's safer and cheaper than football and, frankly, we were better serving nearly half our student body."

There are plenty of U.S. Census Bureau statistics to document the influx of Mexicans and Central Americans into the Midwest. Was this a new one: Count the soccer fields?

Since the 1990s, more than half the Latino migration began opting for rural, instead of urban, America. Harrison County, with the steady loss of younger generations to large cities and other areas, became a popular destination. Here, the lure was prompted by jobs that called for unskilled labor and suitable, available housing.

Nowhere is this more obvious than Liberty, which, at approximately 4,000 residents, is the county's second largest city. The old Thomas Produce & Processing poultry plant, now part of Fairview Brands with its purchase by a Wall Street venture capital group, employed up to 250 persons in its early, high seasons.

In Liberty, vacant stores re-opened as cafes offering full selections of Hispanic-friendly dishes to go with "hot dogs and apple pie" standards. A small, locally owned candy-making plant opened offering traditional Mexican favorites grew to 15 employees and a three-state sales reach.

"Things are pretty lively in Liberty, alright," declared the mayor, Charles "Chuck" Chalmers. "We're growing. Not *many places in this region can say that. We got our problems, too, but we're in better shape than most."*

There are two grocery stores: Raul's Fine Foods, which focuses entirely on the Hispanic market, and Eagle Foods, which began offering new items such as mangos, cactus leaves, and in-store made tortillas, masa, tamales and enchiladas in the deli. Bi-lingual workers always are on duty.

The closest Catholic Church in Harrison is over half Latino, thriving, and offers a Spanish language Mass. There is a Pentecostal church in Liberty that is primarily Latino with many Puerto Ricans.

County schools offer a strong, dual language program where children learn both in English and Spanish. Anglo families have moved to town to enroll children in the programs. The local, public library has significant Spanish-language books in addition to language classes for adults.

The story went on to talk about evolving local politics, public administration, social services, police and fire. The article was peppered with names and quotes and, in the end, had to be a revelation for *Hoosier-Record* readers.

Newt was ecstatic. "Give those students an A-plus," he said, when I brought Kate and Craig to meet him after their work went public. "Is there a higher grade?" The co-authors beamed.

The newspaper saw a healthy sales spike in Liberty and beyond when the article first became available. The headline read: "We give you Liberty." Double entendre? "Made me think maybe I should have had a Spanish language edition printed for this one," said Newt.

Even Nate "The Preacher" Stine---Kate's proud dad and head of the Holy Rollers motorcycle gang, got into the act. He volunteered to make a run to the printing plant in Evansville to pick up 300 extra copies needed to fill the added demand.

Additionally, he took it upon himself to find some new distribution spots---mostly in taverns he and his crew frequented. Who knew? Having a motorcycle gang in charge of circulation could be a good thing. Hard to say no to these guys.

I knew the story was a hit this way: A reporter from the *Indianapolis Banner,* the state's largest newspaper and part of the Gannett empire, called Newt---then me---for some contact information. She wanted to do a Liberty story.

In the news media business, imitation is the sincerest form of flattery. Preferably it comes with attribution.

Chapter 24

Collaboration

"So how did you get this story idea," asked Mary, after I gave her the "We give you Liberty" article to read. "I like it a lot."

"I'd claim credit, but it was Newt's idea," I answered. "It's a change he's observed for several years. I thought it'd work. Good way to build up some readership for the paper in another town, too."

"Maybe you could get it reprinted in Spanish," said Mary, envelope-pushing in her usual fashion. "There's a Spanish-language paper out of Indianapolis that covers the state, you know. *La Prensa.*"

I agreed to check into this. More exposure couldn't hurt. In any language. Could attract some new advertisers, too."

Wait. This newspaper thing was starting to get into my blood. Got to remember I'm an educator first, not a journalist.

"You know," she continued, "I've been to Liberty. Snuck over there a bunch of afternoons. A student from there told me I should check it out. What's going on in Liberty is happening more and more in the Midwest. Iowa, Illinois."

Yeah? You didn't tell me you'd been to Liberty?

"You didn't ask, big guy," she continued. "Met some nice people there. I've been busy this term, too. There've been studies and research on migration to the Upper Midwest. Not much in the mass media. I think there's an opportunity for me for some projects."

"For what?"

"Well, maybe to make Liberty some sort of laboratory for my courses. You're not the only one interested in bringing real life into the classroom. I do actually speak Spanish you know."

"Sounds good to me. Just one thing, though."

"What?"

"Good luck getting it past Dean Brunk."

Chapter 25

Making Noise

Our "this date in history" entries also gained nice traction in the *Hoosier-Record*.

If done right, this could be a popular feature and a good outlet for my students who struggled with writing. For them, it was an opportunity to make contributions via basic detective work by digging through old issues.

Good storytelling does not necessarily mean stylish writing. In this case, the content needed to be only 2-3 factual paragraphs and, at the same time, everyone learns some Harrison County history. The items needed to be lively and have significance, but not long. Punchy. Make the facts matter.

For instance?

> *"Mr. and Mrs. Bradley Moore, on this date in 1998, hosted dinner for out of town guests that included two of Mrs. Moore's Kappa Delta sorority sisters from Indiana University, Louise Gruber and Betty Sutton. A good time was had by all."*

Uhhh, no.
Try this:

On this date in 1980, the Harrison City Council voted unanimously to add a fourth, full-time patrol position to the police department, giving the community staffed 24-hour protection. The decision followed a rash of break-ins and theft of three automobiles, including Mayor Ben Wilson's new Ford.

More like it.

It freaked the class out that *The Hoosier-Record* archives were digitized only as far back as 2000. Everything prior to that was on micro-film, which made combing the files a tedious chore for students used to instant Karma at their fingertips.

"What did they do before micro-film, Professor Doyle," asked one of my young charges during a class.

The real deal, he was informed. Actual print on paper... newspapers themselves, with ink to get your hands dirty.

"Whoa. I can't remember the last time I handled a newspaper."

The murder of Marlene Scott, our last entry for the semester on the "this date in history" feature for the paper, proved to be especially well-read. Touchy, too.

I had no idea how touchy---and far-reaching---it would become for the *Hoosier-Record* and my students in the second semester.

See, every small, rural Midwest community has an unsolved crime, but not often is it a murder. When they stay unsolved and become fodder for cable TV "cold case" documentaries, which this one had, they can grow into monsters and conspiracies that become downright spooky.

Could the killer still be among us?

Fifty years earlier, Marlene's remains were discovered in a wooded patch of farmland owned and operated by Burt Kohl.

She had been missing for months, and no one was prepared for her gruesome discovery---Burt's dog digging up a body part and depositing it at his owner's feet.

"Almost crapped in my pants," was the way Burt, called upon many times to repeat the story, described it.

In the immediate years, the city was consumed with the crime. Theories about the killer ranged from a laser beam shot from a passing UFO to Marlene's boyfriend at the time, Jimmy Bartow.

When Burt passed away three years ago, some Harrison old-timers felt it was the end of the mystery---that Burt was the killer. He never married, lived his entire life as a bachelor in his remote farmhouse, and that, in the minds of some locals, made him guilty of something.

That theory was so absurd that law enforcement officials, who included investigators from the Indiana Attorney General's office, never bothered him with anything but cursory queries.

Rumors in small towns die hard. Up popped a conspiracy theory, naturally. Didn't Burt have a cousin high in local law enforcement circles? Couldn't this person influence the investigation and steer it away from him? And never mind the cousin's identity never was corroborated.

Eventually, Harrison's attention waned. Older residents passed on or moved, newcomers had no interest, and everyone else wearied of speculation.

Marlene had dropped out of Harrison High School after her junior year at age 17. She had transferred in three years earlier, when her mother, Flo, and stepfather, Gene, moved from Indianapolis. She was bright, outgoing, unusually mature, and beautiful, but, perceived as an outsider, and never fit into the school's established social "register."

Worse than that, classmates, mostly jealous girls, loved to spread rumors about her. Today, it would be called bullying.

One especially, humiliating example: It was not unusual for her to find condoms hanging from the handle of her high school locker, which was in a prominent hallway location. She had few friends.

Marlene's one shining moment was her role in a Harrison community playhouse summer production of the musical, "Bye Bye Birdie."

Nicholas (Nick) Walker, the new, energetic director, gave her the star Kim McAfee role after an audition in which she sang, danced, and came with lines memorized. This, of course, triggered gossip among rivals that the audition included a closed-door session in which she demonstrated additional talents to the director.

In what would've been her senior year, Marlene quit school, started work on her GED diploma, and took a job 150 miles away in Indianapolis. The boss was a friend of the family.

Despite the distance, she remained a frequent visitor in Harrison and stayed with her mother and stepfather on most weekends. Also, she remained close to the playhouse scene and theatre-linked pals---her only real friends in town.

She visited rehearsals for the new play, "Brigadoon," as a visitor. This, of course, meant to some that she was continuing private "auditions" with Nicholas.

Marlene never made it to her mother's house on a bitterly cold, windy Friday night in December. Figuring she had decided not to come until Saturday, the mother did not push a panic button until Sunday after repeated, unanswered calls to Marlene's tiny apartment in Indianapolis and known friends.

Investigators eventually targeted three suspects: theatre director Nicholas Walker, boyfriend Jimmy Bartow and Lawrence Charles, a Harrison College freshman who was the last person (allegedly) to see Marlene alive. Walker and Bartow had uncrackable alibis, or at least uncrackable as long as witnesses stood behind them.

Charles? Tough to say. Police, who botched reading him his rights initially, had to toss out testimony that he was, indeed, with Marlene on her last, known night---though he denied wrongdoing.

Within days, Charles withdrew from Harrison College and returned to his home and parents in California. The father, a successful partner in a large Sacramento law firm, surrounded his son with a wall of lawyers too impenetrable to break by local enforcement agencies.

A new round of rumors hit the fan three years later when Gene Brown, Marlene's stepfather, was divorced by her mother. The grounds were physical abuse; Gene, unemployed at the time, was a heavy drinker and known to dip his wick where it did not belong.

Was Brown an abuser?

The short item rekindled long-ago emotions.

"Lot of folks I know got a little riled when they saw that item about Marlene Scott by your students in the newspaper," said Gil Munson, at the first Rotary lunch following its publication. "Just wanted to let you know."

This was an uncharacteristic comment for Gil, never one to question my work.

"The thing is," he further explained, "a lot of rumors flew around this murder. Ugly stuff that damaged reputations. Lots of bad feelings. Some people got burned and, to this day, hold grudges."

The crime occurred in pre-CSI days on TV, of course. Advanced forensic techniques, such as DNA testing and computer tracking, were so much science fiction in rural Indiana. They never came into play.

The evidence (what little there was), reports, interview transcripts and other related files were stacked somewhere in

Harrison County Courthouse's dusty storage. They were untouched for several decades. Until our little item appeared in the newspaper.

To be used in the "this date" feature, we somehow reduced everything we read into three paragraphs to make the item fit the format. There was plenty of extra information to be collected and, as things developed, this was helpful in the second semester.

Chapter 26

Party Time

As it was explained to me, the annual December faculty party at Harrison College to mark the end of the first semester used to be called the Christmas party. Then, noting Jews and a Muslim---not counting atheists---were increasingly in the mix, the event became known as the Holiday Party.

This year there was a new component: The Chinese. Apparently, they'd have to wait for their New Year celebration, which occurred in late January.

The Holiday Party, held in the Milbert Social Center ballroom, did double duty this year as an acknowledgement of our new association with China and Xiamen University. I could tell something was up when I spotted Gil Munson, plus several other trustees, go into the room ahead of me. I'd never heard of board members in attendance.

There also were familiar faces from Rotary with no direct link to the college---the mayor, two county commissioners, Chamber of Commerce executive director Vance Dennis, The Dough Girl bakery owners Mildred Briggs and Dorothy Dotsauer.

Newt Ames told me this was his first invite to the event "and I'm pretty sure that's true of others like me from off-campus." The president's Town & Gown initiative was on the move.

We toasted three exchange faculty members from China, plus 20 students from Xiamen, here in this first year of the Harrison program. Several courses were added to the curriculum and, if everything went smooth as hoped, a full-blown Chinese Studies program would follow---possibly starting next school year.

In turn, a new, rich vein would open for enrollments, faculty, researchers, and investors. A Sino-American Renaissance right here on the Tippecanoe River in rural, isolated southern Indiana!

Several additional, special guests from China---two administrators from Xiamen University---were on hand. They were here for a week-long fact-finding feasibility tour on behalf of their university. Apparently Chinese educators go on junkets just like Americans, too.

President Casey, like a good salesman, was everywhere at the party. Was he twins? He introduced them to everyone, though I noticed he steered quickly from Dean Brunk and several other "old guard" faculty members.

Embarrassingly, it was discovered our lone Chinese-American on the Harrison College faculty, Wang Wei, an assistant Biology professor could not speak a word in any Chinese dialect. He grew up in Milwaukee.

My suggestion to the president to take guests to Whitey's, the rural tavern that was the seat of all local wisdom, drew laughs. "Not so sure that would work in this case," he said. "Maybe after we all get to know each other a little better."

Our little school was causing ripples in higher education in America, and everyone was keeping fingers crossed we wouldn't blow it. There was talk of the *Chronicle of Higher Education*, academia's news Valhalla, doing a feature.

This semester-ending party, my third, was especially festive. The addition of wine helped. Harrison hired an excellent, new food service this year, Bon Appétit, in an obvious (to me) move to help lure the Chinese as well as American business investors. For partygoers at this event, there still were the ubiquitous, boring egg salad and tuna finger sandwiches, carrot sticks, chips and dips, but new additions included Pan Fried Dumplings, Lotus Seed Buns, and Pan Fried Pork and Cabbage Rolls.

"Tasty, eh?" said Mary, as we nibbled away in one corner of the event. "I could get used to this."

Off in a corner, I caught glimpses of a dour-looking David Krugendorff, who obviously still smarted from his "CV outing" by my student, Craig. His smiles looked forced and furtive in his circle of colleagues. As far as I knew, his bogus credentials remained off the radar and our secret. However, there were rumors he was applying for positions at other schools.

One memorable---depressing?---exchange for me came when I found myself in a food line next to James ("not Jim, please") Goodwin, a European history professor and, in my humble opinion, one of the most pretentious Harrison faculty members.

"Well, Mr. Doyle, your writing class seems to have created a bit of a buzz this semester," he said. "I must say that's quite the adventure, interacting with the local newspaper. What's its name? The Herald Record?"

"The *Hoosier-Record,*" I corrected, "as in Indiana. You know, the Hoosier state. Where we live."

"Oh yes, yes. Well, I don't read it. I'm not sure who does. I just happened to see a copy lying about somewhere. I suppose this could lead to *real* writing some day for your students. For a serious audience, that is."

Ah, well. I didn't have an answer before he walked away, but later this thought came to mind: Maybe I should set Craig loose on Goodwin's resume, see what he could discover. Of course, the last thing Harrison needed---at this pivotal point---was a scandal to scare off the Chinese.

Mary and I spent most of the party huddling with the newer, younger faculty, who, like us, were aware we---hand-picked by President Casey---comprised the new wave. Our charge was to help breathe new life into the school.

"I got to say, Flip," said Eileen Kelley, in her first year teaching political science, "you sure know a lot of off-campus people here. Maybe you should run for office."

"Rotary" was my answer as to why I knew so many outsiders attending the party. Eileen was dumbfounded, saying she'd never heard of college faculty members becoming Rotarians.

Maybe not, but it made more sense when I pointed out I was now the local club's college scholarship chairman. She saw instantly how that could be useful. I promised to take her to a meeting after the holidays, which was a lesson in itself. She wasn't aware women could be members.

My Dad is a Rotarian," said Mike Glavin, another new hire who inched his way into the conversation. "I got a scholarship for my undergrad work. Came in handy, too."

In addition to teaching technology courses, Mike was the new, ice-breaking e-sport coach. He also was charged with trying to get Harrison's faculty up to speed on computer knowledge and usage, a daunting assignment in my estimation. He had to be the only faculty member with a visible tattoo---a picture of a laptop keyboard with the word "N.E.R.D." underneath the graphic---on his right wrist.

Obviously, Mike was viewed by the old guard faculty as a novelty, not to be taken seriously. A tattoo? Good God! He and Craig, my resident tekkie, already had struck up a friendship and were in the process of organizing a club. They could compare tattoos, too.

A few, final announcements by President Casey concluded the event. Pointing at a big, bay window, he noted a light snowfall had begun to fall. This was followed by a weather joke, and party goers started to disappear.

"You never asked me to one of your Rotary meetings," sniffed Mary, while we walked back to our apartments just off campus.

"You never asked," I said. "Maybe if you're real nice to me. Like tonight."

"That shouldn't take long. I'll see what I can do."

Chapter 27

Reunited

The mid-December to early January break from school was welcome.

My writing class was a lot of work, staying on top of everyone's projects, helping students develop sources, and shepherding their efforts through Newt at his newspaper. This course became part writing, another part journalism.

I barely had time to look up, and that included up to Mary in the apartment directly above mine. Not once did I hear another set of heavy footsteps in addition to hers, so at least I still had that going for me.

Mary had been busy, too. She thought of her sociology courses as a hands-on experience, which meant vacating the classroom on occasion. Field trips were a big part of the course work and Harrison's location was perfect. Indianapolis and Louisville, two large cities with typical urban problems, were easy drives.

There also were the usual rural challenges---shrinking number of small farms, soil conservation, meth labs---to be plumbed in Harrison County. And, just for good measure, not far away in Terre Haute there was a Federal prison for hard core criminals to study and interview.

Our first holiday break week was spent in Harrison, where we got reacquainted. In fact, the first night we got "reacquainted" twice (tying our record for one night) without leaving my apartment.

We came up for air with several trips to Whitey's bar on the Tippecanoe River to gather a few pearls of wisdom from Whitey. We watched some Netflix films, had several Mexican food outings to nearby Liberty, and, of course, there was morning pastry from The Dough Girls. "I could really get used to this," said Mary.

We got up to speed on Maria, too. She finished Pima school and got her diploma just before Christmas. In keeping with maintaining a shadow existence, she passed up mid-year graduation exercises.

Later, we discovered this was a good thing. I.C.E. ramped up its surveillance in December and, though there was no indication she was yet on any hot list, the Feds were known to be taking closer looks at schools, soup kitchens, churches, bus stations and airports for illegals.

By now, Father Tony at Vincentian House was in full confidence with us. Mary could be a very persuasive person on these matters, though he needed no persuading to give us briefings,

The priest gave Maria a temporary job tutoring at Vincentian House, which gave her another layer of cover before finding something safer or---preferably---the family's status was resolved in a positive manner. She would continue living there.

"We cannot go back to El Salvador," Maria told him. "It would be a death sentence for my father. He made too many important people angry with his teaching and politics."

Mary returned to Phoenix for several days after the first week of our break. Ostensibly, she planned to see Arizona State pals.

If it did not attract attention, she also planned to meet with Maria. She did not dare visit her where she was living in the Vincentian quarters. Too many eyes and ears. Phone calls were being monitored, too. Snitching was an easy way to gain the favor of I.C.E.

"It's getting creepy in Phoenix," Mary told me after returning from Phoenix. "You feel there are eyes and ears everywhere. I.C.E. pays bounties for tips on illegals. Can you believe it? The media has no clue this is taking place."

After my return from visiting parents, assorted relatives, and old pals in Chicagoland, we rendezvoused at O'Hare Airport and drove to Colorado to join her family.

Chapter 28

Some Family History

The annual Christmas gathering for the Jagger Family in Steamboat Springs, Colorado, was written in stone. This was my third.

Everyone made me feel comfortable, especially her brothers Pete Jr., Terry and Mike. They became even more accepting of me after learning I'd been a decent basketball player at Lake Forest College in Illinois.

Mary's father, Pete Sr., became a widower nearly 25 years ago when Mary's mother was killed in a car crash on a Christmas Eve in Garden City, Kan., where they lived. The other vehicle was piloted by a drunken driver who never served one incarcerated day.

"Christmas time never was the same for us, not in our house," said Mary, who was five years old at the time with her three older brothers. "We had to get out of Garden City for the holiday. The pall would've been unbearable."

Her family, which had done a ski trip to Steamboat a year earlier, returned to the Colorado resort a year after the crash---and never stopped going there to celebrate the holiday and ski. It became an annual fixture.

Pete Sr., now a retired school superintendent, never remarried and, though he never said anything to his kids, Mary and her brothers were quite aware that recently he had acquired a "lady friend."

"If he ever said anything to us, we'd say: 'Hey, Dad, go for it,'" Mary added. "It's more than time for him to move on. Maybe he'll surprise us some year and bring her to Steamboat."

As the only girl in the house surrounded by a busy father and three jock brothers, Mary liked to call her upbringing "one, big fart fest." Like many family reunions, the Colorado gatherings were not without drama.

This was my third and, in that span, I saw Pete Jr.'s marriage dissolve. There was obvious tension between his wife and him the first time, then last year there was an outright, very public argument between them that produced their early Steamboat departure. Thankfully childless, they were divorced within two months.

This time? Pete was back with a new girlfriend.... a possible heiress to the throne? "You got me," said Mary. "You'd have to ask him. Go ahead. I dare you. I'd like to know, too."

Interesting to me, Pete was a detective first grade on the Kansas City Police Department. His new squeeze was a lieutenant on the KC Fire Department. Two upwardly mobile, first responders in the same household!

I wondered: How could someone from Garden City, a dinky Dust Bowl community in the far, isolated SW corner of Kansas, became a detective in a major city.

Mary didn't miss a beat. "The Clutter family, and Holcomb," she said.

The what?

"Didn't you ever read "In Cold Blood"? Truman Capote's book, or see the movies?"

Err, yes.

"The book about the slaughter of the Clutter's, a farm family, in the late 1950s. By two drifters, ex-cons looking for money. Real wackos. It was a sensational crime at the time, national headlines and all. Capote's book was about that murder in Holcomb."

So, what's the connection? For Pete?

"Well, Holcomb's only five miles from where we were raised in Garden City. My grandparents were friends of the Clutters. Went to the same church. The crime happened before my brothers and I were born, but Pete was fascinated by it after he read the book in high school.

"The trial, and all the good stuff like that, including the investigation, took place out of the Finney County courthouse in little old Garden City. Put the city on the map, especially when the movies hit the big screens.

"Pete became obsessed, learned everything he could about the crime. Talked to people who knew, or were related to, the justice part. From then on, all he ever talked about was becoming a detective.

"He joined the Kansas City Police Department within a week of graduating from college and then the state's police academy."

Terry and Mike? They were both high school coaches in Dodge City and Chanute, respectively, at opposite ends of the state. Terry also was athletic director, and seemed headed for a full-time administration post, perhaps becoming a superintendent like Pete Sr.

Terry and Mike had solid marriages and three boys among them.

"I'm surrounded by men," pointed out Mary.

Part III: Liberty

Chapter 29

Bonding

In the end, it seemed inevitable that Mary would meet Dorothy Blair in nearby Liberty, and they would become close pals. Never mind Dorothy was more than old enough to be her mother---and maybe that was what generated their karma.

Mary's mother died at an early age. Try as hard as he could, her father could never be all things to his daughter. Then, toss in the hardy dynamic of three brothers to complete the family circle. This meant a long-standing void in her upbringing that only a caring mother could fill.

Mary first came to Liberty to make it a personal, classroom laboratory. With its growth of Hispanic migration in the Upper Midwest, this community had become a major port for migrants for reasons she---in full academic mode---sought an explanation.

Mary was a prospector in heat panning for academic gold, possibly publishing a book on this dynamic that would look mighty, darn good on her CV. She'd organized numerous Liberty class outings, plus arranged related internships, to plumb the community's Hispanic demographics.

All roads seemed to lead to Dorothy Blair. It was the town's librarian who suggested to Mary she contact Dorothy. The high school's social studies teacher pointed her in that direction, too. Even the high school's Spanish instructor.

Dorothy Blair lived on the edge of Liberty less than 10 miles from the Harrison College campus, "stomping" around, as she called it, in her stately Victorian "Painted Lady" home. With its light-yellow base trimmed in white, turrets, towers, iron railings, stained glass windows, and wide, wrap-around porch, the house easily would fit in San Francisco's Nob Hill neighborhood or on St. Charles Avenue in New Orleans.

There was more than an acre of lawn to take in, flowers and gardens smartly spread across the expanse and kept in immaculate, prize-winning shape by a full crew from the local Ramirez Landscapers.

The house once rated a two-page feature in Midwest Living, and the Sunday magazine in the Indianapolis Banner made it a cover story. It was not unusual to see out-of-town vehicles slow almost to a crawl as they passed the Blair house, the noses of occupants pressed to the windows.

Easily, it was Liberty's No. 1 "tourist" attraction unless you counted the Harkin Horse Farms on the edge of town.

Directly behind the house, the property bled into corn fields that stretched endlessly into the horizon. "My sea of green," Dorothy liked to say. "When the wind makes the stalks ripple back and forth like so many waves, you can get seasick if you watch too long."

She was a widow of nearly 10 years. Her husband Jim was a Certified Public Accountant (CPA), who inherited an accounting business from his father. And the business---specializing in keeping books and financial records for farmers---had been very, very good to the Blair family.

The best way to describe Dorothy: almost always she was the smartest person in the room, but not aggressive or showy about it. She was friendly, knew almost everyone in Liberty by their first name, and, according to a few clients, was the real brains behind Jim's business that grew after he succeeded his father.

Civic affairs?

Again, quietly and with no fanfare, she picked her spots and they were meaningful. They included a stint as library board president, garden club membership, and ongoing League of Women Voters participation. She got things done, or, as one impressed ex-library board member once put it, "Makes no difference what it is, she walks the walk."

Though rarely offering opinions, people listened when she did talk. Speak softly and carry a big stick? You just *knew* she was intelligent. It was written all over her, whether or not she was wealthy and lived in that big, old Painted Lady.

It was in her eyes. They registered everything.

In many out-of-the-way communities like Liberty, you can find a Dorothy Blair. Sometimes you wondered: How in the world did they land here?

Not making a big to-do over it, her world also included migrants from South of the border who had transformed Liberty into a destination in the past few decades.

While old-timers griped and complained about "them Spics" and made "Taco and Tamale" jokes over morning coffee in local Lloyd's Café, she paid no attention. She was too busy smoothing the transition for everyone concerned.

As the library president, she made sure its collection of Spanish-language books grew exponentially. Innovative, basic English classes for the newcomers became part of regular library programming---for youth and adults. Area schoolteachers were paid as language tutors, and she made sure there was money in the budget for this.

With the League of Women Voters, Dorothy quietly spearheaded door-to-door voter registration drives targeting the new Spanish-speaking residents, rural and in Liberty. This took time, much effort, and friendly persuasion. Many of these newcomers---though legal---were reluctant to divulge personal information to government agencies. Who could blame them?

No breakdowns were officially quantified, but it was obvious a large percentage of the naturalized Hispanic voters did cast ballots. In time, they became amply represented on local boards and councils as well as in law enforcement ranks.

When Dorothy retired from the school board, Juanita Jiminez was elected to her seat. There was no opposition and, unknown to anybody, Dorothy quietly persuaded Juanita to run. The town's district seat on the county board was occupied by a fine fellow named Arturo Martinez.

Even her husband Jim, undoubtedly at Dorothy's urging, got involved before his premature passing.

As a school board member for two terms, he helped integrate complementary curriculum changes. New teachers with Hispanic backgrounds were hired. Soccer, always popular with Latinos, became an extracurricular activity. There was little public discussion over these moves during his tenure, which helped.

The Liberty school's curriculum now includes a prize-winning foreign language program specializing in Spanish. Taking advantage of the state's open registration policies, several dozen out-of-town students were enrolled by enlightened parents eager to have the best education for their kids.

Just as important: Jim, with the aid of an interpreter, conducted free, monthly workshops giving migrants advice on bookkeeping methods, tax laws, and banking procedures in their new country. They were very popular.

Behind Dorothy's back, there were whispers: Liberal? Socialist? Activist? Or just as bad, Democrat?

To Dorothy, who hated labels, her energies simply were logical. She didn't care what you called her. Not even her closest friends knew her real political leanings. "Life should be about doing the right things, no matter what it's labeled."

So, how did Dorothy end up in a backwater town in southern Indiana like Liberty? What's her story?

She was from Grosse Point Shores in Michigan, a toney Detroit suburb. Her father was an auto industry executive and she had an undergrad degree from Tufts, earning Magna Cum Laude honors in the process.

Her goal was to get a PhD in American Studies and teach in college. In the 1960s-70s, it was an exciting time for this academic ambition. The burgeoning, hybrid subject known as American Studies---an interdisciplinary field gathering history, sociology, political science, religion, psychology and other majors under one U.S. roof---was in its infancy.

Dorothy was perfectly poised to take the dive into doctoral work at the University of Michigan, a school that jumped into this new discipline with both feet. She quickly gained a master's degree (MA) there, and a future husband in Jim.

But the future turned out to be NOW.

They married earlier than planned when Jim's father died unexpectedly, meaning he took over the family business several years ahead of schedule at age 26. He had just squeezed in his MBA, followed by passing his Certified Public Accounting (CPA) examination on the initial try.

All of the above meant moving to Liberty. There would be no soft landing.

Like many women in that era, Dorothy's career ambitions went off the rails. She vowed to resurrect them somehow, three kids later, plus a posse of nine grandchildren---two with special needs, and it was goodbye PhD in American Studies.

Eventually, after becoming an empty nester, a polite query to Harrison College over a part-time teaching job in history was rebuffed. Very coldly, too. The dean, good old D. Nelson Brunk, even more imperious in his youth, simply sent her a rejection form letter---misspelling her name in the process. Her schooling---a MA from Michigan---did not meet his standards even for a part-time or adjunct role.

Dorothy rarely set foot in Harrison or on the college campus from that day on, the exceptions being an occasional theatre production or concert. Her local civic projects kept her busy and content. Furthermore, they were important and made a difference.

Then she met Mary.

Chapter 30

Hatching a Plan

Soon after we returned to Harrison from holiday vacation, Mary popped her plan. Faintly aware of her trips to Liberty and related academic migrant projects there, it came as a big, daring jolt.

An Underground Railroad? To Liberty?

"Here's the deal," she said. "During our break between semesters, I'm going to drive to Phoenix, get Maria at the Vincentian House, and bring her back to Liberty. She's going to move in with Dorothy Blair. God knows she's got the room."

Having been in the Blair home, I knew this to be true. Maria could hide there and never be found.

Furthermore, the stay would be indefinite. If her family got granted asylum, she would join them. If not, well, that bridge would be crossed later.

Is this legal? Can it jeopardize Maria's family? Will it compromise the college?

"Dunno, don't care," was the answer. "I do know things are getting kind of dicey in Phoenix. I never got to see Maria when I was there at Christmas break. Father Tony and I had a good talk about this, though, and he sees her almost every day. He said I.C.E. was nosing around a lot more lately. He suggested it might be a good idea to keep her on the move. Get her out of Arizona.

"He said it may be months before her family gets a decision on asylum. They're going to be stuck in detention until then. Now if it comes out another Lopez family member has been loose in the U.S. all this time, it won't help anybody."

Dorothy would play a big role. Gladly. She and Mary met midway in the first term and there was instant bonding.

Dorothy was thrilled finally to make a connection with an academic interested in border issues, particularly someone worried less about tenure and arcane issues. In her new young friend, she saw someone willing to roll up her sleeves and discover what's happening in the real world---right under her nose.

Her own children lived on the East and West Coasts. Their trips to visit mom were becoming fewer and fewer to Liberty. By all descriptions, Maria sounded like a bright girl who'd fill a void in Dorothy's daily life.

Mary was equally thrilled over the arrangement. Though she met understanding residents in the Harrison area, they either were college faculty who merely paid lip service to the migrant issues or were migrants themselves, shy with strangers.

No one matched Dorothy's resources and smarts. Furthermore, she, too, spoke fluent Spanish. It was not difficult for me to picture them collaborating on something as bold as their plan---most likely late one evening in Dorothy's beautiful home and deep into a second bottle of Chablis Blanc.

Maria wasn't just going to stay hidden away in the attic, like some pre-Civil War runaway slave traveling the Underground Railroad. Oh, no. Dorothy had a job for her, according to Mary.

"She's going to have her assist on a project Dorothy wants to do. She wants to compile a history of Latinos in Harrison

County. Not just some cursory treatment, but something definitive. Something starting with the first migrants to settle here---and why. This is the sort of basic, grassroots stuff that never gets done.

"This could be useful information in some circles, explaining objectively the dynamics of this migration to the Upper Midwest and not just the border states. Her intention is to clear away many of the generalities and stereotypes. I see this as something important. I'm going to help, too. Maria's bright, and we'll find some low-profile role in this for her."

My concern: In aiding Maria, were we breaking any laws? And: Would we be putting the college at risk?

"Not really," countered Mary. "Maria's got a high school diploma from Pima and Father Tony's got paperwork on her employment there. She's building a paper trail. She's 18 now.

"Dorothy's going to sign off on everything, anyway. It's her project. She even got a grant for this, so she plans to give Maria a small salary."

This meant the only connection on our end would be Mary driving Maria here from Phoenix in a car over semester break. Couldn't risk flying and its necessary IDs. And, hey, how was anyone here to know she wasn't legal? She'd keep a low profile, even among the local Latino community.

"You and Dorothy have it all figured, don't you?" was my counter. "There's only one thing you forgot."

"What's that?" asked Mary.

"Your car. It's such a clunker it probably can't make a round trip to Phoenix. You barely made it back last time you did a round trip to Phoenix."

"That's no problem."

Why?

"I plan on taking your car."

Oh.

Chapter 31

Course of Action

Independent Study.

It doesn't take long at Harrison, or any college, to discover that Independent Study can be a valuable format for teachers. It means you can go one-on-one with better students for an individualized, hands-on meaningful learning experience.

The professor lays out a course of action for the student outside the classroom to be completed during a term, which then leads to four hours of graded credit. Students at Harrison can do this twice within their major.

It's rare. Since Independent Study means extra work for professors, who get no course relief or extra pay, the faculty typically shy away. Exceptions generally occur when the student's project is research for the prof.

Me? I took it a step farther. I organized my Gang Of Four (Kate, Craig, Jing, Pete) to work on something decidedly out-of-the-box: Solve a killing. The 50th anniversary of the Marlene Scott murder simply was too good to pass up.

The "This date in history" item had generated much excitement in Harrison. A full-blown story, or series of stories, on the crime would surely create even more ripples.

My students agreed. In fact, it was as much their idea as mine. Several already hinted they wanted to delve deeper into the story after our little "This date in history" item in the local newspaper drew so much attention.

I was more than willing to create an Independent Course around the effort.

Our contributions to the Harrison *Hoosier-Record* had ended at the end of the first semester. I passed out a boatload of A's to my students, enough to warrant a call from the school registrar. She informed me it was rare that such a high percentage of a class received the top grade.

My response---"So?"--- threw her for a loop. Apparently, I was being closely monitored by my superiors. Dean Brunk? Krugendorff? Mary thought I was being paranoid, or, at the very least, a little too sensitive.

Unquestionably my advanced writing class in the first semester was a big hit. Even my Rotary mates took note of their contributions in the local newspaper. "Maybe we ought to start funneling some of our scholarship money to the college," said Fred Jackson, our president. Not sure if he simply was being flip, but I would remember that.

Newt's *Hoosier-Record* circulation did see gains. More important, it drew new advertisers. The Associated Press syndicate lifted several of our efforts, which was a rare happening for a weekly. His paper was not even part of the Associated Press (AP) network.

Newt threw a nice party for my class at semester's end. He was crushed when I first told him our work would come to an end at the term's close. I could only teach one advanced writing class per academic year. My scheduled writing class in the second semester would be an introductory format for new students---to be partnered with another literature class.

Several students expressed interest in continuing to write for the newspaper. They got quite a hoot from seeing their work in print as did, I'm sure, their parents when they saw clippings sent to them---or clicked on the paper's web site.

I encouraged everyone to keep at it, though I would be too busy to get involved. But ever since our "This Date in History" item on Marlene Scott's death, the idea kept percolating. Maybe we should re-visit this crime in some form or fashion.

Kate McDonald got the ball rolling.

"Professor Doyle," she said, "some of us---Jing, Pete, Craig---would like to do more on that Marlene Scott item. A cold case kind of thing. These shows are popular on TV. Why not in a newspaper?

"Not saying we'd solve it. Might be kind of fun to work at it, though. I have to tell you: I don't like to involve my Dad in anything, but he thought it was a great idea. He could be help-ful."

Considering her Dad, Nate (The Preacher) Stine, was head of southern Indiana's notorious Holy Roller motorcycle gang, this could be big. Some of his Rollers had to have experience in the, ahem, inner workings of the criminal mind.

Everything was starting to take shape. Be still my heart.

Newt certainly was hot to publish their effort. "Something like this could win some journalism prizes. Wouldn't hurt," he said.

There was an immediate hurdle, and I would have to act fast with the second semester approaching. I needed the OK from the college's Academic Affairs Committee to proceed.

Four students working on the same Independent Study project? All that extra work for a professor? That was sure to set off alarm bells among faculty on the committee---though my Gang of Four likely would've taken on the project without academic credit.

The tricky part would be crafting the proposal's wording. Academia had its own written language and phraseology, in-discernible as Hieroglyphics to the real world.

Never use two words when you can use four. Never use words with 2-3 syllables when 5-6 are available. Bloviate whenever possible. Leave the non-academic reader scratching his or her head. Make them plow through a fog of unfamiliar terms, phrases, and concepts sure to drive them to the dictionary and known only to a handful of higher ed peers.

Last year, I received a note from a colleague---who shall remain nameless---and he described a seminar thusly: "....*discussion of teaching processes involving photons emitted from energized tubes filled with gas, emitting different colors dependent on orbital jumps.*"

Here is how a communications course is described in our Harrison handbook:

> *Understanding through reading, reflecting, and dialogue of the functions of communication in organizational settings with particular emphasis on the self-defining aspects of the social contract between the individual and the organization in a changing world.*

And, difficult to picture many liberal arts students salivating over this Classic course offered at Harrison:

> *This course will look at several ancient Mediterranean and Near Eastern worlds, examining the many different methods we use to learn about the past and learning how a multitude of modern institutions and ideas are rooted in early antiquity from religious and philosophical ideologies to social institutions to artistic and architectural forms. We will also look at many ways in which we now use the past when we are talking about the present, for example in films and literature, in political and social debates. Our focus will be on the ancient Mediterranean and Near East, and we will examine material from the*

early Paleolithic era up into the Byzantine and Islamic eras. Throughout the course, you will be encouraged to reflect on connections between the distant past and our contemporary world, using the past to better understand the present, and using the present to make better sense of the past.

That's four sentences, 150 words. Is there an editor in the house?

In my mind, the pitch for the collective's Independent Project did not need to say more than this to the academic committee: *"We will work at solving a 50-year old, unsolved murder and write about it."*

If I stretched, maybe I could boost it to something like this: *"We will work in separate, but complementary roles, at solving a 50-year old, unsolved murder that will be the core content for a creative nonfiction writing project."*

While I went with Door No. 2, I added one sentence that I was sure would get a positive reaction. *"...There is a commitment for the final product to be published in a popular journal."*

Well, "popular journal" might have stretched it a bit. The reference was to the *Hoosier-Record*, but there was this going for me: Once committee members saw the word "published," the proposal surely would get rubber-stamp approval.

No matter the audience, nothing makes academicians pee in their pants quite like having work published. The proposal quickly passed. Was someone looking out for me. President Casey?

Chapter 32

A Gamble

The Harrison County Courthouse was built in 1907. The three-story, rectangular classic revival structure, constructed of granite and limestone and fronted by four columns, dominates the entire square in the center of the business district.

The lawn is shady. The trees are a mixture of pine, maple, and hickory. The grass is a bit trampled with scattered, dusty bald spots.

There are benches that get good use over the noon hour by county workers with sack lunches. In warm weather, and I am not making this up, old timers sit there whittling small blocks of wood with knives. Board games---generally checkers---occasionally break out.

The Norman Rockwell appearance is deceptive. Like many county courthouses in rural areas, closer inspection reveals the need of updating on the inside and a facelift on the outside. The elevator creaks, the wood floors sag, and it's 50-50 whether the building could pass a handicap accessibility inspection.

Surely a sign of expanding government, the interior has become crammed over the years with new offices, desks, computers, and file cabinets without planning. Just stick the new stuff somewhere. There is one court room.

The sheriff's office, including the jail, finally had to be re-located several blocks away in a newer---but drab---building that formerly was a grammar school. The jail was a re-purposed gymnasium. "Used to play basketball right here when I was a kid," Sheriff Lester Birnbaum liked to tell prisoners he led to a cell.

The Gang of Four---Jing, Pete, Craig and Kate---got familiar with the local public buildings as they pursued the Marlene Scott cold case, especially the offices of the sheriff, county attorney, and county clerk in addition to the office of the Harrison city police chief, Terry Cronin.

As word spread throughout faculty circles, it also became obvious a certain anatomical appendage of mine was flapping in the wind here. No question.

Once I read a piece that a two-time Pulitzer Prize winning Chicago Tribune reporter taught a university class totally dedicated to learning the identity of Deep Throat, the anonymous source who ended President Nixon's presidency in the 1970s.

Two years after their announcement of the leaker---a special White House counsel, they learned they had the wrong person. The leaker was a source in the FBI, whose identity was made public when he died.

If a Pulitzer winner got it wrong working with students at something with such a high profile, what chance did we have with a run-of-the-mill, backwoods murder that occurred 50 years ago?

No doubt this was a slippery slope. There was potential here for an embarrassing, career-damaging flop that could haunt me. I had a dean who thought I was a pain-in-the ass and faculty members who saw me as a dangerous threat to their way of tenured life. They would be primed and ready for my fall.

Pssst. Isn't he the *dummkopf* who thought he was Sherlock Holmes? Worse, I had a partner, Mary, who'd no doubt toss in an occasional jab. Already she'd referred to me a few times as James Bond. Hopefully I would not be Barney Fife.

Chapter 33

Low Profile

"In a word, emotional. And a little scary since it probably was illegal."

This is how Mary described her quick trip to Phoenix between semesters in late January to transport Maria Lopez to Liberty, where her new, safer home would be living and working with Dorothy Blair.

And the exit could not be too quick and careful. They needed to be inconspicuous. Arizona is in the "zone." A speeding, northbound car occupied by a Latino passenger with luggage and questionable papers would be a red flag to any law enforcement officer.

Mary had to observe speed limits all the way, a real challenge for her lead foot. She also needed to stay off highways at night to avoid further observation and isolation. This added an extra day to the journey. And there was this additional pressure: The car was registered in my name, which might be difficult to explain to a trooper.

"When we left, Maria had tears. I can tell you that. She hated to leave the Vincentian House and Father Tony, who hated to lose her, too," Mary said. "If this thing ever gets straightened out in a good way, she could always return there and have a job with him.

"The thought of moving so far away from her parents and (two) sisters---even if she didn't get to see them? It was a real downer, like she was abandoning them. She's had some real generic notes passed to her from her Dad, and now she won't even have that.

"Living in southern Indiana might as well be Greenland."

Hard to imagine the bonding that gets built within a family that travels for months, much of it on foot, from El Salvador to the U.S. And now, separated and incarcerated, they wait for a decision on their asylum status that could mean life or death.

At least Maria, with her Pima high school diploma and Vincentian employment papers, had a thin layer of protection. And living and working with Dorothy in what figured to be a habitable environment figured to lower the anxiety level a bit.

Distance may make the heart grow fonder, but, in this case, it provided an extra layer of security.

Dorothy's history project, charting and chronicling Latino settlement in and around Liberty, will be perfect as a diversion, added Mary. "She's bright. Seemed to have a good handle on it when we talked. She and Dorothy were having a pretty lively chat when I left.

"There was one immediate problem, though."

What?

"The weather, Flip. The snow and cold. It'll take her awhile to get accustomed to it. Her home in El Salvador is tropical, and then Phoenix. We stopped at a Wal-Mart on the way and I got her a winter coat, some sweaters, and boots."

Chapter 34

On the Road

Maria did not just go to sleep in her new home with Dorothy. It was more like a 12-hour coma. The long trip by automobile totally exhausted her.

The miles---nearly 2,000---ticked off methodically with Mary at the wheel. All the way Maria could not stop thinking, as they drove across Arizona, New Mexico, Colorado, Kansas, Missouri, Illinois and finally Indiana, about the immensity of the U.S.

There were tree-less prairies, snowcapped mountains, and farmland, interrupted by huge, neatly laid-out, large cities. Hundreds of miles got covered in mere hours, distances that had taken her family weeks to accumulate in their brutal trek from El Salvador to the U.S. border.

Albuquerque, Denver, Kansas City, St. Louis, Indianapolis.....places she had read about, but never expected to see in her lifetime. Great rivers such as the Missouri and Mississippi.

Well-paved highways with relentless huge, cargo-carrying trucks and adjoined by railroads with trains bearing even more cargo. Rest stops with conveniences such as clean, public toilets and vending machines that dispensed food and drink.

Her wonderment gave way to stabs of pain and guilt. Each mile into this new-found paradise took her farther from her beloved family, ensconced---for now---in what politely could be called an internment camp in the middle of the Arizona desert.

Would there be a Catholic church in her new home? She would need to find a priest somewhere like Father Tony for counsel. For now, her fate was completely in Mary's hands.

Maria barely remembered the late-night arrival to her new home. There was a warm welcome by Mrs. Blair, who, understanding her exhaustion and anxiety, quickly put her to bed.

"You get some sleep now, child," said Dorothy, after ushering her into an upstairs bedroom. "I've laid out some clothes that should work for now. There's a bathroom through that other door.

"We'll talk in the morning, but you sleep as long as you want."

Part IV: Treks

Chapter 35

A New Day

Maria woke with a start. Her room was filled with bright sunshine streaming through the big, bay windows that faced south. She was wide awake, which seemed weird considering the depth of her sleep just minutes earlier.

Her bedroom was huge. There was beautiful Victorian-style furniture throughout the room including a desk and chair set. The floor-length curtains, a light maroon, completed the décor. Also, the adjoining, spacious bathroom through a door had a huge tub.

This is the most beautiful room I ever slept in, Maria thought. Their home in El Salvador was nice, but it was a fading memory. The family's trek over the past year, from Central America to the Mexican border, diminished or completely purged many items in her memory bank.

Much of the family's northward odyssey was on foot when they could not find buses or hitch rides. More times than she cared to recall they slept in the open, huddling together to stay warm.

Their father was no Boy Scout. Outdoor camping never had been a family pursuit, but he was able to pick up extra money with day jobs and that meant they could rent rooms---rarely with clear, running water and indoor plumbing.

While they managed to dodge thugs and bandits who preyed on the weak, sleeping under the stars in isolated areas meant remaining alert for wild dogs, scorpions and snakes. She never would forget the nights her younger sisters, Sara and Daniela, huddled with their mother and her and cried themselves to sleep. Not out of sadness, but fear.

Often, they rode on the roofs of northward bound railroad cars. Occasionally they banded together with other border-bound migrants for protection. Friendships developed and acts of kindness occurred among the migrants built on a de-moralizing and dehumanizing shared experience no one would want to remember.

After crossing the border with help from a friend, the weeks they spent living in two tents in the Arizona desert near Ajo were almost like a vacation. Their subsequent setup in Phoenix in an apartment was the first accommodation in this entire adventure that resembled healthy normalcy.

Then Maria's thoughts were interrupted by a soft tap on her door. It was Dorothy.

"I hope you slept well," she said. "You needed it, you poor thing. This room---and the house---is going to be your new home until things get straightened out for you and your family.

"Let's go have some breakfast. You must be hungry. Coffee or tea? And then," she added with a smile, "we've got some work to do."

Chapter 36

The Plan

"And that's what we have in mind," concluded Dorothy, having just outlined the plan she and Mary had put together. "Now, let's get this table cleared and on our way. The first thing we do is get you some more warm clothes. Our Indiana winters are probably like nothing you've experienced."

Maria's response was totally unexpected.

Burying her face in her hands, she started to sob. Quietly, but with great tears creeping slowly down her cheeks.

"Why? Why?" she said, between catching her breath and the sobs.

Dorothy let her cry. And cry.

Finally, Maria, gaining composure, looked up and asked between sniffles: "Why are you doing this for me? You're an angel, but is this not something that could be trouble? For you? Why should I be so fortunate? Why?"

After a long pause, Dorothy answered: "Well, from my standpoint, I guess because it's the right thing to do. Almost that simple. For me, I cannot say it's something complicated. That I've been taken over by some great spiritual cause.

"A friend, Mary at the college, came to me in need of help. I guess it's that simple. I would have trouble understanding why anyone would not do something. And to be honest, you can be helpful to me, too."

Maria said, "But I feel so guilty. All these good things for me, and my family sits in a detention center."

Dorothy responded, "Mary told me the whole story. How you stayed overnight with a friend and missed getting caught in that sweep in Phoenix. I can't help with reuniting you with family. But you're 18 years old, soon to be 19. You need to keep moving on, building credentials through your experiences. No one can take those away.

"You are bright and have a future, whether it is in this country or some other place like Canada or wherever. The stronger you are the stronger you will be for your family wherever they go or what they do. From what I hear about your father, this is what he would want."

Indeed. Dorothy's plan---a project actually---did seem a good fit at this juncture. And, as they continued to converse, Dorothy became more and more impressed with Maria's understanding and knowledge. She would be perfect.

Before Maria came into the picture, Dorothy was the point person for a grant-supported study awarded the Harrison chapter of the League of Women Voters. The sum--- $25,000---was not stupendous, but nevertheless significant.

The money was coming from the U.S. Citizenship Foundation, a progressive, private D.C.-based think tank dedicated to targeted studies of contemporary American demographics, trends, and histories among ethnic groups in America. Their work provided objective, well-researched content that became basis for impactful decision making by outside groups and causes.

The topic: Latino Migration in The Upper Midwest.

Ostensibly, the grant was awarded to, and funneled through, the University of Michigan's American Studies department, which in turn, after a preliminary inspection, picked Liberty and Harrison County in Indiana as one of four areas (at $25,000 apiece) to be put under the microscope. The others: Muscatine County in Iowa, DeKalb County in Illinois, and Calhoun County in Michigan.

The local League of Women Voters chapter in Harrison became one of three groups with a pitch for the Harrison segment, but the only applicant in the county.

Mary, who would become a co-manager in the project, helped Dorothy load the formal proposal with academic verbiage. With the selectors being faculty members of a major university, there would be a need for inflated wording.

Undoubtedly, it also did not hurt that Dorothy was a University of Michigan alum and a healthy contributor over the years.

The goal was a complete study of Latinos in the county. A definitive, historic timeline for migration---its reasons, impacts (commercial, cultural, social), stereotypes and myths would be produced and published.

This would entail a close look at migrants themselves, highlighting in part their ethnicity, pre-U.S. statuses, and related anecdotes. There was much to be plumbed. Hundreds of interviews lay before them.

Juan, the guy who sells tacos from a food cart in Liberty? He had owned a restaurant in Veracruz.

Pablo, the Uber driver? He had a successful auto repair shop in Guatemala.

Consuela, the babysitter? She was a nurse in Mexico City.

Pedro, who works in the produce section of a grocery store? He raised, harvested, and sold bananas in Honduras to Wal-Mart.

That sort of thing.

There had been noticeable growth in the local Hispanic population in recent years. Forget stereotypes. Residents knew this was not some overnight phenomenon spurred by recent illegal crossings as some mis-represented. There were many migrant families in the county already into a third generation of residence in Liberty.

Still, the work ahead in and around Liberty would be tricky business, Dorothy pointed out. Lots of meetings to monitor, door knocking, and getting people to talk about something they were wary of being used against them or members of their community.

Little would they know, of course, that Maria was more vulnerable for deportation. The 10,000-pound elephant in the room was her status. She was illegal and, to protect her secret, only Flip, Mary, and Dorothy would know it.

I.C.E., in its aggressiveness, was known to have agents make occasional passes in Upper Midwest communities like Liberty and Harrison. There were standing rewards---bounties?---for tips that led to illegals.

"We don't want you to lead a life here as a recluse, hiding in the attic," said Dorothy. "That would be even more suspicious. We'll find some social outlets. I suspect Mary can help. She's around bright, young students you'll meet, but you must never, never let your guard down.

"You went to high school in Arizona and you came here to be part of a work-study program at the University of Michigan. That's as far as you go. As hard as it might be, you must invent something if and when it comes to talking about family."

Dorothy and Mary spoke fluent Spanish. Mary also could get by in Portuguese. The participating Harrison College students spoke passable Spanish, but they---like Maria---would not be point people in any interviews. They would know nothing of Maria's background. She would be regarded simply as a college student.

And Maria's job?

"You know what I mean when I say it'll be organic?" said Dorothy.

She answered, "Not really."

"It can change and, I suspect in your case, grow," said Dorothy. "For now, you'll be a record keeper. Help me gather materials, transcribe---and translate---interviews we record. Filing, too. That sort of thing."

In time, Maria would graduate to tasks that became more important. She would be assigned to pore through back copies of the Harrison *Hoosier-Record* and other journals looking for stories and tidbits related to the dynamics of the county's new residential wave.

This part would be daunting. Newt Ames was happy to give access to his files, but, with only a small percentage digitized, it would require maneuvering through mostly microfilmed newspapers.

Dorothy further explained that an hourly wage would be paid out of pocket to Maria. This meant avoiding Federal income tax paperwork. To Maria, the whole experience was becoming a real civics lesson, something she hoped would be helpful when---and if---her family was granted asylum

More layers of protection: Maria would be given business cards now at the printer's office describing her as affiliated with the University of Michigan. This would be one more form of identification to go with her Pima School diploma and Vincentian House employee paperwork.

"Hey, as someone from El Salvador, we'll appoint you as manager of our Central American Division," said Dorothy. "Maybe we should put that on your card."

Her own business card. Maria smiled. No more tears.

Part V: Journalism 101

Chapter 37

Briefed

At about the same time Maria got oriented, Newt and I, in our first meeting with the Gang of Four students, developed ground rules for our cold case adventure. We were in new territory here, sort of a Hardy Boys' mystery on steroids. We were writing a story, not making an arrest, 50 years after the crime. This had to be made clear. In all likelihood, shedding new light or producing a very readable rehash would be the result of our efforts. A trip down memory lane hopefully with new facts.

In our dreams, we would solve the mystery of Marlene Scott's murder.

Since this was for academic credit, the school was vulnerable if we overstepped. The students needed to be reminded---repeatedly---they were journalists, not the police or even private investigators. This was not Law & Order or Criminal Minds. No one should get hurt.

It got the students' attention that another adult was in the room for the initial planning session. When he was introduced as Guy Troyer, attorney for the *Hoosier-Record,* there was a look of surprise in their eyes. Yes, this project was to be taken seriously.

Guy went over ground rules, paying special emphasis on libel and defamation. Here's more of what was stressed:

1. The work could be quite boring. Forget what you see on TV. We weren't real "detectives" and had no authority.
2. We may not succeed, but we would produce an in-depth paper of our effort. Part, or all, of our writing would be used to craft a narrative to be published in the *Hoosier-Record.* Maybe a series.
3. Newt would be the middle person to handle direct contact with persons needed for, or facilitating, interviews. This included officials whose offices would be impacted in any formal capacity.
4. Most work will be digging through past investigative materials, fact-checking, and updating material with new, improved technological advances. Write down everything.
5. No one leaves the campus or courthouse to pursue the mystery without my permission or, for that matter in a case-by-case basis, without Newt accompanying them.
6. We would meet weekly with updates on assigned tasks.
7. We weren't to talk about this project with anyone outside our circle.
8. Nothing would get published until Guy Troyer said OK.

We asked, "Can you live with this?"

"Yes," came a resounding reply.

"One thing, though," inquired Craig. "Am I free to hack or you want me to stay legit?"

This time it was Newt and Guy with surprised looks, until they saw my smile. Craig's sense of humor was an acquired taste.

Newt said, "I think you know the answer. I don't want anything obtained illegally to be published in my newspaper.

That could be big trouble for me, for sure. It's also a good way to taint anything that could---if it comes to this---be used in court."

Our regular "staff" gatherings would be in the newspaper office, away from campus. First and foremost, we dedicated ourselves to learning as much about the case as possible from old newspaper clips and official records.

In the second meeting, we started outlining tasks. Guy also gave a short lecture on the Freedom of Information Act (FOIA), which he and Newt thought would be a useful, needed tool. This gave us access to public records.

Normally public officials are reluctant to open files to outsiders, let alone a bunch of college students. As it turned out, I had a secret weapon: Rotary. Every county and city official, including the clerk, was a fellow Rotarian willing to cooperate with my quiet requests.

"I think I'm learning more about America with this project than any class I've taken," said Jing. "It's too bad some others from China could not be part. I feel lucky."

Chapter 38

Just the Facts

Our first order of Independent Study business was to detail the crime, and we had to be careful here. Had a crime taken place? A body was found and, though plenty of circumstantial evidence indicated there was foul play, there was nothing legally proven to that effect. Forensics were not high science in those days.

What remained of Marlene's body was badly decomposed, bones scattered around fields apparently by four-legged animals. An autopsy produced no scars, knife cuts, or bullet penetrations. If a murder did occur, strangulation seemed the probable path. Or freezing to death. The area experienced record cold temps at the time.

We reviewed the bare facts:

Marlene left Harrison High School after her junior year, which was the only full year she lived in the town. She moved there from Indianapolis when her mother married her stepfather, Gene Brown.

Marlene returned to Indianapolis a year later, with her mother's approval, to take a job in an auto parts store, live in a studio apartment by herself, and work on a high school diploma through correspondence courses. The store was owned by a family friend, Tommy Edwards.

Marlene, who had several friends in Harrison, returned most weekends via Greyhound bus to stay with her mother and stepfather. On a bitter-cold Friday night in January, she was last seen in the 24-hour Monarch Café, a popular truck stop, on U.S. 231 on the town's edge.

She was with a young, adult male, eventually identified as Harrison College freshman Lawrence Charles Jr. A waitress recalled them leaving together, minutes later becoming remotely aware of raised voices and slamming car doors in the parking lot. She was too busy to pay attention.

On Saturday, after repeated calls went unanswered by Flo to Marlene's apartment to learn her daughter's weekend plans, Indianapolis police and Harrison County law enforcement agencies were alerted.

Since Marlene simply disappeared, and there were no signs of foul play, a serious search never was mounted. Where would you look? Few people in town really knew much about her. She lived only a year in Harrison. Her reputation among high school peers, colored by jealousy and gossip, was not good.

Maybe she borrowed a car and left for Hollywood to get "discovered." That had always been her dream, to become a movie star. Fifty years ago, the legends surrounding actresses getting "discovered" on the street or in drugstores were alive and well----and mostly bogus.

Tongues wagged. Classmates, who basically ran her out of town a year earlier with their bullying, let their imaginations run wild. They were quick to relay the most scandalous themes to anyone who'd listen.

"Marlene got knocked up and ran away to have her baby" was the most popular scenario. There were plenty more, all unflattering and unconfirmed. It was all speculation.

But three months and about a thousand rumors later, Marlene's remains were discovered on Burt Kohl's farm property. The prime suspects:

Nicholas Walker, 24, at the time director of the Harrison Community Theatre. Surprisingly, he gave Marlene the leading role in a production of "Bye Bye Birdie" and that turned a lot of heads. He was known to be close to her, helping Marlene find roles elsewhere in Indiana community theatre.

Walker moved on a year later, but that was not unusual. His theatre position was entry level with paltry pay. His predecessors' tenures were equally short, so seemingly there was nothing suspicious about the departure. At last word, he was semi-retired and teaching drama part-time in a small Ohio college.

Jimmy Bartow, a boyfriend and classmate from her year at Harrison high school, was a solid candidate. Their relationship was known to be strained, disintegrating with Marlene's move to Indianapolis. They had been seen arguing in the Monarch during her returns to town.

Jimmy graduated from high school several months following the body's discovery, enlisted in the U.S. Army and---almost to the day a year after her body was found---he was killed in combat at age 19 in Viet Nam.

Lawrence Charles Jr., was a Harrison College student and last person known to see Marlene alive sitting with her in the Monarch on what could've been the night she went missing. An arts' major, he had a small part in "Bye Bye Birdie" and befriended Marlene in the process.

Lawrence's parents---his father a big shot corporate attorney in California---pulled their son from college before the end of the semester when the body was found. By then, Junior had one in-conclusive, legally botched interview with the Indiana state law enforcement bureau.

Later, additional suspects surfaced with no results. In many local minds the best of the rest was Gene Brown, Marlene's stepfather who divorced Flo several years later. The grounds were physical abuse. "If he was a wife-beater," went the reasoning, "it wasn't a stretch for him to set sights on an attractive step-daughter."

Edwards, her employer in Indianapolis, also was questioned. He was the last person known to see her before she boarded a Greyhound bus for Harrison on the fateful night. Did they meet later in the evening? His alibis proved solid.

Our Gang of Four plan was to spend two weeks simply reviewing everything already documented or gathered as evidence. Look for loose ends that, through the course of a half-century, might take on a different meaning or yield new clues gleaned through new technology.

There'd be three stacks of data to attack: Official files, evidence already gathered, statements; read every account written for outside publications; and watch every obtainable, archived TV news coverage of Marlene Scott's murder including a lengthy, documentary produced for a cold case show on cable TV.

Kate was quick to note, "Wow! There's a lot here to cover. This will be work."

Added Pete, our only Gang of Four townie, "I'm going to know a lot more about my home before we're done. My folks used to talk about this, but mostly I think people in Harrison just wanted to move on. Now it sorta seems like ancient history."

Jing, of course, approached in typical fashion---as a sponge, eager to soak up everything "American." Apparently, our bootlegged TV crime shows were popular in China. Occasionally she wore a "CSI" t-shirt.

Craig?

Well, the sober expression on his face and furrowed brow told me all I needed to know. His wheels were turning and processing. Obviously, he saw this as a supreme test of his web skills---exactly as I hoped.

I did not need to worry about him. Or did I?

Mary was totally excited and supportive, though she did seem to weary a bit of my almost daily updates on our progress. Her limp "Yeah, Flip, got it" comments, with her eyes suddenly looking skyward, were the tipoffs.

Chapter 39

Dead or Alive?

The immediate question for my Gang of Four was obvious.

How did we handle interviews? Were students mature enough to do this? Would they ask the right questions? Worse: Would they be in harm's way if the interviewee did just happen to have this murder on their resume?

As their professor, my obligation was to not take risks. These kids had parents who loved them and trusted the school. From my limited experience, I knew anything could happen when talking to strangers from my days writing newspaper stories and, more telling, tending bar in Iowa City, a college town.

Kate dropped a bomb the first time we discussed the question of safety. "I could ask my Dad to join us," she said, quickly adding she was joking.

Considering her Dad was leader of the state's baddest motorcycle gang, The Holy Rollers, he would provide security. He was 6-foot-5 and 240 or so pounds of sculpted muscle. The image of him as a bodyguard was fun to picture, though.

Seriously, no person had to cooperate with us. We had no leverage. If the students did secure some promising time with a subject, it was decided Newt or me would conduct the interview with a student present. What we gathered and might use had to be scrupulously collected, recorded and sourced.

Then on the other hand, our angst could be moot.

Since it had been 50 years since Marlene's body got discovered in Burt Kohl's field, who could still be alive among prime suspects? The youngest would be in the late 60s. And if not the suspects, what about others---relatives, friends, law enforcement officials, lawyers, journalists--- we might meet connected directly to the crime?

Already we could cross off boyfriend Jimmy Bartow, killed in Vietnam. At last word Nicholas Walker, Marlene's theatre director, as a college professor in Ohio and presumably alive, should be easily traced.

The question marks were Lawrence Charles Jr., the Harrison College student whisked away to California by his parents, and Gene Brown, her abusive stepfather. If alive, no one had a clue of their whereabouts. This would be Craig's challenge.

Flo Brown, Marlene's mother, moved from Harrison shortly after the memorial service. Following a quick check with several obituary search sites on the web by Craig, we learned she died 20 years ago of cancer. She had been a heavy smoker.

Chapter 40

CSI

If there was one thing Lester "Bernie" Birnbaum, the county sheriff, considered his pride and joy, it was his evidence storage facility. Most big city police departments call it the Property Room. His was a repurposed and upgraded small barn on the Harrison city outskirts.

The facility---officially called the Harrison County Sheriff Crime Authentication Center---was fulfillment of a pledge by him in his first successful election to modernize crime fighting procedures in office.

Lester, never without an unlit cigar in his mouth, now was in his fifth four-year term. His initial win was a landslide against an incumbent who'd held the job when Marlene's body got discovered.

Lester's campaign slogan: "Hope For Tomorrow." Supporters of his opponent, 81-year old Nick Nichols, criticized Lester for being ageist. They conveniently overlooked, of course, that dozens of cases in Sheriff Nick's tenure got tossed for lack of evidence that had been misplaced or lost.

Lester won big and it did not hurt that when, at the start of their only joint appearance of the candidates a week before balloting, the incumbent tripped on the last step to the platform, did a face plant that broke his prominent nose, and required a doctor in the audience to step forward to stop the bleeding.

There was close to 10,000 square feet in The Center taken up by filing cabinets, computers, lockers, closets, freezers and a laboratory. The heating and cooling systems were state-of-the-art, installed by a contractor imported from McLean, Va.

The modernized premises were so good the F.B.I. regional office in Evansville occasionally stored items there on a temporary basis. There was plenty of room. The county had its share of crime, but rarely required an abundance of property to be stored.

The items related to the Marlene Scott case remained the single, largest collection. They included many personal items---diary, magazines, phone bills, clothing---gathered from her Indy apartment and Harrison bedroom.

Zach Campbell, a young, ambitious deputy in the sheriff's office, managed the facility. Truth be told, the pace was slow and that was fine with him. This allowed Zach time to read journals and stay abreast of developments in law enforcement. In another year or so, he hoped to enter law school.

Lester, from one Rotarian to another, was quick to grant access to my Gang of Four "as long as nothing left the building and they put it back where they found it." They also were permitted to take pictures of items. He gave Zach instructions to keep a close eye on things.

The sheriff's office was no closer to solving the crime than it was 50 years ago, but Lester was open to anything. After all, he didn't want to be criticized for failing to close the case. Her death occurred on his predecessor's watch and the investigation was badly botched before handed over to Lester.

The process of sifting through Marlene's items was eerie for Jing and Kate, who got the assignment. After days spent reading about her life, they now were touching her clothes and other personal items.

They itemized everything, comparing their notes with what law enforcement officials recorded 50 years ago when the evidence was first assembled. One thing slipped through the cracks though---Marlene's yearbook, The Eagle---from her junior, and only, year at Harrison High School.

Interestingly, there was no record of it on the inventory list. How could that be?

The best guess, forwarded by Zach, an interested observer, was that it was obtained from Flo at some point after the early crush to collect evidence.

"Flo probably hung onto it for sentimental reasons," he said. "Hid it from the officers, maybe. Marlene was her only child, don't forget. She needed some attachment, something to treasure."

When it finally did land at the sheriff's office, however that did actually occur, it simply got tossed in the property room and never properly recorded. "Things got pretty sloppy under Sheriff Nichols toward the end of his run," said Zach.

Kate and Jing were pumped. Had they made an important discovery? A game-changer? It was just a high school yearbook, but until now not part of the chain of evidence.

Zach was excited, too. After he and Kate explained the high school yearbook concept to Jing, the three of them thumbed through the 80-page publication. They paid particular attention to the signatures and notes written to Marlene by classmates.

Innocuous stuff, really. "Have a great summer!" "Enjoy the break." "We had a ball!" "We're going to be seniors. Can you believe it?"

Kate and Jing weren't quite sure what to do with their find. Since it wasn't to leave the The Center, Zach, totally into it now, had an idea: Photograph all Eagle pages with personalized writing as well as those with class pictures and additional pages with shots of Marlene.

Little could they realize then the surprising lead to the crime this would produce.

Chapter 41

Turkey Time

Dorothy, with Maria in lockstep, attacked her grant-supported project full bore.

First, she reduced everything to a simple, informal title and acronym: Patterns in Population, or PIP.

This was a noticeable simplification from the University of Michigan's title for the project---"Migrants, Borders, and National Security Issues: Case Studies, Settlement Experiences, to Guide U.S. Immigration Policy."

"We use mine, PIP, for now gathering our material and doing our local research," she said. "It might seem a little simple, but I want to be generic, avoid buzz-words and academic foofoo no one understands. We'll make it warm and fuzzy for people we interview. Non-threatening."

Maria thought: If nothing else, I am getting some good lessons in the English language. This is great.

Dorothy added, "We don't want to seem at all confrontational, or make it sound like we're singling out anyone when we do interviews. We're not lying or using false pretenses, just being careful. We need people to be forthcoming about their roots."

The starting point, or launching pad, for the influx of Latinos to Liberty and the county did not seem to be in doubt. This was the purchase in 1950 of a local, moderately successful tomato canning company by a regional turkey processing firm.

The re-purposed facility became Thomas Turkeys, or simply Tom's Turkeys, naturally, by everyone but those in the corporate board room. Business was good and grew. A shift foreman, tasked with building a bigger workforce to meet the seasonal growth, traveled one winter to Brownsville in Texas---where he had relatives---to recruit workers.

Though salaries mostly were minimum wage with minimal benefits, the situation was appealing enough to lure a steady stream of Mexican-American employees from Texas.

The jobs were subject to periodic layoffs without much notice, but there was one unpredictable, sure-fire attraction that came with employment: air conditioning. Well, not AC as we know it today.

Those lucky enough to have jobs inside the plant, which was 70 per cent of the employees, were kept cool by the steady opening and shutting of freezer doors. The temperatures indoors rarely left the 70s, summer or winter.

This was thanks to one clever assembly line worker. He figured a way to channel escaping freezer room air throughout the building with strategic opening and closing of doors, windows, and shafts.

"That person was a hero. You ever been to Brownsville, you'd know why," one transplant explained to Dorothy, who promptly made a note to explore weather as a contributing migratory factor.

The Liberty turkey plant went through several, early owners. The location in southern Indiana was compatible for the business, decidedly rural but close to large markets. U.S. highway 231 connecting the town to the outside world saw a steady stream of Thomas Turkey trucks headed in each direction to Indianapolis and Louisville.

Then fifty years ago---late 1960s-early 70s---new money was pumped into the business. A giant, more modern plant was built, a huge garage to house the growing truck fleet followed, and buildings were added on the company's three farms in the county.

The construction work took nearly a year and engaged almost as many workers---luring more migrants---as the turkey processing business itself.

"Liberty was a boom town then before I got here," said Dorothy. "From what I heard a bunch of residents converted their homes to boarding houses. There were 2-3 more taverns, too. So, it got pretty wild on weekends. The town started to gain a reputation."

Liberty had barely a thousand residents in 1950. This more than doubled by 1960, nearing 3,000 and hopping over two other towns to make it No. 2 in population in the county.

The numbers seem modest, but not for the rural Midwest. Over the years it grew to approximately 5,000 residents, where it has held steady through the last two censuses--- making it one of the few, non-metropolitan towns in Indiana to not lose residents.

"Many of those turkey jobs, and others they created outside the Thomas operation, got filled by Latinos," said Dorothy. "We'll get to them with our research. There's a lot of official, corporate histories on the big picture with the turkey people. We can rely on them for more context when the time comes."

There were there other turfs Dorothy was anxious to plumb in her PIP plan: The Harrison County school superintendents' records for Latino impact on enrollments, curriculum, and extracurricular activities; churches, in particular Immaculate Conception in Harrison, the county's only Catholic church;

and the county historical society, which had newspapers and other, more personal data on file.

Though most of Liberty's migrant population morphed into almost every facet of daily life, there were traditional white-only social and cultural organizations that resisted mixing. Rotary was not a resister.

But, at the same time, there were newer Latino-only groups formed that stuck to themselves in Liberty and less so Harrison. The most prestigious was the Cinco de Mayo Club, sort of a country club without a golf course. There also was a community Mariachi Band that performed in local festivals.

Dorothy---again due to her library board years---also knew of two Spanish-language book clubs, in addition to scattered, more informal knitting, card, and cooking clubs. There also was an exclusively Latino Cub Scout Pack, but, in the early years, nothing for girls.

"I want to hit everything, sit in on meetings, the works, and pick up all sorts of tidbits," said Dorothy. "We don't have to have a finished product done until the end of summer. That gives us the upcoming Cinco de Mayo festivities, too."

As they progressed, they would interview Latinos from a cross-section of backgrounds. "You can be a big help," Dorothy told Maria. "Already you've seen and experienced a lot that should help you relate. More than most."

Chapter 42

Lay of the Land

Maria's first, real day "on the job" helping Dorothy was, fair to say, surprisingly delightful. Not at all what she expected.

On a grand, overview tour of the county and its communities, all targets for the study, she felt herself de-compress with every outstretched Latino or Gringo hand warmly welcoming her. At this rate, her past year's nightmarish existence could be reduced to smaller, occasional bad dreams.

Dorothy's intention was to build a comfort zone for Maria, make her more relaxed, less paranoid. A wider circle of new friends and contacts could only help. Her disposition---smart, quick, funny, attentive, respectful---was perfect for their project, much of which was simple interaction with area residents.

No one asked for papers. The closest it came was this: A handsome 20-something bachelor in the local police department, obviously a bit smitten with Dorothy's Spanish-speaking, comely friend, asked for her telephone number.

"You've got to feel comfortable," said Dorothy. "Fortunately, you're among people mostly who won't be asking much about your background. They'll take you for what they see in front of them. It's enough you're from El Salvador and associated with the University of Michigan.

"The rest? I doubt anyone will ask. The Americans are too polite, especially in the Midwest. And Latinos certainly don't want to get that conversation started."

On the surface, Liberty's Latino influence was easily discernible.

The Main street was dotted with three Mexican restaurants, two bars, taco stand (closed in the winter), three hair salons, grocery store, coffee shop and dental and law offices. Surnames on all the signs indicated south of the border roots---Lopez, Fernandez, Herrera, Diaz, Castro, Molina, Ortega.

The grocery store offered mangos, cactus leaves, in-store made tortillas, imported candies, masa, and tamales and enchiladas in the deli. Every business they visited, even those without Latino ownership, there seemed to be a Spanish-speaking employee.

To Maria, the confidence of those she met, relieved of not looking over their shoulders and making heads-up eye contact, was palpable. Would it be contagious?

Maria purchased a spiral notebook on one stop, started adding names, businesses and a few notes as they made the rounds. She was an excellent listener. In turn, Dorothy encouraged Maria to give everyone she met her new business card. An inside joke between them, the recipients nevertheless always seemed impressed, especially when they read: "Central America Division, manager."

"We are just skimming the surface here," said Dorothy. "There are many Latinos working at the turkey operations. Those people we'll interview in homes. But there are many others, too. For one thing, maybe 20 or so work at Harrison College, everything from janitors to administrative assistants.

Next to the turkey jobs and those in government, the college is probably the county's biggest employer."

Dorothy concluded their tour in nearby Harrison, where top on the list was showing Maria the insides of the county courthouse. She introduced her to a Liberty resident, Olivia Martinez, manager in the clerk's office.

"Olivia's an old friend," said Dorothy. "At some point, you may be digging through files here. Just come to her. She'll set things up for you. Right, Olivia?" They laughed.

Slowly and surely, Maria was beginning to believe Dorothy had a never-ending pipeline of local Latino and Hispanic friends. She thought: How could I be this fortunate? In Indiana?

At one point, the tour took them to the county sheriff's office, where they met two Mexican-American deputy sheriffs. At first Maria hesitated, a natural reflex considering anyone wearing a badge could mean a ticket to deportation or worse. Dorothy insisted they meet.

They drove around Harrison College, where its historic, landmarked buildings created a postcard appearance even in February. They parked the car, strolled the campus, and stopped at Mary and Flip's offices, only to learn they were conducting classes. Too bad.

They visited the Grabbe Library, perusing a periodical section that included familiar Central American publications. Also, there was a small collection of Spanish-language novels. Maria, thanks to Dorothy's library card, checked out two books.

"This school makes me homesick," she told Dorothy. "My father was a college professor. He would take me to his office, and I would sit there for hours reading while he conducted classes. Sometimes he would let me sit in his classrooms while he taught, too."

There was one, last surprise remaining for Maria on the tour's Harrison leg. It was unplanned.

When Dorothy stopped to do a little grocery shopping, Maria noticed the local Catholic Church---Immaculate Conception---just a block away. "While you shop, do you mind if I go visit it for a few minutes?"---a request quickly agreed to by Dorothy, who said she would pick her up when she finished in the store.

Not seeing her in front of the church a half-hour later, Dorothy parked, went inside, and spotted Maria deep in conversation with a young priest in the nave's front row.

"Father Campanelli," said Maria on the ride back to Liberty. "He was so kind. He explained about some of the church activities. And there is a Spanish-language Mass."

As a Presbyterian, Dorothy still knew one thing for sure about Immaculate Conception. Like most Catholic churches, it would have good records. Tracing the growth of Latino membership could produce valuable data. This would be a good portal for Maria.

And there was a bonus that undoubtedly would help her get good access.

"Father Campanelli is Vincentian," added Maria. "That is the same order that runs the homeless shelter where I worked and lived in Phoenix. There it was Father Tony. There are only a few hundred Vincentian priests in America.

"This is a very good sign."

Chapter 43

A Love Story

Maria most enjoyed the home visits she and Dorothy made, interviewing fellow Latinos, hearing their stories, and plumbing details to become part of the county's official history.

On one hand, it made her sad to be with families in these comfortable settings. Her family was locked up in the middle of the Arizona desert. She had not seen them, or had direct communication, going on four months.

On the other hand, she was inspired listening to the challenges courageously met by the interviewees. Could it be true, Maria wondered, that her new home in the Midwest was some sort of Utopia? That Latinos and Hispanics, community builders at heart, could find a slice of the American Dream so far north of the border? In a remote, rural and small farm town in southern Indiana?

Not completely. Dorothy warned that old biases die hard. "It's the older generations here, people resentful 'outsiders' took jobs, crashed the local culture, speak a different language. They see a threat. Their thinking isn't logical, of course. The good news the old die-hards are doing just that, dying."

In fact, one visit---with Diego and Marianne Escobar---gave both Maria and Dorothy pause. Though not farmers, the Escobar's rented home was a farmhouse surrounded by a large acreage owned by outside investors and cultivated by a renter.

The Escobars were in their 70s. Marianne, a retired schoolteacher, was a Harrison County native of Scotch-Irish descent with three generations invested in Indiana. She met Diego at Immaculate Conception. At the time, he was close to returning to his former home in Orizaba near Veracruz in Mexico. His full head of now silver hair, neatly styled for the interview, and large, silver streaked mustache gave him a distinguished look.

"Marianne changed everything for me," he said, a quick, wide smile brightening his face, lifting his otherwise droopy mustache.

Diego, a little over 50 years ago, connected with a large U.S. contractor, Butte Construction, on a recruiting tour it conducted for non-union laborers in Mexico. The pay was minimal, but acceptance meant a free trip to America and possession of a valuable, but temporary, work permit. They were easier to obtain in the 1960s.

"Butte was very big, with many sites," he said. "I worked in Illinois, Iowa, and other places before coming to Harrison. Here, we built the new turkey plant for Thomas."

Here, also, were problems.

By the time he reached Harrison, many co-workers from Mexico had returned home. Others were scattered to different Butte construction projects.

His then-weak English language proficiency became a bigger burden.

"I got all the bad jobs, things that I did on earlier work," he said. "I was able to do more skillful things. No one cared. They just assigned very heavy, dangerous jobs to me. I could not make myself understood."

Making conditions worse was a foreman, a bigoted bully, Ben Cooper, who relished tormenting "Dago" as he referred to Diego. By then, he was the only worker left imported from Mexico and working in Harrison.

Cooper's apparent goal was to drive "the little Beaner" back to Mexico, too. "We got enough Spics in this country," he'd tell others behind Diego's back---but loud enough for him to hear, too. "He can't even speak English good."

Diego added, "He was very bad man. There were rumors he had committed crimes. He beat up people. Butte did not seem to care about this. He got the jobs done on time."

Diego said he made up his mind to quit and return to Mexico.

"I decided to do it on a Monday, maybe 50 years or so ago. The winter was here. It was very cold. That made my decision easier. When I came to work that day to quit, this man Ben did not show up for work. He never came back. No one really knew where he was. I did not care. I stayed. I felt like a free man. Butte gave me more important jobs."

Good for me, too, Marianne added.

Diego finished the Thomas project with Butte. Because he had met Marianne, his future wife by then, he remained in Harrison and got hired by Thomas to assist the building's operations chief. Eventually, he became a foreman.

"They knew I was very familiar with the new buildings," he said. "Also, with Marianne's help, I took some courses that helped me advance. My English improved with her help."

Chapter 44

Familiar Autograph

Not long after my Harrison College students' pursuit of Marlene Scott's death got launched, a discovery was made that was stunning, something so unexpected that it gave me pause whether we should drop this entire Independent Study exercise.

In looking at notes and photos gathered by Jing and Kate from "The Eagle" yearbook late one night in my apartment, these few handwritten words touched off alarm bells:

"Always, Gil M."

Gil M. Gil who? Surely not Gil Munson, who I knew to be a Harrison native. Thumbing through class pictures, I found him. Yep. Gil Munson, a member of the HHS senior class when Marlene was a junior. More hair and darker, but no question the same person.

Surely there were other Gil's in the high school then. I looked at the index. Nope, not one. Next, a cross-check of the handwriting, though not conclusive, bore resemblances to a note he once passed to me in a Rotary meeting.

It could be meaningless that he signed the yearbook--- there were several dozen more signatures, but "Always"? That was curious. What was their relationship? This one word hinted of something more than casual between two teenagers.

Gil and Marlene? No, no, no, no. Don't go there. Or should I?

Plowing forward: Gil's name never came up anywhere else in the research into Marlene Scott's death done by my students. Still, I recalled that furrowed brow of his several months ago when my students' "This date in history" item about Marlene first ran in the *Hoosier-Record*.

In fact, he initiated the subject. He seemed uncharacteristically concerned. A sort of dark cloud passed over his face. What were his words..... "think twice"..."bad feelings," "damaged reputations," "old grudges."

Gil was a Harrison icon, both in the community and campus.

Past president of the college's trustees, champion of President Casey, generous donor, and, in addition to former Rotary chapter head, someone who had been on almost every municipal board or commission in the county and town. He personally befriended me early after I was hired, paving the way for my involvement on different fronts.

Ruin a reputation? Who were we? A bunch of college people on an academic exercise. Was it our obligation to cast doubt on him?

"Always, Gil M." did require some explanation. A quick Google search showed no statute of limitations on murder in Indiana. Whoa, slow down.

What to do? This could blow up in my face. For now, this would remain between Mary and me. Not even Newt would be told of a possible connection, and certainly I would not brief my students. This had disaster written all over it.

Chapter 45

Signing Off

Mary and I slept on it. In the morning over coffee, we agreed: This "Always, Gil M." tidbit needed to be broached with him. There was a chance it could lead to something important besides Gil.

The fallout could be bad, perhaps me losing my job, and for now I'd keep Newt and the students out of it. At the very least, I could say to Gil any input for our final project paper would be appreciated. He lived in Harrison through the entire drama, then and now. We'd wait for his insights. He could take it in any direction.

Then, off-handedly, I'd bring up that we had her copy of "The Eagle" and noticed he was a grade ahead of her. Also, that he signed her yearbook. Then, I'd wait for the response. I was prepared to totally ignore he wrote anything in the publication.

My rare call to his home 20 minutes later undoubtedly was a flag-waving of some sort to him. When I finished the first half of my song-and-dance, there was total silence at his end.

The clock ticked, and ticked, and ticked.

Finally, I broke the silence. I mentioned a new piece of evidence---Marlene's copy of "The Eagle"---had turned up after

50 years. Might be fun to go through it with him, see if it could spark any memories that might help us flesh out our re-search.

Did he guess that I'd seen his signature? The silence wasn't long this time.

In a voice that was terse, "Can you meet me at 4 this after-noon? Say at the Monarch?"

No problem. I hoped. A lot could be at stake.

Chapter 46

New Development

I arrived at the Monarch 10 minutes early.

Gil, stirring coffee, was waiting. His smile was thin, not too convincing. There were few preliminaries.

"So, you found Marlene's Eagle, eh?" he said. "That should've been interesting. I'm in there somewhere. Signed it, too. I guess I had a bit of a crush. She was only in school here a year, but she covered a lot of ground. The girls in school mostly hated her. Saw her as some kind of threat, I guess."

What was she like?

"Pretty. Smart, but a bit different, and for sure ambitious. Just ask me. I dated her a few times, though no one really knew it. That's the way we both wanted it. I already had a commitment. She didn't want one. I was a senior, a year ahead. She was playing the field. Poor Jimmy Bartow. He was overmatched as her boyfriend. He had no clue, then dies in Vietnam."

How did it end for you?

Gil answered, "Kind of ugly, I guess. We sort of had an informal date set that last Friday night after she got back in town from Indy. I called her house a bunch of times. No answer. No voice mails either in those days.

"So, I called a buddy. After a few beers in my pickup, we stopped at the Monarch. I can point to our parking spot from where we're sitting now. We were getting ready to come in the door when I spotted her through a window. She was in a booth with some twerpy looking guy I figured for a local college student.

"I decided we'd wait outside. Then I could ask her there why she stood me up. I wasn't mad or anything, and I don't have a temper. I just wanted to know if we were done. Hell, we never really got our relationship going. Nothing else. Wouldn't have bothered me either way. The parking lot seemed like a better place to have that discussion than inside, in front of an audience."

That was the last night before she disappeared, and you never got called by authorities to give an account?

"No. I figured I would and never did. The sheriff then, Nick, wasn't exactly Sherlock Holmes. I waited for days. Wasn't going to raise my hand, though. Since I never set foot in the Monarch that night, no one really knew I was there except my buddy, John. We sort of made a promise to each other to stay mum. That's John Martin. He lives in Evansville. He can corroborate everything.

"When we did connect outside in the parking lot, we got a little noisy, raised our voices. That college kid knew he was in the middle of something. He just got in his car and drove away and left her. We offered Marlene a ride to her folks' place. She didn't want to get in the car. Stomped off."

Gil never wasted words in the few years we'd known each other. Now he was on a roll, becoming relaxed as he unloaded.

"Gil, I'm your friend here. I'm not the police and I'm not trying to trap anybody. But did you give any thought to volunteering to cops what took place?"

"Truthfully, not really. You've got to understand what it was like then. A murder in Harrison? This was poison. Anyone connected to it---in any way---could see their reputation ru-ined. Besides, between you and me, I had another reason."

What?

"Barbara, my future wife. She and I were an item almost from our first day in high school. The All-American couple. We were hot and heavy. She would've killed me if she knew I had anything to do behind her back with Marlene and her rep-utation. I could kiss Barbara goodbye.

"Look," he continued. "I'm not sure where you're going with this project. I don't know exactly what the students and you are doing. I do appreciate you coming to me like this. Feel free to use anything I said, though I'd be mighty pleased if my name was left out. It's up to you.

"I admire what you're doing at the college. I trust your judgement. You're a great hire for the school. Been a long time since I could say that about a Harrison professor. You've given our stagnant faculty a booster shot.

"If you see fit to use what I said and my name, so be it."

And Barbara?

"She knows everything. When I first saw that item a few months ago in the *Hoosier-Record*, I figured you might be coming my way. We talked."

And?

"Really, she could care less at this point. We're too old to get bothered. In fact, she regrets being so mean at the time to Marlene along with the others."

Chapter 47

Alibi Time

Mary could hardly wait for me to get back to my apartment. "How did it go with Gil?"

Excellent. Two birds with one stone.

"Gil explained to me about his signature in Marlene's yearbook," I answered. "Turns out they'd been an item, briefly---unknown to others---in high school. His *'Always'* was just a case of teenaged hormones."

She wondered, "Doesn't that mean something? Couldn't he be a suspect then? His name never gets mentioned as one."

I said this is where it got interesting. "Turns out he was with Marlene briefly at the Monarch the night she disappeared. He was with a friend, male, and she had stood him up. She was with that Lawrence Charles, the college student who's on our list as a prime suspect.

"They bumped into each other in the parking lot after Marlene and the Charles kid were leaving the restaurant. So, no one saw him there. They had a bit of an argument, Gil said, and the college student apparently got scared. Drove off and left her.

"That would seem to eliminate the college kid as a killer. Then Marlene refused a ride with Gil and his buddy. Stomped off, too. After that, who knows. That's the mystery's real starting point.

"If he needed to, Gil could confirm everything at his end. His buddy that night is alive and well in Evansville. He witnessed everything. Gil even gave me his contact info.

"So now my students have new information to add to the mystery, and this: Apparently, we can cross two suspects off the list. Gil, who never really was one, and Charles, who lawyered up and was yanked from school---and is out West somewhere. If he's still alive.

"This narrows things down."

"Or," countered Mary, "opens them up to new possibilities."

Chapter 48

Take a Letter

On an unusually crisp, late February day, Maria sat in the Harrison County Courthouse kitchenette eating a sack lunch before anxiously opening the envelope. A few, braver souls who worked in the building, had ignored temperatures in the 40s and took portable meals outdoors to be in the bright sunshine.

Maria still could not get used to winter weather in the Midwest, but that was not why she was indoors now. The envelope carried a message inside written by Father Tony at the Vincentian House in Phoenix. It had been sent to Dorothy, as pre-arranged by Mary.

Maria wanted to be alone while she read. The content was brief and cryptic. Mary, Maria and Father Tony had worked out generic wording, a sort of code, in case the mail got read by I.C.E.

Maria needed a few minutes to work through the content, then she broke into a smile---her first genuine, deep and heartfelt smile since arriving in Indiana. The message said her family was well and that her sisters, Sara and Daniela, were keeping up their academics.

Her father, Roberto, a history professor in El Salvador, and other detainees who were teachers, had organized classes for youths also incarcerated in the Arizona camp. Books were supplied by several U.S. charities sympathetic to their plight. "There is no shortage of reading material," said Father Tony.

The best news, the message said, was that a decision on the Lopez family status seemed close at hand. Several families in the camp had been sent back to their native countries, but her father thought this might be a good sign that his family's status was taking longer.

The reasoning, according to Father Tony, was "more time was needed to find where Roberto's family can be placed in the U.S."

This brought a big smile from Maria, who, a second later, almost jumped off her chair when a hand from behind was placed suddenly on her shoulder.

"Hey, how you doing? Maria, right? You're here today, too?" Pete Gray greeted her with a smile and a friendly nod.

Probably it was inevitable that some of the Harrison College students on the 50-year murder cold case would run into either Dorothy or Maria, or both, in their PIP efforts. They already had been informally brought together by Mary to air their projects and quests to each other.

Who knew? They might discover common ground.

These introductions were Maria's first, real interactions with American students. Dorothy, old enough to be her grandmother, understood that socialization with others the same age should boost her morale.

She certainly had caught Pete's eye in those meets. Hard not to with her trim figure, dusky skin, jet black hair, and brown eyes that lit up the room with her smiles.

"Well, Dorothy thinks it would be good to go to the county clerk's office and look a little deeper into past census figures," said Maria, quietly tucking away Father Tony's letter in her purse. "She wants me to look and see if there is more than what was posted on the government web sites."

Pete said, "That's a good idea. Dorothy really seems to know what she's doing. She's cool."

Maria would like to have said cooler than you'll ever know. She asked about his mission.

"Well, Flip, I mean Professor Doyle and Mister Ames wanted me to check on exactly when the county went digital," he said. "Then, we'll use that date to see if anything got left out in digitizing data related to the case. Kind of a needle in a haystack. But who knows?"

Needle in a haystack? Pete, seeing the look on Maria's face, then explained what he meant by the phrase.

"Ah," she said. "Do you speak Spanish? No? Well, here is a phrase for your task: 'Echar lena al fuego.' You are going to raise the intensity."

"Something like that, yeah," he answered. Which drew laughs from both.

Pete, taking a chair, joined Maria as she finished her lunch. There definitely was chemistry, though Maria was careful to steer away from being detailed about her family. Also, to avoid specifics about her supposed University of Michigan connection.

From a distance, anyone paying attention saw two young adults locked in friendly conversation. Maybe two generations ago, this---a darker-skinned Latino with a local Gringo---might have drawn more attention. Not now.

Though they kept their chatter mostly about the respective projects, even that was liberating for Maria. She could not remember the last time talking with such a confident person so close in age. Maybe Pima School in Phoenix.

Pete was enthralled, for sure. To him, Maria was the most exotic girl he'd ever met---and never mind how few personal details she divulged. As a townie, she made him aware of just how little he understood of the world outside southern Indiana.

And what a day for Maria. First, the note from her father. Now this.

As they exchanged updates on their projects, it was obvious to Maria and Pete they would cross paths again on their journeys. The Gang of Four's efforts---in detailing events that occurred 50 years ago---could easily turn up facts helpful to Dorothy's mission as well.

But whoever would think the study of Latino migration to the county could be helpful in solving a 50-year old cold case?

Chapter 49

The Chase

The next Gang of Four, plus Newt, meeting was on a week-night in the back room of the *Hoosier-Record*. The location was becoming headquarters for us, cozy, but large enough for a table to gather around and a coffee maker---for me---in one corner, a small fridge in another.

We also had our own file cabinet, but most findings got stored in our computers with a password (*Marlene50*) known only to us. Craig protested this was too simple and got over-ruled.

The meeting room was a morale booster, reinforcing for my students that they were part of something special, something above and beyond their peers playing cards in dormitories. They had one foot on the campus, but the other was squarely in a real-life drama emanating from this off-campus room.

The stakes seemed high, which, of course, was exactly the case. We had a private clubhouse, and this was an important gathering.

Every time I visited the space thinking I'd be alone, I'd also discover Kate, Jing, Pete, or Craig there on their own, working on Independent Study or another course. This was extremely satisfying.

Everyone had a key to the private, side alley entrance to the newspaper. It would be hard to give up this space at semester's end.

Now, on this mid-point in the term, we started to plan a stretch run.

Beforehand, I consulted Newt on my update with Gil without giving away his identity. As a journalist, he respected my suggestion: We should use what I was told, spread what I learned in appropriate places throughout our report, and identify him, if needed at all, as an anonymous source.

Newt was on board. He said he did it all the time when he worked for larger newspapers in Louisville and elsewhere. It was legitimate. We were becoming journalists whether we liked it or not.

Up to now, the students' efforts were to confirm details from investigations by Harrison city police, county sheriff's deputies, and the state's attorney general's office.

Aside from a few discrepancies, and my update from Gil withstanding, there was nothing earthshattering. Next came more interviews we hoped to conduct. I smelled lots of work here.

The initial level would be people indirectly involved with the crime and victim, such as Marlene's few known pals, then-neighbors, high school faculty who taught her, employer---Tommy Edwards---in Indianapolis, relatives, law enforcement members part of the investigations, etc.

We built a list. The students gathered the names, and Pete, our only townie, figured big in this exercise. "I know a lot of these people, or at least their names," he said. "I know a few you can cross off the list. They're dead. My parents were only in grade school at the time. They had some of the same teachers as Marlene, though. Maybe my folks can help."

The students put together appropriate questions for each interview, designed to tap into specific connections. For those still living in the immediate area, we'd try to make it in-person interviews. The more detail we could see and use, the better.

For those who didn't live here, we placed Craig in charge of tracking them down---dead or alive---via Internet searches. He loved the challenge.

Another reminder to my Gang of Four: tread softly.

They would tire of this mantra, but our interviews were not to be interrogations. We simply were seeking reminiscences for a "looking back" feature. We were not solving a crime. We had no legal standing. We were writing a history to bring readers "up to speed" on an important story. Don't be confrontational.

I knew, from my limited experience, people tend to be more forthcoming when a session is casual. The trick is to be a good listener, take cues from responses and don't simply rattle off from a list of prepared questions. Don't take notes, which can be intimidating. Use a tape recorder. Also, stay away from asking anything that can be answered with a simple yes or no.

Since we had no budget, anyone outside our area would have to be contacted by telephone or via the Internet. This was why I was especially relieved to cross Lawrence Charles off all lists. California, where he returned after leaving Harrison College, was his most likely address. No way could get I get money for that trip and he could easily duck us.

But we would try as hard as possible to interview in person the two remaining, prime suspects: Gene Brown, Marlene's abusive step-father, and Nicholas Walker, the local community playhouse director known to be tight with her.

And, of course, who knew? There still was time for someone else to appear on the prime suspect scene.

Chapter 50

New Developments

We did not have to wait long to locate Nicholas Walker. With a few clicks on his laptop, Craig had his address before the meeting in the *Hoosier-Record* was concluded.

"Not a big deal," he said. A few more clicks and Craig had added a telephone number. At this rate, Craig would be looking at his bank statements. Hey, this quest might be easier than I thought.

Turns out Walker, still alive---let's establish that first---according to Craig's most current references, was an easy drive north to Crawfordsville in Indiana. He was an emeritus professor in drama at a local college and, according to the school's catalogue, still taught an occasional course.

The phone number turned out to be correct. Later, the same would be true of the address.

A call the next morning was answered by Nicholas. My rehearsed and finely crafted explanation was not all that necessary. As a career college professor himself, he grasped what we were doing and, though punctuating my remarks several times with sighs, did not cut off the call.

"I think it's been 25 years for me since Marlene's story last came up with some TV crew," was his immediate, cynical reply. "I didn't realize now that it's already 50. I guess time flies when you're a suspect in an unsolved murder, or something like that."

He snickered, indicating, I guess, he had a sense of humor.

"Pretty sure I won't be available when it's the 75th anniversary. So, let's get it over with, maybe my last chance to clear myself."

Now there was special emphasis on the word "clear." Another good sign.

Figuring this was a little out of Jing's ballpark, being from China and all that, I asked Kate and Pete to make the trip to Crawfordsville with me.

Craig, though a computer genius, too often came up short on social skills. No problem for him to stay behind. He had more things he wanted to run down, namely finding Gene Brown, the stepdad and another prime suspect. He already had provided an important boost locating Walker.

"Come in, come in, we were expecting you," said the man who opened the door when we arrived a day later at the Crawfordsville address.

"Nicholas?" I asked, sticking out my hand to shake with this trim, fair-haired man looking a wee bit young for someone who should be in his early 70s.

"Oh, no, no," he responded. "I'm Paul. Nicholas is my husband. He's waiting for you inside."

Husband? I'm sure my momentary pause did not escape his---her?---detection.

My mind did a 180 as we entered---and I avoided serious eye contact with my students. Well now. This could put an entirely different spin on everything, opening a new set of questions needed to be asked.

Gay? Were people gay 50 years ago?

Of course, but how did that impact the mystery. There was nothing in our research that indicated anything about this. Or did it have any impact at all? Why should it? Hopefully, we'd get answers. Perhaps it would provide a fresh narrative, a topping for our final draft.

Nicholas came out of the kitchen, and he also did not look to be in his 70s. We shook hands, and he invited us to sit down after offering us something to drink. Iced tea all around.

"Well, now," he said. "Marlene Scott lives on, I guess. Oh, sorry that was inappropriate. Do you mind if Paul sits in on this? I've told him about this tragedy many, many times. Now he's getting a taste, up close."

First, Nicholas had a question for us: Had we studied the reports and statements in the official investigation? Yes, we had.

"Good, and let me say I stand by everything I said at the time, and you can quote me on that," he said. "I've read them, too, and saw nothing to change. Let's not waste time reviewing that ghastly material.

"I stand by my alibis for the night poor Marlene disappeared. And I hate to even use the word 'alibis.' That word sounds so limp, like they're fabrications."

Then Nicholas turned the tables, asking us for updates. He was unaware that Flo, Marlene's mother, had died. He had heard, but did not know for sure, that Jimmy Bartow, was killed in Vietnam.

And what about that California kid who was a Harrison College student? Lawrence Charles? "He was my candidate, as if anyone cared," he said.

Cleared.

"Cleared? How so?"

This was our update for him. I explained how, according to a recently discovered, new witness at the Monarch, they were seen separating in the parking lot and going their own way. The observer was positive they left independent of each other, and that was a missing link in the initial investigation.

"Well, then," said Nicholas, his eyes going into a squint, "if we are to believe this account, that narrows the field of the early, prime suspects to me and who else?"

Gene Brown.

"Oh, yes, the father, or step-father," he recalled. "A real Neanderthal, according to Marlene. She didn't like him at all.'"

This was my cue. I asked him about his relationship with the teenaged victim. Picking Marlene for the starring role in "Bye Bye Birdie" was one thing. They also spent considerable time together after the production, even at the start of her last year when she was commuting back and forth to Indianapolis. This was crucial to him becoming a suspect.

Did they have a bitter, lovers' quarrel? Marlene was known to be flighty. As soon as I asked, I regretted the question.

Nicholas laughed. "Good God! Look at me," he said. "I'm gay. I'm a homosexual. I was then and I am now. There was nothing intimate. Connect the dots."

Well, there was that.

"Do you realize what it was like to be gay 50 years ago in rural Indiana? Or queer as it was called in some of these hick towns? A fairy? Paul and I have been a couple for nearly 25 years, but we couldn't get legally married in Indiana until 2014. Even then, we had to do it in a courthouse. We couldn't find a pastor or church willing. Not in Indiana."

Kate and Pete, silent throughout, were getting a real-life, up close history lesson with this interview. Undoubtedly, we'd have an interesting conversation on the ride back to Harrison.

"I will tell you one thing that never got mentioned in those reports, probably because the deputies and others were too ignorant to ask the right questions," he said, a growing trace of bitterness in his voice.

"Marlene thought *she* was gay."

Whoa. Marlene gay? That goes against everything we've read.

"I know, I know. The poor kid---what 16? She was confused. She didn't know what her sexuality was. Kids experienced that then, just like now. Only now it's acceptable, transgender and all that. Then, it was something not to be discussed. Especially in a small, rural school where you get tagged and bullied.

"Everyone thought she was screwing every boy in sight. Not true. She didn't want to be intimate, have sex, or whatever with boys when she was in Harrison. She resisted it. We had many talks about this.

"Jimmy was her beard, a cover. He didn't get anywhere with her. But he wanted to be in her company. That was enough for him, and enough for her. Her reputation? What's that movie? *Mean Girls*? Her loose reputation came from pure jealousy. Other girls in high school spreading rumors. Probably saw her as some sort of threat. Some threat. They never knew."

This was touchy territory, but here was the question needed to be asked: How did you two become close?

"Ah, yes," he responded. "On stage, she was talented. Maybe because she was playing a real-life role, trying to fit in despite all her self-doubt and confusion. Picking her for that lead role in "Bye Bye Birdie" was a no-brainer. But she was very, very bright in other ways. I'm sure you checked her report cards to learn that.

"But she also was sophisticated, though maybe that's not the right word. Advanced? She had a certain knowingness, or understanding, of the world beyond her age group. Big city girl in Podunk. Her maturity was beyond that of the girls who tormented her.

"Somehow she had a sixth sense about me. To most of the people I met in Harrison then, I was just some flighty, effeminate young male. Light in the loafers, and all that. It came with my work---drama. Not exactly what a man's man does for a living. I didn't drive pickup trucks to work.

"One night after a rehearsal, she came right out and asked me about sexuality and gender and all that good stuff. Apparently, she'd had some sort of squabble the night before with Jimmy. His hormones were flowing, and she still wouldn't give in.

"She admitted this to me. Now she wanted to know if something was wrong with her. Was this the way it always would be for her? More to the point, she wanted to know my attitudes. My proclivities, my leanings. Whatever. Next thing I know, we're best buddies sharing a foxhole. That's all."

Nicholas said he wasn't sure that she was gay, that perhaps she was going through a "phase." That was the usual explanation for any youth acting "strange" in those days. There certainly was no deep thinking applied by police, not 50 years ago. No profiling, no Psychology 101. Not even a school counselor.

"I loved our conversations, though," said Nicholas. "It was very cathartic for me to be discussing these things with Marlene, even if she was just 17 or 18. It was such a relief. I had no one I could be honest with until then. There was a bond. We could trust our listener. Finally.

"There was no Paul in my life then," he added, nodding towards his partner. "It's a whole different world today."

There was a pause, a pregnant one, before all eyes turned toward Kate, who---in her first comment since entering the house, blurted: "Bullying! Marlene was bullied."

Nicholas smiled. "You got it, young lady. Pure and simple. That's what it's labeled today, but that's what it was 50 years ago, too, no matter what it was called. I'm not sure anyone thought she was gay, if she really was. I think even Marlene wasn't sure."

Then, after a few polite comments, we parted company. Nicholas and Paul both stood at the door and wished us well when we left.

I always will think, deep down, Nicholas---a teacher at heart---was pleased that he could be helpful for my students. Relieved, too, that a more complete picture could be painted of what happened so long ago.

"Send me a copy of what gets published," were his parting words. "Use whatever I said. I've got nothing to hide."

No problem there.

Now, we had to locate our last prime suspect. Even if Gene Brown didn't pan out, I was sure we had some revelations that painted a more complete picture of what transpired on that cold, winter night.

We had some real updates for the story. Newt would be pleased.

Chapter 51

New Angle

The car ride back to Harrison was lively.

Kate started it. "Don't you think this puts a whole new spin on things, Professor? At least a new approach for what we write. Even if we don't have an answer to who killed Marlene?"

So, what's the spin?

"Bullying, just like we heard in Nicholas's house," said Kate---with a slight tone of impatience.

How so?

"Well, can't we say the crime might not have happened if Marlene wasn't bullied? She wouldn't have transferred that last year? She might not have even been in the Monarch that night?"

Lots of speculation, I noted.

"Well, everything's speculation. Isn't it? Now we've got new facts and, at least one person---Mr. Walker---to confirm. He told us, in effect, that's why she transferred. We can't do better than that. Her Mom's dead and her stepdad's missing."

Pete, our homeboy in all this, chimed in with this: "Maybe we should check the school calendar for that year. Maybe we find there was something taking place that night at the high school---a play, a basketball game, whatever. Something that she likely would have participated in, or at least attended if she didn't feel like an outsider."

These guys were sharp. I'm thinking about papers to grade when we get back to Harrison, and they've already got serious wheels turning. A new narrative sure to get attention for the *Hoosier-Record?* Newt's going to love this.

Pete added, "Being from Harrison, it's kind of hard for me to know this. The bullies would've been parents---or grand-parents, I suppose---of some of my high school friends. Mr. Walker made them sound pretty cruel."

Maybe, maybe not. I reminded them: We needed to lo-cate---and hopefully interview---our next suspect, Gene Brown. Then we start sifting through our findings.

"Who knows?" added Kate. "Maybe we'll get another angle with him."

What's that?

"Maybe he knew she was gay, or queer in those days. Maybe it was a hate crime."

Killing his stepdaughter? That seemed a stretch.

Chapter 52

Time for a Break

Spring break was nearing and Mary and I, taking a night off from hectic schedules, went for beers at Whitey's. We got caught up on other matters, too.

"Haven't seen you guys for a while," said Whitey after we came through his swinging doors. "If my frozen pizza kept you guys away, I got a new supplier. Not as many complaints. I'll put one in the microwave for you. On me."

I brought Mary up to date on our Marlene Scott efforts, with special emphasis on the Gil Munson and Nicholas Walker developments. "Wow! That's major," she said. "Gives different twists. That gay angle is intriguing."

As far as I could see, there were two remaining, major missions.

"We've got to track down Gene Brown, interview him. As Marlene's stepfather, there's some evidence he was abusive. He's been a prime suspect since Flo divorced him. He just went off the grid, possibly spent time in prison. He'd be in his 80s now, and, from what we know, a real hard-ass."

What's the other mission, Mary wondered?

"Not something major, but I'd like to visit Marlene's grave---if there is one. I'm not sure what they did with her remains. There never was a traditional obituary, which tells us where she's buried.

"Of course, I'm not even sure she was buried. This may sound a bit ghoulish, but, if she were, I'd like to have my Gang of Four pay a visit to the site. It could be a way to make this whole experience more meaningful for them. Me, too."

Mary said, "Newt's readers are going to get their money's worth when this gets published. At the very least you'll have fresh info, stuff that wasn't reported before."

Speaking of readers, I relayed that Newt's *Hoosier-Record* circulation grew a bit over the winter, likely helped by the writing my students contributed in the first semester. Better yet, several students---not in my Gang of Four---have queried him about continuing to write on a part-time basis under his direction.

"You know what you really need to do," Mary quickly pointed out, "is create some sort of internship program. Link it to the writing classes you teach. Keep it small and selective, though. Don't want Newt to end up babysitting. He's busy enough as it is."

Taking it a bit farther, there could be other opportunities here too. Since its advertising that drives his newspaper, perhaps an internship for a business major to help on the sales side? That was an idea worth scribbling on the blank scrap paper I always carried in my pocket. Hey, maybe the school should take over the newspaper.

Mary's sociology classes were doing well, too. They were becoming involved with Dorothy's PIP efforts.

"At the rate we're going with interviews and everything, I don't think there'll be a Latino in the county we haven't talked with for this project. Maria is a real gem. Hard to believe she's only 18."

"And in a foreign country," I added.

There were other updates, gossip, and news to be discussed.

The rumor had Klugendorff leaving Harrison, moving to another small, liberal arts school in Pennsylvania---at best a lateral move. "Wonder if he cleaned up his CV," was my unfiltered response.

Apparently, our school's new e-sport program was off to a flying start, which did not surprise me a bit since Craig was a participant. There was talk of awarding scholarships to the top performers.

We agreed that Harrison College's exchange with Xiamen in China was going swimmingly, too. The stakes were expected to be ratcheted up next academic year, with additional students and teachers exchanged.

"I hear President Casey will be turning over the first shovel of dirt to start a new science building right after spring break," Mary added. "And speaking of spring break, I suppose you want to go somewhere? Make it a real break from school."

I told her that I could use the time here, get caught up on paperwork I'd been putting off. It was OK if she went to Arizona, though she'd be missed.

"No, actually, I'd be happy to stay here and get caught up, too. We could slow down and get re-connected."

She paused, saw my smile. "Yeah, yeah, big boy. I was talking about another sort of connection. But I'm sure we can get in plenty of what you have in mind, too. I'm game."

As it turned out, Mary had another reason for staying in Harrison.

"My brother Pete, the detective on the Kansas City police force? He's been hinting around he'd like to pay a visit," she said. "No one in my family's ever been here for a visit.

"We'd be hard-pressed to find something interesting to do, but I'm sure he wouldn't mind just relaxing. Being a police detective's got to be stressful. We could always go down to

Louisville or up to Indy for something. I think he's got an ul-terior motive, though."

What?

"Well, he wants to bring his girlfriend, Brenda, the one who's on the KC fire department. They're living together. I think, in an odd sort of way, he wants me to get to know her better since it looks like they'll get married. His first wife was a shrew. Good riddance."

So, like he's seeking your blessing?

"In a way," she answered. "Don't forget I'm the only female in the family. We were just kids when our Mom got killed in that crash. I may be the youngest, but my brothers are a wee bit---just a wee bit---more respectful of me. He doesn't want to make another mistake.

"His first wife didn't do much for me, and he kind of sus-pected that was true with the rest of the family."

Chapter 53

Restless

A clock was ticking. Maria could hear it in her head. Two clocks, really.

She'd heard precious little from her father, only three generic notes passed indirectly to her from Father Tony to Mary at the college. Then, on to Dorothy and, finally, her.

As the incarceration of her family dragged out, she wanted to interpret this as a positive sign. Then, one day that outlook turned gloomy when she came across an article on the *Arizona Republic's* website about the status of asylum seekers.

The story struck a sympathetic tone for refugees, but it noted that 97% of those seeking asylum were rejected. Those who didn't were sent to their former homes, regardless of the reasons why they left. For some, it was a death sentence.

This was chilling news.

A rejection would never do for her family, Maria reasoned. Her father, a university history professor, simply could not return to El Salvador. His politics were wrong. His enemies were powerful government officials, and death threats prompted their hurried and harried exit. He had family to protect.

If he were not granted asylum, Maria would be needed more than ever. She simply could not stay in the relative comfort of Dorothy's home while her family scrambled. She was aware there were Lopez relatives in parts of Mexico and Honduras, but how would she connect with anyone living off-grid in southern Indiana?

The other ticking clock?

How long would she be welcome in Dorothy's home? Their PIP project, moving nicely along, had an early summer deadline. They expected to meet it without a problem. Soon, they would begin writing a final draft.

Then what?

Maria was confident Dorothy and Mary would find something suitable for her, and a transition would result. When? That was the question.

Her options were extremely limited even with these two wonderful women for support. Maria would always be indebted to them. But she wanted to extricate herself from this limbo, start working at something with a future. Gain control of her fate. Get some traction.

These thoughts were on her mind while sitting in what had become, for all practical purposes, her private Harrison courthouse workspace in the basement.

How private? One night she accidentally left important research behind and found everything undisturbed when she anxiously returned early the next morning---something that never would happen in her former home.

This afternoon would be devoted to sifting through more building permit records, looking for additional evidence of Latino investment in the county. She was pleased when the work got interrupted by Pete Gray plopping down beside her. He, too, was there to research another angle to the Marlene Scott case. Something about confirming identities of the Scott neighbors.

Maria was beginning to wonder. This was her fourth or fifth trip to the courthouse, all but once he had been here, too. Coincidence? Who cared? She welcomed it. She was starved to talk with someone close to her age. They may have grown up in starkly different environments, but some subjects for young adults were universal.

Pete was a good listener. Good looking, too, she couldn't help noticing. The last time they bumped into each other, they recessed for coffee. They were so relaxed she had come close to revealing her true background.

At the same time, Pete was dying to tell her about his experience several days ago with the Nicholas Walker interview. No go, though. There was a Gang of Four pledge not to get into specifics of the Independent Study project with outsiders.

On the other hand, there was this: was it possible some of Maria's research about the local Latino community could be helpful in the Marlene Scott project? Was it another stone to be turned over for new evidence?

Chapter 54

Lost and Found

As the search through records for the remaining suspect, Gene Brown, continued to draw blanks, I gave more and more thought to unleashing our secret weapon: Craig Conley.

Our resident computer genius assured me he could track Marlene's stepfather down with no sweat—if I didn't mind a little illegal hacking into Federal records. This was especially true, he guaranteed, if the target spent time in the military.

Even more frightening to me, Craig made everything sound as if this was familiar turf for him. We needed to stay within ethical borders, I assured him. This may be only for the local *Hoosier-Record,* but no way could the content be tainted. This likely would get me fired and give the school a PR nightmare at a crucial point in its history.

Headline: "Harrison College teacher supervises illegal hacking."

Still .....

...... and then a funny thing happened.

You know how the presence of another person can be felt, even before he or she can be seen? Like you have a sixth sense? Especially in a small, cramped space like my Durham Hall office?

With my back to the open door, bent over and fishing papers from the bottom drawer of my file cabinet, I could just *feel* someone behind me. This was easier given the person standing in the doorway was 6-foot-5 and 250 pounds. Of course, he was Nate "Preacher" Stine, leader of the Holy Rollers motorcycle gang and Kate's father.

"Katie tells me you're looking for someone, some dick named Gene Brown," announced Nate. As he tossed an envelope on my desk, he said, "Try this."

And there it was: A location for the elusive Gene Brown. He was a resident in the Shawnee County Care Center in Illinois. The facility was on the outskirts of Lawrenceburg, deep in the rural, southeastern corner of the state---just a few hours from Harrison in Indiana.

All this time, he was right under my Geek squad's noses. I asked, "How'd you find this Nate? We've been looking all over for Mister Brown."

"Yeah, well, let's just say I put the word out to some of the more elderly members of my esteemed organization," he said. "Members closely acquainted with some of the Midwest's finer institutions of correction and rehabilitation---otherwise known as prisons.

"Turns out your Mister Brown has been a bad boy on occasion. In two states, Indiana and Illinois."

Brown's most recent stint was in the Big Bend Correctional Facility, a medium security prison for repeat offenders. His record showed multiple, career convictions for assault, forgery, auto theft, receiving stolen goods and illegal possession of a firearm.

Nate added, "Nothing big time. Piss-ant stuff, really. Most of it occurred late in life. Guess things weren't going his way by then. Or maybe he just needed a roof over his head. Jail."

The records further showed Brown, divorced two times, worked at a variety of jobs---auto mechanic, ironworker, and, amazingly, as a security guard at the Lucas Oil Sports Stadium in Indianapolis. He would be 86 in two months and, thanks to Medicaid, was for all intents a charity case at the rest home.

"Wow! This is incredible," I said. "Thanks. It's a real help."

"No problem," said Nate, as he turned and walked out the door. "Just one thing, though."

What?

"I wouldn't wait too long to pay him a visit. I heard the dude's ready to check out. Lung cancer. My associate who found him said he's all hooked up with tubes and oxygen tanks. Like I tell people: You shouldn't smoke."

With that, Nate pulled a pack of cigarettes out of his pocket, put one in his mouth, and lit up as he turned and exited Durham Hall.

A deathbed confession from Gene Brown? Was this too much to hope for? What a perfect topper for our writing. We solve the crime with Marlene's stepdad clearing his conscience. If he were in terrible shape, it's not likely he'd be prosecuted. Everyone wins.

Chapter 55

Rush Job

The next day I couldn't get to the care center quick enough. There was only time to locate one of my Gang of Four, Pete Gray, to accompany me when I took off following Nate's gift.

At first, Pete did not quite grasp the reason to be excited. Then, as we crossed into Illinois in my car, he started to get pumped, too. Even though it was strictly county roads, I'm sure we set a land speed record getting to Lawrenceburg.

"You're right, now that I think about it," he said. "It's almost like solving the crime would be performing a community service. People in town have been talking about this forever. What would be the headline?

"Marlene's mystery solved!"

We'd worry about that later. Now, we needed to get access to Brown. This would be the first order of business. We needed just the right comments before we could pop some meaningful questions.

Of course, Brown's condition could eliminate any chance for dialog. For all we knew, he could be in a coma.

Chapter 56

A Last Chance

No question Gene Brown was dying. It was only a matter of weeks, or less, and he would take his last, ragged breath. There was no escape from the cancer ravaging his body.

For sure, the finish would be lonely and not graceful. No known relatives would be on hand and, if any were, probably wouldn't recognize him.

Nurses were giving him maximum doses of painkillers and, told he was down nearly 50 pounds, his decimated body was a maze of tubes and bandages. His face was half-covered with an oxygen mask.

The Lawrenceburg hospital, a small, rural facility deep in southern Illinois, had few resources. High end hospice care for those on public assistance, like Gene, simply was not available.

Realizing the end was near, the hospital decided to send him back to the Shawnee County home a few miles away in the countryside. This is where he resided the last few years. The bleak brick and peeling wood facility, not a high priority for county administrators, was at the end of a blacktop road in the middle of farm fields.

In the years he lived there, not long after being paroled by the Illinois Department of Corrections, his only visitors were an occasional pastor and social worker. At first, Gene would have nothing to do with these "do-gooders" wanting to build a relationship. "Tell 'em to go fuck themselves," was his standard response.

Eventually, the rest home's boring, low budget existence, softened him a touch. Occasionally he joined in card games in what passed for a recreation room, joked a bit with nurse's aides and, joining others, became a regular "Jeopardy!" viewer on the county home's lone, 21-inch TV set.

And right up to his cancer reaching Stage IV, he would go outside three times a day to smoke a cigarette. Preferably a Marlboro, but he took whatever Darnell, the janitor, had to offer.

Would he be missed? Hard to say. Deaths were not unusual in the facility. At least 1-2 occurred monthly. He made few friends up to this point, but it was obvious they were interested in what could be pilfered from his meager possessions after he kicked.

This day figured to be a good one, we were told. He slept a solid, six hours during the night. Though he was beginning to occasionally slip in and out of awareness during the days, he felt strong and alert this morning.

Then, Mark, the home's director, came into the room Gene shared with another resident. He had a question: "Do you feel up to a visit later in the morning from two people from Harrison? Your call."

Gene, his eyes suddenly snapping wide open, answered, "Someone wants to see me? A little late, ain't they? Sure. What've I got to lose? I'm not going anywhere."

"They'll arrive a couple hours from now, around 11 o'clock."

Gene knew what this meant. It had to be something to do with Marlene's death. Though he'd lived in that butthole of a town Harrison only a few years, the death of his stepdaughter was like gum on his shoe. It followed him everywhere.

Flo divorcing him soon afterward didn't help, just as his later brushes with the law made him an even more suspicious character. Never mind that his alibis held up with police.

In his pre-cancer days, he would never have consented to this visit. Now, with the Grim Reaper knocking on his door, he'd been thinking a lot about his wasted life. He had nothing, or nobody, to show he existed. Just a death certificate, court records for his divorces, a paper trail left by arrests and incarcerations, and a pauper's grave in some unfamiliar cemetery.

Pretty sad. Maybe this visit would be his last opportunity to do something worthwhile. Set the record straight.

Chapter 57

Just the Facts

We were 15 minutes early when we pulled into the Shawnee County home's graveled parking lot. Two attendants on the front porch, spotting us, quickly put out cigarettes and went back in the front door. Apparently mid-day visitors were scarce for this out-of-the-way facility.

Pete and I sat in the car, going over our Gene Brown notes, talking points, and objectives. In talking on the telephone with Mark, the home's director, we were left a bit on edge.

"He's not the most popular resident," the director said. "Old Gene can get a bit cranky, but we're used to it here. We've had worse. He's a little mellower lately. Phase 4 cancer does that. I've seen it before. I just hope he's strong enough to get through your visit. He nods off a lot."

Still sitting in the car, we took a few minutes to review a timeline for Brown that was noticeably short of successes or highlights. The sad looking, middle-of-nowhere and end-of-the-road rest home seemed a perfect metaphor for his life.

*Flo was his second wife when they married in Speedway, an Indianapolis suburb; he was 31, she was 36 and a divorcee, too. Marlene, her only child, was 13 at the time.

*No college. Gene, a high school grad of Indianapolis Manual, worked a variety of jobs, mostly auto parts and repair related. His early ambition---never realized---was to get hired by an Indy 500 racing team as a mechanic. He idolized racing legend A.J. Foyt.

*Less than two years before the marriage to Flo, he spent 60 days in the Marion County jail in Indiana for drunk driving following a collision that left a passenger in the other car partially paralyzed. This was his second DWI conviction.

*The move to Harrison, according to Flo, was to put distance between her husband and his drinking buddies back in Indy. He grew increasingly unhappy with the new location, made frequent return trips on weekends, and occasionally took out his frustration on Flo with physical abuse. Though never charged, police records show periodic calls to their homes to referee domestic disputes.

*There were no reports Marlene, Flo's daughter, was physically abused.

*Flo and Gene left Harrison for Indianapolis a little over a year following the discovery of Marlene's body. In two more years, they parted and divorced.

*Gene, now 86, went into free-fall following his divorce from Flo. He held a variety of jobs, none for more than a year. There were two stints in a substance abuse center/halfway house in lieu of jail time for forgery convictions.

*Brown also served a short term in a minimum-security prison in Indiana for auto theft. After moving to downstate Cairo in Illinois, he was arrested for receiving stolen property---he was part of an interstate auto theft ring---and did a 5-year stint in that state's Big Bend Correctional Facility.

*Marlene's biological father? The official designation belonged to Flo's first husband, John Semler, but this was debatable. Flo was popular. The grounds for the first divorce was adultery on her part. Semler lived in Texas by the time Gene and Flo married.

"Gene's alibi on the night Marlene disappeared---and presumably died---seems solid," I told Pete. "He said he went back to Indianapolis late that afternoon, spent most of the night drinking with his best buddy in a bar. This guy, Al, corroborated it. Never flinched. The bartender in Indy recalled Gene that night, too.

"Of course, Gene never said it, but it was assumed he spent the weekend with a girl friend at the time. He denied it, and nobody had a name to chase down. He had several lady friends at the time, according to Flo."

Pete said, "So, is this going to be a waste of time? Sounds like he's the weakest suspect."

True, but I explained that it's important to take every opportunity to get up close and personal with those connected to the crime. At the very least, we may pick up a few, previously unreported details. They'll improve our story, flesh it out a bit more.

"People are familiar with the facts. We give them something new, they'll be more interested. And there's this: Not to sound too mercenary, but from everything we know, Gene is on his death bed here. Not long to go.

"Maybe he'll want to get some things off his chest."

Chapter 58

The Visit

Mark led us down a long, first-floor hallway that was well lit and lined on both sides with dormitory-style rooms. Some doors were closed, some were not. Each door had a number, but no other distinguishing marks. In each room, there were two single beds separated by a curtain, two easy chairs, a single window and tiny bathroom with another curtain as the door.

There was a steady, quiet hum of activity in the air as you walked the hallway, punctuated by bursts of coughing, snoring, an occasional moan, and scattered laughter. The lighting inside the rooms was dim or totally dark. In a few, visitors were packed inside. There also was an unmistakable, stale odor that was partly medicinal, as if we were in a hospital.

There was a trace of shock in Pete's eyes. For a 20-year old college student who grew up a in a prosperous, middle class household, this was the dark side of the moon. The furniture, furnishings, and plastic flowers in pots barely reached rummage sale quality. There were no bright colors to break the gloom.

"You OK?" I whispered, as we followed Mark.

His "No problems" reply, a little higher pitched than his normal tone, seemed a mite too quick to be authentic.

Gene's room was barely lit, with what light there was produced mostly by glow from bedside medical equipment. He was the room's lone occupant. There were tubes up both nostrils.

At first, it was not evident he was awake. It was obvious his body, skin and bones, had taken a beating. The craggy, deep lines on his face signaled he was, or had been, a heavy smoker. There were patches of dark hair, but splotchy and more evidence of his cancer. It was almost impossible to distinguish the tattoos on his arms from otherwise splotchy skin blemishes.

Opening his eyes with a start, Brown blurted, "They moved my roommate out. You get a single when you're dying. At least I got that going for me."

He laughed at his own joke. Our responses were forced smiles.

"Not much room with all the hospital crap they say I need," he added. "When I'm gone, my roomie, Tommy, will come back and he gets a new roommate. Who knows? Maybe it'll be a broad."

Brown's comments drew more smiles, though Mark's tight grin clearly was an effort. After introductions, the director and Gene huddled for a few minutes. Then Mark exited. "I'll be back in 20 minutes or so," he said, apparently giving us a time limit.

"So perfessor," Gene said, in a hoarse voice barely above a loud whisper, "what brings you here? Let me guess. I'll bet it's something to do with Marlene. You cops or something? You're a little late if you are."

Not sure he fully grasped my description that followed, given his failing condition. I explained it was part of a class project for a college. Figuring he did not have fond memories of Harrison, I did not mention the location of our school.

On the 50th anniversary of the crime, I told him my students were interested in writing a feature story on the mystery surrounding her death. We wanted to see if there were new developments or insights to bring readers up to date.

This would be a factual story. In the process, we wanted to talk with as many people as we could directly connected to the mystery. We were not trying to solve, create, or repeat rumors and conjecture. It was likely our final work would get published in a newspaper.

This was met with no response from Gene. Total silence, and just a blank stare past our shoulders. A minute of silence seemed like an hour as his brain---hopefully---processed my message.

Finally, he spoke: "People will read this? What you write?"

Yes. That's the intention.

"You know, I've never been back to that shithole of a town since I got divorced, moved away," he said. "I don't even like to say its name.

"No, wait," he corrected himself. "I take that back. I went to Flo's funeral there. How could I forget? "Some asshole, I think he was a retired farmer, gave me a hard time, too. Came up to me after we put her in the ground, said I had a lot of nerve being there after the way I treated my family. A real turd. We'd never even met."

Gene's face began to gain color---from a pale gray to a light pink---as he continued.

"He blamed me for what happened to Marlene. Said I should be arrested. Mind you. I never even knew this guy. I came close to throwing a punch. But I didn't. Somebody stepped between us. Never forgot that."

Gene told us that he was interrogated about Marlene's death by police several times after her body was discovered.

He had an airtight alibi. He was in Indianapolis drinking with buddies. Nothing ever happened following that, though he certainly was aware people in Harrison remained suspicious.

After an awkward silence, he continued: "I ain't been no angel, that's for sure. I know you probably seen I did time behind bars. I'm not proud of a lot of things. Booze. Broads. Guess I just couldn't stop drinking. Smoking, too."

Gene turned his gaze to Pete. "And who are you, kid?" he asked. "You part of this thing?"

Pete explained that he was, indeed, a student in the project. He assured Gene that he and the others were open-minded. They didn't consider themselves "some kind of police."

Who were they to make judgements on something that happened 50 years ago? This seemed to calm things down, until Pete's only mistake---mentioning he grew up in Harrison, went to high school there, and knew the story from his parents---seemingly torpedoed everything.

"Wait, wait! You saying you're from Harrison?"

"Yessir."

"Didn't you hear what I just said? I hate that dump. End of story. I don't want nothin' to do with this. Go to hell."

As if on cue, Mark, apparently hovering just outside the door, suddenly materialized. And, as if he hadn't heard a thing, said calmly: "Time's up, fellas. Let's let Gene get some rest."

End of conversation. In a flash, we were ushered out the door and escorted down the corridor.

"I had to do that," said Mark, as we retreated. "I'm sorry, but Gene's an irascible old fart. I know the signs. We want him to stay calm. Too much excitement would---and I mean this--- kill him. He doesn't have much time left as it is; my duty is to make him as comfortable as possible."

Pete felt he ruined everything. The car ride back was somber. To be honest, we didn't come away with any more information regarding what happened 50 years ago. But we did get an update on Gene. Some quotes, too.

I said, "I want you to write down every detail of what you saw at the rest home. Write down everything he said, even if it didn't pertain to the crime. His confrontation at Flo's burial site, for instance. Do it now while it's fresh in your memory. We'll sort it out later, use it for a little color we can sprinkle in our final writing."

After assuring Pete he shouldn't feel bad about what happened, the car ride to Harrison was quiet the remainder of the trip. Only his tapping of laptop keys and a few questions to confirm a few details broke the silence.

Chapter 59

Second Chance

"Crap." That was Mary's response at dinner later that day. Hard to argue.

"All that effort and driving to find him, then it turned out like it did," she added. "Sounds like your interview didn't last long enough to learn anything. I guess he was the last chance to really solve this thing."

My response: "That would've been nice. What a great feather for the school, the kids, my class.... We'll still put together a piece of work, probably a two- or three-parter for the paper. That's what Newt says would work best. We've got some new material, plenty of updates. The crime was so long ago that telling it again will be new for lots of readers."

While mostly stream of consciousness, I laid out a rough outline of what would be our highlights---how there was a witness to what took place at the Monarch, which eliminated Lawrence Charles, the Harrison student, as a suspect; Gene's innocence updated by his bad health (which would have to be monitored in case he died before publication); and highlights from the session with Nicholas Walker.

"I know this is your baby, but you might be missing a bigger picture here; forest for the trees and all that," said Mary, cautiously. "Something that makes it a little more current."

"What's that?"

"Bear with me, but I'm thinking two themes kind of run through this. Well, maybe one-and-a-half themes. Bullying for one thing, and maybe to a lesser degree sexual identity.

"Think about it," she said, before I had a chance to do exactly that. "No question you've built a case for bullying, hearing how classmates---especially the girls---were so cruel to Marlene. It's not likely she would've transferred if she'd been treated better. That could've changed everything."

Could've, should've. Interesting. Her narrative certainly should resonate with any of her old classmates---and taunters---who read our work. Just as I was about to hear her theory on gender, my cell phone rang. Looking at the ID, it had to be answered.

The caller was Mark from the Shawnee County Rest Home. The conversation was brief, with me reduced mostly to one-word responses. After I clicked off, Mary asked: "Gene dead?"

"Just the opposite. Seems he had a change of heart."

"How so?"

"Mark said Gene felt bad after we left. That he lost his temper. Wants to know if we'll come back. He wants to clear the air."

We both grinned at the implication. Knowing he only had days to live, maybe he *was* ready to confess.

We'd soon know. I would head back early tomorrow morning to complete the interview. There wasn't enough time to alert Pete, who I knew had classes. I'd go by myself and take a tape recorder. Probably just as well I went solo, too. I wouldn't want to touch off another rant by Gene."

"And speaking of Pete," said Mary, "I have a bulletin for you. My brother Pete and Brenda, his new squeeze? They're definitely coming for that visit I told you about a while back."

"When?"

"Next weekend, and probably be here 3-4 days. Then maybe go back through Chicago for a few days. Frankly, I figured they might go to Las Vegas and get married. It's the second time for them so no need for any bells and whistles."

For the next five minutes we tried to come up with some things to do with her brother Pete and Brenda during their Harrison visit. There was Whitey's for local color, a tour of the campus, Whitey's, maybe sit in on one of our classes, Whitey's, and they could get in workouts in the field house. Oh, and Whitey's."

"Where they staying?" I wondered.

Mary answered, "With us, of course. They can have my apartment and I'll stay with you."

"Really? You won't be self-conscious? It's your brother."

"Hey, grow up Flip. We're all adults. Besides. Your place is a pit. I'm used to it. They'd probably choke to death on the dust. Pete was the fussbudget in the family."

"Thanks."

Chapter 60

Learning Curve

Dorothy thought she was plugged into Liberty's Latino community as well as any outsider or, for sure, any gringo. Through Maria, she came to understand she had only scratched the surface. She had much to learn.

"I've never seen anything like it," Dorothy said to Mary, when the two met for coffee one afternoon in Harrison College's Milbert Student Union. "That girl can really get people to open up about themselves. Of course, her Spanish is better than mine. That helps."

This was a rare appearance on the campus for Dorothy, who never quite got over the school's brusque---rude?---brushoff of her application for a part-time position years ago. They met to coordinate PIP material. One of Mary's sociology classes was devoted to Latino migration at macro level while Dorothy (and Maria) was busy at micro level.

"Sometimes she's made a few return trips to pry things loose from subjects, but she seems to win everybody over and get them talking," Dorothy added. "She's gathering much more than I can actually use. It's a shame she really isn't a student at Michigan, or wherever."

The key: Maria was a good listener. That helped. And while holding back on her own perilous route to America, her quiet, smiling face and soft and caring brown eyes radiated warm, trustworthy empathy. You could let down your guard with her. You *wanted* her to know your background.

Maria loved it, too. For sure, she was contributing valuable content---statistical, logistical, demographical, familial---to PIP regarding the local Latino scene. But it was the unofficial, anecdotal material she loved the most. She felt she could write a book.

In particular, she loved the stories she heard of personal heroism, hard work, entrepreneurship, and perseverance (especially in unfamiliar winter weather) it took for families to create households and a community in this region. It was the American Dream, pure and simple, and she prayed someday her family could have this experience.

Some of the stories she relayed to Dorothy, whose admiration of Liberty's new faces grew greater with each revelation. Some she would not repeat to anyone, even Dorothy.

Maria met Rodrigo, the new, bilingual teller in the local bank. He was quietly working on an MBA at Indiana U. which meant two nights a week he hustled from work to drive 100 miles to classes at Bloomington that started at 7 p.m. Meanwhile, Teresa, his wife and full-time mother of their three children, left a teaching job in Mexico to join her husband in America.

Maria met Jose, a former member of a Honduran secret police death squad who, as a born-again Christian, renounced his background and came to the U.S. to avoid his own assassination. He became an ordained deacon in El Rey Cristo, a fundamentalist, Spanish language church several miles from Liberty.

Maria met Irina, a 17-year old Liberty High School senior originally from Mexico awarded a full-ride scholarship for next year to play soccer at Indiana University.

Maria met Valentina, the long-time assistant office manager at Thomas Turkeys, and single parent with four children, who hosted Tupperware parties on weekends to make ends meet. Three children graduated from college, and now teach in public secondary schools. The fourth is a Navy SEAL.

Maria learned more about the Evangelical Free Church in Liberty, a gathering that spooked Dorothy due to its fundamentalist beliefs. The congregation was almost exclusively Puerto Rican. One of its missions was an ecumenical meals-on-wheels program for homebound invalids.

Maria befriended three persons living under false names with fake documentation, which she learned was easily obtainable for a small fortune. She kept this information from Dorothy.

Maria met at least four persons who got to the U.S. by swimming the Rio Grande River. Ironically, the son of one was on the Liberty High School swimming team.

Yes, there were many homes where welcome mats now existed for Maria. It would be difficult to leave this. A dream perhaps, but some day she would love to bring her family to meet people she interviewed.

Chapter 61

Final Words

The visits with Gene Brown in the Shawnee County Rest Home were only 24 hours apart, but was this possible? Could someone's condition deteriorate overnight so quickly?

Apparently.

In just a snap of fingers, poor Gene appeared to have double the number of tubes connecting him to oxygen tanks and assorted, bedside medical technology. His face, ashen enough yesterday, now was an even a darker gray, which only deepened the craggy, dark lines on his cheeks and forehead.

For sure, he had the look of a heavy smoker who'd paid dues.

"Gene's not having a real good day," said Mark, who met me at the Shawnee County home's main entrance---and escorted me to his resident's room. The director gave no hint of what was in store for me.

Gene's lips started to move when he saw me come through the door. Nothing could be heard, however.

"You'll have to get close, and speak loud to be heard," said Mark. "He can only whisper."

I walked to his bedside and bent over.

"Closer," said Mark. "Get your ear down close. We could have him write out what he wants to say, but not enough strength left for that."

I leaned nearer, my ear no more than two feet from Gene's lips.

"Perfessor," he said, then pausing to wet and smack his lips several times before taking a long, wheezy breath and continuing. "Is that kid with you?"

I answered, "No."

"What?"

"NO!"

There was another long pause. Gene processed my answer. His Adams apple bobbed up and down on his skinny neck.

"Too bad," he whispered, finally. "I wanted to tell him something. Can you tell him for me?

"YES, NO PROBLEM."

Gene's eyes drifted upward. He looked at the ceiling for another minute, as if a script was there for him to read. He collected his thoughts, then continued.

"Tell him I'm sorry. I shouldn't have flipped out like that. He didn't have nothing to do with what happened to me 50 years ago."

I was eager to hear more. "ANYTHING ELSE TO SAY?"

Gene resumed looking at me. He stared at me for a minute or so. Then, tears started to roll down his cheeks.

"Yeah, I'm just sorry," he said, after taking a long breath.

"FOR WHAT?"

"For everything."

Were we getting closer to what I wanted to hear? A confession?

After another long pause, again followed by Gene's deep breath that sounded more like a sigh.

"You tell that kid not to forget me."

"OH, HE WON'T."

"Don't forget what can happen if you don't do right. I ain't got nothing to show for nothing. I ain't got nobody. Look at me good. Whatta you see. Nothing. A loser."

"WE CARE," I said, a twinge of guilt running through my conscience.

"You tell that kid to do right. Helluva thing. All I got to give is telling someone not to be like me."

"ANYTHING ELSE YOU WANT ME TO TELL HIM?"

I held my breath.

"Yeah, I guess."

"WHAT?"

"I didn't do it."

"What? I MEAN WHAT DIDN'T YOU DO?"

"Kill Marlene. I never touched her. I told the truth."

There was another pause, before Gene added, "Can you do me a favor?"

"WHAT?"

"Tell people that. Tell 'em in that thing you and the kid are writing. It's God's truth. What've I got to lose at this point. It's all I got to pass on."

As if he was cued, Mark jumped in and told me it was time to go. I couldn't argue.

Gene definitely was tiring---dying?---fast. I said my good-bye and exited.

"Well, I guess you could call that a deathbed non-confession," said Mark, who accompanied me to the county home's entrance. "He's not going to make it through the night."

And he didn't.

The next day there was a call from the Shawnee County Rest Home. Gene passed away at 7:37 that night, only hours after I departed.

Chapter 62

First Night

The first highlight of the Harrison visit by Det. Pete Jagger, Mary's brother, and Brenda did not take long to materialize. After an early morning start in their car from the condo they shared in Kansas City, they arrived in Harrison late-afternoon ready to "see the bright lights" that night.

"Calm down," said Mary, quickly assuming the grownup role with her sibling. "Go take a nap."

"I'm still going on adrenalin, Sis," said Pete. "Dazzle us."

This was going to be interesting.

I knew from the Jagger family Christmas gatherings in Colorado I attended to expect the unexpected when Mary, the only female, was with her three brothers. Fart Fest, as she called it. There would be countless jabs among them, each trying to gain the last word. None liked to lose.

The "dazzle" we came up with that first night was dinner at the Monarch Cafe---the $10.99 chicken special, y'all come--- and then a trip to Whitey's, which turned out to be lively.

It was Friday. The place was jammed and, with spring warming up, the weather was warm enough for the crowd to spill into the parking lot.

There was live music by Frankie & The Bar Flies, a local All-man Bros. wannabe group that never-would-be. They did sound better as the night progressed, relative to the rate of beers consumed.

Whitey was thrilled to discover Pete was a detective on the Kansas City police force. A 6-footer, with a lean, athletic-look and crew cut, he looked the role, too. All that was missing---I hoped---was a shoulder holster with a pistol.

Then, after learning Brenda was an officer in KC's fire department---looking every bit too stylish to run into burning buildings---Whitey, a Law & Order man, could barely contain himself.

"Two 'first responders' from the big city!" he declared, loud enough for almost everyone in house to hear. "Doesn't get better than that."

When Whitey had a picture taken of our table to put on his VIP wall, the attention we received spilled across the crowded room. We didn't pay for another drink the entire evening.

"You're earning your keep, Bro, finally," was Mary's reaction. "About time."

Brenda seemed to fully enjoy the atmosphere. Either that, or she should've been nominated for an Oscar.

Though raised in a toney Minneapolis suburb, you figured she did receive a formal education in barhopping as a graduate of Wisconsin in Madison---one of America's premier, beer-guzzling campuses.

The pace picked up decidedly when "The Preacher" wandered over to our table. He---leader of the Holy Rollers motorcycle gang, and looking every bit the role this night---definitely got Pete's attention.

"Alright, which one's the cop?" asked Preacher, when hovering above us.

"Take a guess, Reverend," said Pete.

"Preacher," he corrected. "Am I under arrest?"

"Only if you try to give a sermon," said Pete.

The two continued to exchange quips, with their repartee quickly devolving into a regular conversation that included the whole table.

Pete found that Nate, or the Preacher, was a witty, well-read fellow---definitely a cut above the average motorcycle gang. Or at least any motorcycle gang he was familiar with in Kansas City.

Everything thawed nicely even more when they got to the subject of Kate McDonald, his daughter, a star on the Independent Study team.

The highlight of the visit to Whitey's? Preacher and Pete squaring off for a game of 8-ball at the pool table.

"Let's call it cops and robbers," said Preacher.

"For a round of drinks for the house," added Pete.

Their heated match drew a ring of spectators. Pete would've bought, losing to Preacher, but then Mary stepped in with a challenge.

"Double or nothing," she said, "and I break."

Preacher grinned. "You got it, Little Lady," he said.

His grin slowly evaporated. Two balls found pockets on Mary's opening blast. In two more turns, she ran the table---quickly knocking in the 8-ball with a called shot that included three banks before the target ball dropped home in a corner pocket---to the cheers of at least 30-40 spectators drawn to the competition.

"You haven't lost your touch, Sis," said Pete. "You're still the family champ."

"That's two rounds for the house," she said. "You guys can split the cost. Set 'em up Whitey."

Chapter 63

A New Angle

The visit at Whitey's was the first highlight for Pete and Brenda, but the best was ahead of them. This highlight, or at least its launching pad, took place the next day in our Independent Study "conference room" in Newt's newspaper.

After explaining the project to Mary's brother and how this was to be a final wrap-up session before starting to write about the Marlene Scott case, he insisted on attending. "Hey, don't forget I'm a police detective," he reminded. "One thing about cold cases. New techniques, technology, DNA, whatever, can be a game-changer."

So, while Mary and Brenda took a spin to Evansville for a little shopping, and to get better acquainted since they were likely to become sisters-in-law, I filled in more details for a curious Pete on our walk to the meeting.

"You covered a lot of ground with your students, I'm impressed," he said. "A big thing had to be keeping the kids out of harm's way. You never know when real trouble can materialize.

"You were breaking new ground, too. They had to learn things aren't like they see on TV. Oh, and good you got a computer geek in the group. The nerds always come in handy. Lots of ways they can be useful."

The room was jammed for the gathering. Crowded around the table were Newt, two Pete's (Mary's brother and Pete Gray, our resident townie), Kate, Craig, Jing, and, for the first time, Maria.

Maria was invited by Pete Gray because, as he told me earlier in the day, she had done "a ton" of research on Harrison County history for PIP. "She might have some background details we can use for our writing. They could flesh out things. Add some color."

Or maybe even a new suspect? My students were learning. Always a good thing.

We went around the room with everyone reviewing their division-of-labor efforts and highlights of what they extracted. It seemed to me our series was beginning to take shape. Logical storylines were developing. The installments were writing themselves, which generally is the case with good content. Keep it simple.

Each prime suspect in the 50-year old cold (freezing by now) case could, as it turned out, be accounted for with significant updates. The fresh news, of course, would be Gene's deathbed comments and Marlene's encounter in the Monarch restaurant parking lot. There were lots of good quotes from Nicholas, too.

In addition, we collected many interviews with Marlene's old classmates, past and present city officials, and neighbors. We found a lot of contrition, much of it coming from her antagonists---including Barbara Munson, Gil's wife. This would fit quite nicely into a bullying angle.

It was agreed, enthusiastically, that Kate should do the bulk of the writing. Having one lead person would help with continuity, I explained, though everyone would contribute prose. I wanted to generate ownership in the final product.

In his spare time, which was not much, Newt had been reviewing some material as it crossed his desk. He was particularly enthused about pursuing the "bullying narrative," as he
called it.

"Bullies always are with us," he said, "but now it's become a
very topical issue. More defined. I think we can all agree Marlene likely would have remained at the high school with a
warmer reception. Then, who knows if she dies?

"Bullying gives, I dunno, a sense of currency that makes
everything more relevant for today's readers. There's a chance
your work could get picked up by some news syndicates.
This'll help sell it."

My students' ears perked up with mention of that possibility.

"Oh, and speaking of updating," he added, "you'll need to
get in some info on Nicholas being gay. That's another topical
theme. I've never seen that in any of the old stories.

"And frankly, it's probably doing him a favor, exonerating
him to some degree since it made him less likely to commit a
crime of passion against someone of the opposite sex. He certainly sounds up front about everything."

At first, Kate objected to singling out his sexual identity.
"What's the big deal? This is the 21st Century, Newt. When do
we let these old hang-ups go?"

Time for me to intercede.

"But society was a lot different *then*," I countered. "You
kept those things hidden. People just did not accept homo-
sexuality like today. Now his marriage is part of the public
record.

"Nicholas wasn't hiding it from us when we were in his
home with his spouse. We use enough '*nuance*' so readers in-
fer he's gay without making a point of it. Mentioning that his
spouse is male should do just fine. I'm sure it'll be an eye-

opener for some of the older readers. We'll drag them into the 21st century, kicking and screaming."

Kate grumbled a bit more, but Newt chimed in with an old, standby argument: "Kate, this is one of these things you're just going to have to take our word. Trust me. It'll strengthen the overall narrative. We have to write to our audience."

We went at it for about an hour, exchanging more ideas and prioritizing information. Everyone pitched in, a statement of sorts for their work ethic.

The hard part, as always happens when the reporting has been prolific, was this: What should we leave out? We couldn't use everything.

Then, it occurred to me. We hadn't heard from the expert in our midst---Pete, Mary's brother. After all, he was a real, live big city detective. My students had been sneaking quick peeks in his direction throughout the evening. I'm sure they were curious about having a real, live detective in their midst.

"Sure, I'll jump in," he said, when I asked for input. "You guys have done a great job accumulating data. You talked to the right people, asked the right questions, and, from what I'm hearing, drawing excellent conclusions."

"Am I hearing a 'but' in there somewhere," asked Newt, following a pause.

"Forest for the trees," said Pete. "Forest for the trees."

He went on to explain that sometimes investigators can spend too much time on the obvious, small details, and miss bigger pictures. While the information they gathered was usable and well-corroborated, did they give some thought to indirect factors.

"You interviewed her friends, looked at obvious tangibles like school schedules, and followed her interests that were documented, but what were things taking place that, residually but not obviously, could've spilled into the picture? Think outside the box. Work from the outside to the inside, instead of the inside to the outside."

"Like how?" challenged Craig.

Pete answered, "You have to remember this was the late 1960s, early 70s. A lot of things were taking place in society. The Viet Nam war. College unrest. Drugs. Trips to the moon for the first time. Beatniks. Woodstock. Kent State. Look at newspaper stories that, at first glance, may not be connected to the death of Marlene Scott---but perhaps contributed in an indirect way to the environment."

The problem, he further relayed---with Newt nodding in agreement, was that local newspapers tended to shy from stories that were not formulaic. Small staffs made it tough to do much more than cover meetings and events.

Not much time to be concerned with anything but the facts. Local newspapers were reluctant to do more than be papers of record, when, in fact, good stories lurked between the lines of a meeting's minutes, he explained. There could've been local controversies and rivalries at play during the time Marilyn lived here that, on the surface, did not seem to have a connection. But there *were* connectors.

"Here's a good example," said Pete. "Say there was a blizzard on the night before Marlene disappeared. What about the roads where her body was found? Were they passable? If so, who plowed them?

"Or what about some big event at the college the night she disappeared? One that brought lots of visitors to town. Or did something that happened in a neighboring town have a connection? Something that you, with the help of time and perspective, can spot?

"You've got context. Use it. Look for new and different dots to connect."

The room got quiet.

Then Maria, who'd yet to speak one word, slowly and shyly raised her hand.

"I'm not sure if this is what you mean, but Dorothy and I have found something interesting taking place in Harrison at about the same time Marlene disappeared. I have not heard it mentioned here."

Chapter 64

Bombshell?

If there was an invisible, everyday wall that separated Harrison College and faculty from life and residents with the rest of the community, there was a third grouping totally ignored by the other two: The local Latino or Hispanic community, which made up nearly a third of the county's population.

Mostly this demographic was concentrated in Liberty, the county's second largest community and just a short drive from Harrison. Its impact was spreading.

Liberty had the largest concentration, but in recent years more were living in Harrison as well as the county's smaller towns (all 1,000 residents and fewer). This co-existence was cordial, though not exactly warm, fuzzy, and inclusive.

There was inter-marriage. They shared public schools and municipal programs and institutions, but that was about it. A handful were sprinkled among governmental jobs, including the sheriff's department and Harrison and Liberty police departments.

The most significant indicator of a shifting dynamic was at Immaculate Conception Catholic Church, where a Spanish-language Mass was added in recent years.

So, what does this have to do with the 50-year old, un-solved Marlene Scott death?

"This may not mean much," said Maria, "but, in listening to Officer Jagger, it made me think of something. In the research my friend Dorothy (Blair) and I do, the greatest time for Latino migrants to move here was in the late 1960s---right about 50 years ago."

Pete (the detective) said, "Are you suggesting Marlene was murdered by a migrant?"

"Maybe, maybe not," she said. "All I am saying is this could be an example of what you said tonight. To be creative and find new---how do you say---dots to connect. I have not heard one word here tonight about Latinos in the area at the same time. Is this not something to be explored? They were not in-visible. Well, maybe they were to some people living here."

"That is a terrific idea," jumped in Newt. "I've read all the reports like the rest of you, but I've never heard of a possible connection, even a slight one, with this segment of the popu-lation. Any suggestions, Maria?"

"Si, I mean yes," she quickly responded, drawing laughs from us---and a blush from her.

She went on to list numerous cultural intersections, in-cluding businesses where Latino workers might've overheard incriminating comments or field workers who might've spot-ted her body before Burt Kohl, and were too intimidated to step forward. Perhaps a busboy at the Monarch witnessed Marlene getting into a car on the fateful night.

"A new people in a new country," said Maria. "They would not be volunteering very much. Dorothy and I found this to be true with us, too, sometimes. After all these years of living here!"

Nevertheless, Maria and Dorothy had managed to accumu-late impressive amounts of material from a hundred or more interviews conducted with Latinos and Hispanics. Many were here, or just arriving, in the late 60s.

Households had taken in the PIP researchers and frequently relayed confidences, anecdotes, stories, indignities suffered, slights, facts .... whatever.

"And another thing," Maria, on a roll, continued.

"Newcomers came here for jobs in the Thomas Turkey plant because it was expanding. But there was a big wave that came in the late 1960s to work at constructing the many new buildings that came with this growth. They moved on when projects were done.

"Could there be a connection there?"

Maria paused. Everyone was staring at her. She wondered: Had she been too outspoken? She was a guest, after all, and one who should not be drawing attention to herself.

Little did Maria know her input could prove so valuable.

Chapter 65

Leaving a Trail

On paper, it was the Butte Construction Co. that built the new Thomas Turkey plant additions in Liberty. The work lasted from mid-1968 through most of 1970. The final result covered over a million square feet of enclosed space in two adjoining, multi-story buildings.

At the time, the Thomas plant thus was Indiana's single, largest construction project for one company before the Fort Wayne GM auto assembly plant surpassed it in 1986.

The mammoth, new Thomas structures were subjects of cover stories in trade magazines. The company hired a full-time employee to coordinate tours. Engineering firms sent reps to study its design features.

But Butte, the construction company itself, was not there to receive accolades. The firm's investors quickly folded the firm after completing the Herculean project, claiming bank-ruptcy in a blizzard of pre-arranged, creative accounting strategies that included revenue diversion and resource trans-fers.

The overall object of these moves, bankruptcy, was to ab-solve the company of any liability not covered by insurance. You want to sue Butte for, say, a shaky beam installation that caused enough damage to delay turkey processing for a day or two? Asbestos siding? Faulty wiring? Leaky roof? Fine, then be prepared to work through a mountain of paperwork that would take years, maybe decades, to get resolved in court because Butte, now bankrupt, no longer existed. Only lawyers will get rich.

The U.S. still was a year or two away from instituting strict Occupational Safety and Health Administration (OSHA) standards in construction work. Shoddy, faulty work was not rare before this tightening in the industry. Instead, the bankruptcy ploy was a shell game, common in the building industry. One company gets formed for a project, completes the work, evaporates, and infrastructure (equipment, foremen, laborers) reappears with fresh paperwork in hand with a new name for the next job.

"It happened," said Gil Munson, a successful contractor himself before retirement and his trustee work at Harrison College. He did not elaborate on whether the strategy was in his playbook. I did not ask.

Gil and I chatted while we were tablemates at the Rotary luncheon following Maria's observations at Newt's office. In my role as scholarship chairman, I was on the meeting's agenda with an update on plans and candidates. Each year our club generously doled out $10,000 to a worthy recipient.

I also brought Gil up to date on the Independent Study group project. After contributing valuable input about his own connection to Marlene, he had taken quite an interest in the series we planned.

And he knew first-hand a little something about Butte and its creative bookkeeping.

"Rough crew," he said. "I spent a couple summer breaks from school working on that turkey plant. The money was good, but there were a lot of---pardon my French---assholes on the job. Most were career laborers who traveled around the country and worked project to project.

"And yeah. Things got tough for the Spanish language guys. Cruel, really. Butte imported dozens of them from south of the border. Many didn't last long. The foremen were really hard on 'em. Picked on them, really. Probably resented them because they were non-union and worked for less.

"To this day, I haven't forgotten some of the meaner guys. I learned a lot about how not to treat employees."

Gil went on to describe instances when tempers flared on the job, resulting in fights, injuries, and cover-ups. There was spillover off the job, too, he pointed out. "Some of these guys hit the bars hard, especially on Friday nights after they got their paychecks," he continued. "Like a swarm of locusts."

In its wake, he said, Butte workers considerably enriched the Harrison municipal piggy bank with significant fines for misdemeanors and traffic violations. At least two laborers he knew did short stints in the local jail for assault.

Gil said you could bet the journeymen workers, many married with families living elsewhere while they moved into motel rooms during the work week, left a few pregnancies in their wake when they moved to the next project.

"They were a horny bunch, too, that's for sure."

Chapter 66

Waiting Game

Ricardo Lopez, Maria's father, could feel it. Something should be happening soon on his request for asylum at the Mexican border.

He and his family---minus Maria---had been living in the Federal government's detention camp for nearly five months. They saw others come and go. Now, in some twisted way, the Lopez's were considered the facility's wise, old senior detainees.

Since the overwhelming majority got returned to native nations they fled to avoid serious, and often deadly, recriminations, the departures were highly emotional. It was better to not become too friendly with neighbors. They might be gone the next day. Besides, they could be agents masquerading as migrants to spy for the U.S. government on the refugees.

Ricardo's request for asylum was expected to take 3-4 months. The fifth month was not far away. He knew the numbers were not good, something like a 95% denial rate.

Perhaps their longer wait was a good sign, Ricardo allowed himself to rationalize. Maybe Federal officials giving his request more consideration. He had been a college professor, teaching history, in El Salvador. How could this be considered subversive, that he was a threat?

The camp's daily life was tedious, but bearable---though no one wanted to be here in the approaching summer, when 110-plus degree, sun-blitzing weather arrived with rattlesnakes and scorpions more noticeable scurrying for shade.

None of the tin-roof buildings had air conditioning. They were hastily built in 1942 and filled with Japanese interns shipped from California for the duration of World War II. There were 5,000 detainees at one point, with space designed for 4,000.

At least the current Latino occupants had beds, an upgrade from what many endured on their treks northward to the Promised Land. Restrooms were public. There was acceptable food, soccer balls to play games, and Ricardo, finding several other teachers in the mix to help, organized informal classes for youth.

Almost anything was better than what his family, and almost everyone around them, experienced on their 2,000-plus mile trek from Central America to the U.S. border in Lukeville, Arizona.

His daughters Daniela and Sara were fortunate to be close to each other in age (12, 14), meaning they always had a friend. There were others that age, but it was difficult to build relationships with so much uncertainty hanging over everyone. They dearly missed big sister Maria.

Incredibly, Isabella, Mom, had struck up casual friendships with several of the female security personnel. The Americans were happy to get her recipes for several dishes done Latino-style.

In the end, Ricardo had to be content with this: His family, minus Maria, was lucky to be together in one spot. This was not the case for the majority of migrants, their families coldly, tearfully separated by border patrol at most entry ports.

For someone like Ricardo, affable and outgoing, the isolation from colleagues and friends, was most difficult. And he missed Maria. His only real pipeline to the outside world became the weekly visits by Father Tony from the Vincentian House in Phoenix. What a wonderful man.

Maria's name could never be mentioned in their monitored conversations. If it became known a fifth member of the migrant family was somewhere in the U.S. under false credentials, it would mean a one-way ticket for everyone to their old home.

Ricardo was anxiously awaiting Father Tony's next visit. On his previous stop, he hinted of a positive update on his status.

Chapter 67

The 'Asshole'

The search was concluded.

Maria, with Dorothy pitching in mightily, had no idea just
how much work would be created by her suggestion: Was
there anything in the local Latino community that could be
tied to the Marlene Scott case?

The pair spent hours reviewing notes and taped interviews
taken during their field work. They searched for anything, or
anyone, mentioned or hinted about in the late 1960s, early
70s that could provide the slightest link to Marlene's death.

In the more promising instances, they returned to the original sources for additional details. This created some degree of
suspicion, making those interviewed a second time less forthcoming.

Would the interviewees get drug into something that
threatened their comfort zones? Life in the U.S. was tough
enough if English was your second language.

"The *el carbon* search," was Maria's description late one
night while she and Dorothy pored over printouts scattered
about the living room floor.

This drew a cackle from Dorothy. She may live in a little
town in Indiana, but she knew the Spanish words for "the ass-

hole search" ---Maria's label for the effort to find the perpetrator---when she heard it.

Since they did not know exactly what they were looking for, the digging and reviewing---became especially exhausting as well as frustrating. "This is what you call a pin in the hay," said Maria.

"Needle in a haystack," Dorothy quickly corrected. They were getting giddy.

They did note that several, ex-Butte employees got mentioned more than once as bad apples, especially when it came to behavior toward Latino laborers. Considering things occurred 50 years ago, Maria and Dorothy thought it significant the cruel behavior still resonated---though names sometimes were lost.

As best as anyone could recall, the bullies tended to be itinerant, journeymen laborers who, with permanent homes in distant locations, took up temporary housing in motels or boarding houses as they traveled job-to-job.

The Thomas Turkey expansion project had been a plum project for the town. The main thrust lasted nearly two years, Butte employed at least 100 workers at different points, and required both skilled and unskilled labor.

Names were hard to dig up. In the late 1960s, Liberty had three motels: The Starlight, Budget Inn, and Thunderbird. Unfortunately, none still were in operation. A check of *Hoosier-Record* advertisements undoubtedly would turn up boarding houses, but they surely would've been temporary lodging with sketchy---if any---recordkeeping could be located.

The Butte workforce was a community within a community. Was anyone in it bad enough to cause harm to Marlene? Did her path cross with anyone capable of that on the fateful Friday night when Marlene, in a state of high anxiety, stalked off the Monarch parking lot?

On paper a man named Ben Cooper, hands down, emerged the No. 1 candidate.

There were other incidents and Butte laborers in the running, but no one matched Cooper's "resume." His name popped up in interviews in six, different households.

Dorothy summed it best: "We simply don't have resources to track everything. He's the obvious person if we pick a single person for a follow-up. There's things we learned about him that did it for me."

Maria had first gleaned Cooper's name from Diego and Marianne Escobar, the delightful, elderly couple willing to recall additional details from their experience with "an ugly man."

Marianne was a decisive, retired former middle school teacher. She had no hesitation reciting their remembrances, naming names in the process. In good detail, too. This man almost cost her meeting Diego, who would become her beloved husband.

Diego? He slowly warmed in the repeat interview. He recalled harsh treatment by Cooper, a foreman, toward him and other migrants. It got bad enough that he was within days of returning to his native Mexico. Others had preceded him.

But things turned completely around when the racist, bully Cooper suddenly did not show up for work 50 years ago one Monday, having abruptly quit his Thomas Turkey construction job and apparently moved on---to who knows what and where. Few cared, even Gringos who'd become disgusted with his behavior.

"This was like a very dark cloud disappeared, and the sun came out for me and others," said Diego. "*Un milagro,* a miracle. Not much longer I met Marianne. Everything became good."

What was most interesting was this: After they dug deeper into their memory banks, rifling through documents and as-

sorted collectibles, the Escobar's pinpointed Cooper's vanish-
ing act occurred on the Monday following Marlene's last
sighting on a Friday night.

"Is this important?" asked Maria.

Had they found *el carbon*?

Chapter 68

Emotional Day

Father Tony was due later in the afternoon for his weekly visit, but the news Ricardo received several hours beforehand hit hard. It would be good to consult a priest, he thought.

The bad news got delivered after the stoic security guard, this one known as "El Burro" (the donkey) behind his back, escorted Ricardo from his living space to the office of the detention camp director.

There he was handed an official looking envelope containing this 2-sentence notice:

> *"In the matter of your application for admittance to the United States as an affirmative asylum seeker, the request is denied. You are directed to meet with the camp director and resident legal counsel if you wish to pursue the appeal process according to the bylaws of the U.S. Citizenship & Immigration Service (USCIS).*

After catching his breath, Ricardo asked the director: "What do I do? Does this mean we go back to El Salvador? Now? My family and me?"

"Not exactly," he was told. "You can file an appeal. It'll be fast-tracked, and you and the family can stay here through that process. That buys you a little time."

"And how much time would that be?"

"Unfortunately, a lot less than the application judgement process you just went through," he was informed. "Figure 10 days to two weeks. Max."

"And if I get turned down again?"

"Within a week after that determination, Federal officials will escort you from this camp to Phoenix. You'll be taken to the airport there and put on an airplane. At our expense, of course. You might stay there another day or two in a holding center, depending on seating availability."

"Do we have to be flown to El Salvador? Can we fly somewhere else? I face much trouble in my homeland. That is why I left. I would prefer to go to Veracruz in Mexico. I have family there."

"As far as I'm concerned, I'd fly you to Helsinki if that's what you wanted. But USCIS rules say we take you to your last place of residence as a citizen before coming to the U.S."

Isabella knew as soon as she saw the expression on husband Ricardo's face when he returned to their cramped quarters. Immediately, they stepped outside and out of their daughters' earshot. After he explained the options, her immediate solution was simple, "Pray!"

There never was question about Isabella's faith, but Ricardo, was, to say the least, a very casual Catholic. This latest development was a supreme test. By the end of the day, he would be ready to renew any vows. Father Tony's visit did the trick.

Chapter 69

Talk About Timing

Later in the day when Ricardo Lopez learned his U.S. asylum application was rejected, a golden opportunity surfaced that could solve everything. A job.

"It's for one year, but there is always the possibility this could become permanent," said Father Tony, as he sat down in the Lopez's living quarters and looked at the anxious faces surrounding him. "For now, it should be an answer to the problem. I'm pretty confident you will get it. Your credentials are a good match."

For several weeks, the priest, who had grown quite fond of the Lopez family, a connection starting with Maria, had worked quietly on a situation he thought could answer prayers. The position: Teaching at DePaul University in Chicago.

Father Tony had scoured job sites on web pages like *Inside Higher Ed* and *Chronicle of Higher Education* before finding the perfect stopgap solution with DePaul.

"I have heard of this school," said Ricardo. "Being in a big city like Chicago is very attractive to me."

Father Tony laughed. "Wait until you experience one of Chicago's winters."

The position was not certain yet. But it was an immense plus that DePaul is one of a small number of global universities run by the St. Vincent DePaul Order, or Vincentians, in the Roman Catholic Church.

Father Tony, a Vincentian priest running the Vincentian House for the homeless in Phoenix, had accumulated many friends throughout the Order's international network. The school was big on social work and border issues.

"Would they be willing to hire someone like me, someone whose asylum status was denied?" asked Ricardo.

"They wouldn't blink," laughed Father Tony. "In fact, knowing some of the faculty and administrators as I do, it might even help. They are not easily intimidated."

The position was a one-year visiting professorship in the History Department. If he got it, there would be no guarantees beyond a year, which would be the limit of his still-renewable U.S. work permit.

His credentials should be helpful, though American universities often were not willing to acknowledge the quality of educational backgrounds outside of U.S. borders---with the exception of European schools. DePaul was an exception.

Ricardo had undergraduate degrees from Panamerican University, or UPAN, in El Salvador. He had a master's degree from Inter American University in Puerto Rico. Then, he earned his doctorate in Central American history from the University of El Salvador, where he taught for several years.

It was there, in his homeland's own university where he hit a dangerous wall by refusing to adopt the ruling political party's perverted interpretation of local, historical events.

Furthermore, in this new setting in the U.S., Ricardo could simply list his home as El Salvador. He still was a citizen, after all. And he could add Maria as part of the family, giving everyone a green light to legally accompany him to Chicago for at least the next year.

The DePaul job was not a done deal. There would be the matter of how---and more important, where---he spent the summer before starting. The regular school year was months away.

"Let's get the job first, then worry about that," said the priest. Besides. There's always summer school and other opportunities at DePaul to keep you busy before the school year gets running."

If he did get the position, this would add another layer of documentation to his resume and a more secure work status outside El Salvador. At DePaul, visiting professors often morphed seamlessly into permanent, tenure-track positions.

"I would love to let Maria know about this fine development," said Ricardo. "I know I cannot do this now."

"Like I said," said the priest. "Let's be quiet for now and get the position first."

Part VI: Big Ben

Chapter 70

Another Chase

No doubt Ben Cooper was worth pursuing by our Gang of Four, one totally new---thanks to Maria---and viable suspect if, indeed, someone was directly responsible for Marlene Scott's death.

But Newt and I also could feel the Independent Study group's energy start to wane a bit. Running out of gas? You can hold college students' attention only so long. For over two months, a ton of effort was put into this project---interviews, poring over old newspapers, writing, and researching government records.

We agreed Craig and his computer skills were the logical starting point in locating Big Bad Ben. He could use them to unearth useful, preliminary data quicker than any gumshoe methods. He was quite anxious to get started. He had a summer internship lined up with Google, and it would start as soon as he could put this semester behind him.

Jing was headed for a trip home to China, not having seen her family since the school year began last September. Then she planned a quick return to a job waiting for her in Chicago with its Chinatown Chamber of Commerce.

With a waitressing job waiting for her in a golf resort, Kate really did not mind the chase of another suspect. On the other hand, she needed to make as much money as possible in the summer. She was headed for China next school year as an exchange student.

I was not going anywhere until July, when I would head back to Phoenix to do volunteer work at Pima school and the Vincentian House. Undoubtedly, Mary would have other projects in mind.

In the meantime, I had a growing mountain of papers to grade in addition to completing some Rotary business: Picking a recipient of the local chapter's annual, substantial scholarship. This would be a pleasant chore. Not so pleasant, I suspected, would be chasing down Ben Cooper.

Maria hoped to be headed for Chicago and DePaul. While the Gang of Four was not briefed with the tentative news at this point, Mary, Dorothy, and I were made aware she could be joining her family in Chicago as soon as Ricardo, her father, finalized a teaching offer.

There was emotional investment, too. The students had come face-to-face with unfamiliar worlds. They learned things weren't so easy for past generations, altering many images. Mostly, as a shared experience, they learned that life can be a bitch.

In one case, they witnessed Gene Brown, an important figure in the Marlene Scott mystery, die a lonely, pauper's death. I am sure Pete never will forget time spent with him in the Shawnee County rest home.

In the interview with Nicholas Walker, Pete and Kate learned that being gay 50 years ago was not the same as today. His stigma---homosexuality---was the scarlet letter of its day, something that needed to be hidden. If not, there could be serious consequences.

Of course, they had no idea of Maria's backstory, starting with her family's perilous trek from Central America to Arizona. The journey's life-and-death challenges would've been totally alien to them, considering their mostly privileged middle-class backgrounds. Maybe someday they'd become aware.

The four Harrison students had easily invested 3-4 times more effort than they would've for a regular class. In my mind, this was graduate school level work. And they still carried full academic loads in addition to our Independent Study project. They'd each get an A grade, of course, and see their work have a real-life impact.

Furthermore, there was this fast-approaching rite of spring that occurs on college campuses: As temperatures rise with warm, sunny breezes, the student body's attention spans shrink. Hormones flow faster than the nearby Tippecanoe River currents.

Final exams and graduation loomed, too. And both students and faculty generally are on the same page: Let's get the academic year done.

"You really expect to get much more from them?" asked Mary. "Isn't it about time to start composing the final stories for Newt? Go with what you've got?"

But when the question was put to Jing, Pete, Kate and Craig, there was unanimous consent to turn over a final "Ben Cooper stone." Or as Kate, our resident sage, put it: "We'd look pretty stupid if we didn't and it came out eventually that he killed Marlene."

The search for a dead-or-alive Ben Cooper would be a challenge. It had been tricky enough locating Gene Brown, and he lived not far away. With Butte Construction claiming bankruptcy after finishing Harrison's turkey plant project, employee records likely would be impossible to locate and provide clues.

And so what? That was 50 years ago. We had to assume he'd covered much ground since his stop in Liberty---if that, indeed, was his home when he worked on the plant. And how long was he here?

Chapter 71

Tracking Ben

Once again there were several angles launched in a search, this time for Ben Cooper. Maria's PIP work for the University of Michigan was nearly completed, and she joined the hunt.

She had Dorothy's full blessing. "You need to be around people your age, not oldies like me," she was told. On that front, Pete Gray was quick to volunteer as her driver since she had no license. Something was brewing between these two, no question.

Maria was given the important task of re-combing the county's Latino population for additional details that could be recalled about the Butte foreman, Cooper.

Did anyone interviewed have knowledge of Ben's permanent home? Did anyone recall Ben mentioning his wife's name? Did he have a wife? A family? Who were his on-the-job buddies? Could they be found? Where did he hang out when not working?

Maria's Spanish language skills, and the rapport acquired in her earlier rounds of PIP interviews, proved valuable. When she came calling again, she was remembered by many as that "*nina adorable*," someone to be trusted.

Since Pete planned to stay in Harrison for the summer, helping with the family grocery business he would inherit, he didn't care how long the chase took with Maria. And this part of the entire saga was an education for him not to be forgotten.

The town's Latino segment was new to him, but he was amazed at the hospitality incurred on their rounds. Despite being born, raised and educated in the same county, he became more and more startled at how little he knew about this segment of the population under his nose---including high school classmates.

"Alberto, sure I remember you," said Pete, quickly racking his brain for memories after they shook hands at the door. He and Maria were just invited into the home of Hector and Lucia Rosario, a small, but very tidy bungalow on the edge of Harrison in a neighborhood familiar with the Spanish language citizenry.

Alberto was there to greet them, too. Hector and Lucia were Alberto's grandparents. He moved in with them after high school. His parents' three-bedroom home---filled with Alberto's four younger siblings---was just around the corner.

Maria had these interviews down to a science by the time they were at the Rosario home. A little friendly patter on PIP progress to start, then a gentle transition into her questions. Typically, they got interrupted by coffee and a proffered sweet snack.

In this case from the initial interview, she had learned Hector worked alongside Diego Escobar---hence, Ben Cooper. In the end, this second go-round offered no real, factual background details about Cooper aside from his browbeating of Latino workers.

The same could not be said for Pete, who learned a lot about former classmate Alberto.

"So how are you doing," Pete asked Alberto as they prepared to leave. "I haven't seen you for a long time. You must be near your last year of college like me."

"No, no. I work at Thomas Turkey," he said. "I am on a night shift, so that is why I am home now."

"So, you're taking some time off from school? A gap year?"

There was an awkward pause before Alberto answered, "I never went to college. I am saving as much money as I can now to afford it someday. I hope to go to the University of Indiana's branch in Evansville, or maybe start junior college."

Pete would later learn Alberto's father had abandoned his family after the fifth child was born. His grandparents, Hector and Lucia, made room for him in their home. Not only did this ease the burden, this gave Alberto an opportunity to save money for school as well as help support his immediate family.

Alberto worked nights so he could be available to help his mother get his siblings off to school. The night shift also paid more, which helped the college fund.

"Makes you think," said Pete, as he and Maria walked to his car.

"About what?" said Maria.

"I used to see him almost every day in classes for four years," he answered. "I had no clue he was going through all these family problems. I saw him, but I never really took the time to know him.

"The thing is," Pete added, "Alberto was the smartest kid in my class. He ranked No. 2 behind a nerdy girl named Lucinda Flowers. She's going to Princeton."

"Makes you think."

Chapter 72

Newt's Business, Efforts

Hoosier-Record business was looking up, no question.

Since his Harrison newspaper began publishing stories produced by the local college students---first by Flip's class, then through an internship program that resulted---Newt Ames saw circulation grow. He found it gratifying the improvement was due apparently to actual editorial content, not some tricked-up subscription giveaway or cuts in rates.

The gains weren't monumental, but significant enough that he could justify raising advertising rates a smidgeon. Maybe there was a way to additionally package some of the new content and syndicate it to other papers. A fantasy? More income would be good. He did have a family to support, after all.

That he was thinking like a businessman annoyed him, though. Newt could feel himself getting jerked farther and farther from his love of reporting and writing stories. True journalists, like Woodward & Bernstein, could give a rat's ass about their industry's business side.

In a perverted way, that's why he left his Louisville *Courier-Journal* job as a feature writer---to buy a paper and call the editorial shots himself. Before the business side took over his life, the grand plan was to hire someone, or take in a partner, to handle ledgers. That idea went up in smoke with the economy's collapse in 2008.

His pals back at the *Courier-Journal*, and they were becoming fewer with each gut-wrenching layoff there, assured him he wasn't missing a thing these days in his old newsroom. Reporters were saddled with ball-busting, real time deadlines that prevented in-depth work and follow-ups.

Editors insisted on pictures with almost every story. His old colleagues were being turned into clerks with cameras. A picture worth 10,000 words? In this new age, it was the other way: The word, if you could get beyond captions, equaled 10,000 pictures.

Feature stories had been Newt's real love. Forget it. Who was left to do them? The writers of articles that required a reader to turn a page generally were the first to get tossed aside by the number crunchers. Three days to turn out a well-researched story. No way.

Papers like the *Courier-Journal* and nearby Indianapolis metros belonged, or subscribed, to syndicates that supplied content from outside sources. Cheaper, and no benefits to pay which thrilled the corporate bottom-liners. Freelancers had a better shot at getting something thoughtful into print than regular staffers.

Newt was envious of the Harrison students, and Flip, throughout their Marlene Scott project. They were engaging in real journalism, whether they knew it or not. It was tough for him to remain on the sidelines and play his ancillary role.

Maybe that's why on a Friday afternoon, when things got slow at the *Hoosier-Record* offices, he jumped in his car and headed toward Indianapolis. His destination was Mooresville, a community on the southwest exurban side of Indy.

There was a simple reason for Newt's destination. Marlene Scott was buried in the Mooresville Cemetery next to her mother, Florence "Flo" Brown, and he wanted to see her grave. Not that he doubted she was dead and buried there, as her obituary stated. Instead, he knew from experience that sometimes final resting spots can provide clues and maybe answer a question or two. It was worth a shot.

Besides, Newt was itching to contribute something reportorial on this project. After much thought about how to get involved, it occurred to him this was one stone---a gravestone at that---left unturned. It never got mentioned in one of Flip's meetings.

Mooresville was one of Indiana's older towns, which saw steady, almost predictable, growth as a bedroom community to residents working in and around Indy. No one truly newsworthy came from this city of 10,000 unless you counted John Dillinger, the notorious midwestern bank robber of the 1930s.

As it developed, Mooresville was only two hours away, and the miles flew by after he hit Interstate 70. The cemetery was a few blocks off that highway, hidden behind groves of trees lining the city's Indiana Street.

When it came to locating Marlene's grave, he winged it after parking on a lane that meandered through the quiet grounds. There was no office, public map or directory for guidance, and his checking of several "locate a grave" web sites were not helpful. Probably should've put Craig, the Gang of Four's computer nerd, on the case, he thought.

After a mile of tramping up and down rows of graves, Newt spotted a maintenance worker on a tractor lawnmower. The poor guy, intently concentrating on keeping his rows straight, jumped and almost fainted when Newt came from behind with a startling tap on his shoulder.

"Yeow, scared the hell out of me," he said. "Give me a second for my heart to stop pounding. Coming up behind someone like that in a cemetery ain't the best idea, friend."

Eventually, Newt and Nick, who had all the looks of a retired farmer with his suspendered overalls, matching John Deere cap, and red handkerchief dangling from a rear pocket, exchanged pleasantries. They retreated to a maintenance shack near the end of the same lane where Newt was parked. This is where the cemetery's map of plots was kept.

It took 10 minutes or so---the plot registry was not alphabetized---before Marlene's grave was located on the chart. It was just off the graveled parking lot of a garage housing assorted municipal vehicles

After they left the shed, Nick pointed across the cemetery to the approximate location of Marlene's grave. Was he familiar with Marlene Scott, Newt asked? Did he know her mother? For that matter, did he know anyone in the family?

"Never heard of 'em," was the response, "and I been here maybe 20 years or so. I know no one's ever asked me about them. Kind of surprising. You always get curious people when someone's buried who's been in the newspapers. I see it all the time. We got close to getting (John) Dillinger buried here. That would a been something, but he's over at Crown Hill in Indy.

"Well, better get back to my mowing. Good luck."

The graves were not that easy to find, even after the general location was pointed out to Newt. The headstones mostly were flat, ground level tablets, dark imitation granite, and looked inexpensive.

On the left was the mother, with "Florence 'Flo' Scott" the chiseled engraving. She was 53 years old when she died, just four years following the death of her daughter and only child.

Curiously, she used the surname of her first husband, Scott, who was Marlene's biological father. The divorce from her second husband, Gene Brown, apparently was bitter enough that his name got ignored.

But that wasn't the biggest surprise.

A closer look at Marlene's tombstone engraving showed that her birthday would've been Thursday---yesterday, the day before this trip---and she would've been 68 years old. Furthermore, an expensive-looking bouquet of red, yellow, and purple flowers fronted the marker with a card. It read, "Never forgotten. God be with you."

This was a surprise. Newt looked up and around. Where was Nick? There, parking his tractor in the maintenance shed across a row of tombstones. He hustled over, catching the caretaker just as he was locking a door to the building.

Nick had no idea of who might've left flowers on Marlene's grave.

"But I can tell you one thing," he said. "I sort of remember this happening before several times 'bout this time of year. Kind of funny when you think about it."

How so?

"Always thought it was unusual flowers got left on Marlene's grave, never on her mom's."

Chapter 73

Just the Facts

In cobbling an image of Ben Cooper, the students' labors produced a disparate collection of facts surrounding the man. Bottom line: Not exactly someone you invite to dinner.

We already knew Ben Cooper was a bully, racist, and used his role as a foreman to verbally abuse workers, especially Latinos. "A really bad guy," noted Kate, who, given that her father, Nate, was head dude for a motorcycle gang, knew something about bad guys.

There also was indication from several interviews that he had coerced several wives of immigrant underlings---worried about deportation---into sex, sometimes with their husbands in the next room.

"He come one night to a home I know, very late," one elderly woman whispered to Maria in an aside. "He pound on door. He was very drunk. The wife answered. Her husband was not home that weekend. This bad man knew it. He made the woman do many things. Terrible things, she tell me. They no live here no more."

It did not take long to uncover what a disgusting person he was, but we needed specific facts about Cooper's moves. Even if word-of-mouth, the goal was to learn if he was alive and could be located for an update. Here were some nuggets that went into the profile we assembled:

*While working on the turkey project, he lived in a Harrison rooming house during the week and most weekends, though he was known to "go home" on the weekends he didn't stay in Harrison;

*His hometown? Not much luck there. No one knew for sure, but among candidates mentioned were Hammond or Hobart in Indiana, Danville or Chicago Heights in Illinois, Paducah or Mayfield in Kentucky or possibly Lima, Ohio.

*He was an ex-U.S. Marine with "Semper Fi" tattooed on his right forearm;

*Loved old automobiles, and owned a much-prized, light blue Studebaker pickup truck most likely from the early 1950s;

*A heavy drinker, he hit Harrison's bars straight from work almost every work day;

*Married? He never wore a ring or mentioned a wife or family;

*Got bailed out of jail by Butte management on at least one occasion after involvement in a barroom brawl.

Now it was up to Craig and his computers to track him. He assured us there appeared to be a strong trail to follow.

Chapter 74

The Chase

"Damn! Well, forget that. Now I got real work to do."

I was in our *Hoosier-Record* workspace when Craig launched his Ben Cooper chase. I'd never heard him swear. This did not sound like a good start judging by the outcry after he opened his laptop and, in a blur of fingers, typed a few keys.

"What's wrong?"

"The White Pages didn't have him," he answered.

"White Pages? You mean the online phone book? You're trying to find Ben Cooper by dialing 411? Maybe there's hope for me yet."

Craig answered, "Yeah, sometimes it can be that simple. Believe me. It's always my first step when I start these things. The first time I did it for money, I wormed my way past more firewalls than a Chicago fireman. Couldn't find this person. The guy who hired me? He finally said, 'Why don't we just do the White Pages? You never know.'

"Bam! There was the guy I was looking for. Pretty embarrassing. Ever since then, it's how I start---the White Pages. But there's no Ben Cooper that fits our general demo."

Craig had a bunch of formulas up his sleeve. Some were very clever. This kid had a big technology future. Go get 'em, pal.

Did Cooper ever re-join Butte, or its shells, after his abrupt departure in Harrison following that last Marlene sighting? One techie program he used had Butte as the magnet. It showed locations for its major construction projects after the Harrison turkey job. The journeymen tradespeople often followed work best matching their skills. He was a heavy equipment operator, bulldozers, pavers, forklifts, and the like. The pay was good.

Then, Craig accessed newspapers in those communities where Butte had jobs, looking for Cooper's name to materialize on police blotters during the project's time in those cities. If he was brutal enough to murder Marlene Scott, it was no stretch to think he could get in additional trouble with the law---and caught---somewhere by now. If his name did pop up, then it would be easier from there to find pertinent, personal details like a hometown off public records.

This was complicated, of course, by the fact Butte changed its name and paperwork a few times in re-organizational efforts to smother lawsuits left in the company wake. Also, we soon discovered the company rented its equipment to firms, with some employees following the machinery.

Going way deep in Butte's files, Craig got registration numbers for the heavy equipment pieces---most states required them in contracts---to stay on the trail to other projects and locations.

One problem to overcome? Many of the back issues of newspapers in the work site towns were not digitized, available only on microfilm. Luckily, he could turn to Lexis-Nexis, ProQuest, American Journalism Review archives and the U.S. Congress's Chronicling America search micro-filmed files for help.

Was all this a stretch? Craig's legwork did pay off, sort of. Turned out Cooper worked a job several years later after Harrison in Kirksville, Mo., where he got arrested for an assault that took place in a local bar.

According to the Kirksville *Express* back issues, Bad Ben was charged with beating up a bartender, a college student, at closing time. The newspaper did not have many details. Reading between the lines, it was obvious he did not wish to leave the establishment without another round of beers with pals. And, when rejected, made feelings known with his fists.

There was no mention in the *Express* story, but a little additional digging found Butte had a major highway and bridge project taking place locally at the time. Furthermore, Kirksville was home to a university. The name of the bar was the Varsity Club, an obvious student hangout. Not a stretch to figure Ben liked being around all those young coeds.

We got a hometown for Cooper off the Kirksville report, but not without much prodding of a desk sergeant slow to go into the back files "fer a bunch of college kids." It was listed as Fort Madison in Iowa, a beat-up Mississippi River town that had been belted by one too many floods over the years.

Nice, but no go. We couldn't find Ben's name connected to Fort Madison in any fashion. Craig even surveyed the county clerk's files for real estate records and birth records at the local hospital.

He must've been faking it in Missouri with a bogus ID when charged. Pretty ballsy to scam a court. We never found any record of him living in Fort Madison, but it was home to the Iowa State Penitentiary. Was he playing some sort of joke?

Furthermore, back in Kirksville, there was precious little information on the outcome of the arrest. The Express did no real follow-up---standard practice for most small daily newspapers---and, after our not-so-friendly desk sergeant was prodded a bit more, we learned from court records the charge was settled with a $200 fine after he spent a night in jail.

"This guy does a nice job covering his trail," said Pete Jagger, involved in similar searches in his work for the Kansas City (Mo.) police department. "You'll need some luck finding him. Your student techie's doing a nice job, though. Let's hope he stays on the right side of the law. No hacking."

Craig had more search programs and ideas he put into play.

At one point, knowing Cooper owned a vintage Studebaker from the 1950s, he accessed membership lists of organizations such as the Antique Auto Club of America and Class Car Club of America. Didn't work. Knowing he was a U.S. Marine, he also plumbed data related to veteran groups like the American Legion. Zero results.

In what had to be one of the oddest combinations in law enforcement history, we recruited Nate "The Preacher" Stine to work the incarceration angle with Pete, whose access as a detective figured to be helpful. Was Cooper ever in jail? While Mary's brother took care of perusing official prison files in Missouri, Nate worked the other side of the street. He put word out on his less-than-official prison grapevines, which he used in our earlier Gene Brown quest.

"I'm at a little bit of a disadvantage," noted Nate. "The (Holy) Rollers' prison enrollment's down a bit now. We've been good little boys and girls lately."

Craig did uncover a Ben Cooper, who figured to be the right age and lived not far away in Central City, Ky. But it was a false alarm. A quick telephone call and we learned this Ben Cooper, in addition to being deceased, had been a school superintendent in Kentucky.

"Close," I told Craig, "and I think we're getting closer. I feel it in my bones."

"I hope so," he said. "I'm running out of ideas. I may have to reach back for something extra to find him."

This made me nervous. By dipping deeper into his kitbag, I was sure he meant something illegal---as in hacking government files. There was no shortage of data banks waiting to be cracked, such as Internal Revenue Service records, Medicare or Medicaid files, credit cards, Social Security, U.S. Department of Defense records, etc.

This would be illegal, which Newt and I definitely did not want to happen. It could taint everything. But what to do if Craig, who had the talents to breach KGB emails, found our man in this manner?

Time was running out. The school year was nearing a close, students were packing bags, and the fate of Ben Cooper---an excellent suspect---still was unknown.

We already had enough to put together a nifty series for Newt and the *Hoosier-Record.* On the other hand, I sure would hate to have our work published---and then have Cooper materialize later as the person responsible for Marlene's death.

On what figured to be the last search day before we began writing, I walked into our *Hoosier-Record* workspace and immediately things looked promising. Craig, who had not smiled since first striking out with the White Pages, sat at his usual spot with a huge grin on his face.

Got him. "Everything's rosy," he said. "Literally. Not only were there roses, but snapdragons, lilies, and button pompons," he added. "Yellow, red, blue, gold, green. I'm probably missing a few colors. And one, big, beautiful bouquet."

What? Care to explain?

Craig said, "I found our elusive Mr. Cooper. And he's not that far away and he's not going anywhere and, better yet, he's alive. The flowers were the clue. A bouquet. They gave him away, on probably my last shot."

Craig explained that, out of ideas short of hacking, he recalled Newt talking about the flowers he saw not long ago on Marlene's grave in the suburban cemetery. Furthermore, the caretaker indicated they were there every year on her birth-day.

"I wondered. So where did they come from? Was this some-body feeling guilty? Who'd still be arranging a bouquet for someone dead 50 years? Her mother was dead. So was her stepdad. There was no name on the card.

"On the other hand, someone had to pay for them---didn't they? And likely it was from a florist in the area. I whipped up a search. Did you know there are 19 floral shops that deliver in a 20-mile radius of Mooresville and its cemetery?"

Craig, working it the old-fashioned way, personally tele-phoned each florist. He struck oil with "Flowers by Dewey" in a nearby community, Danville.

"Took some talking with the clerk," he continued. "This was the third year she'd been the one to fill it, so she remem-bered some details. Guy used a credit card over the telephone. His name was Ben Cooper. Only one thing bothered me, though."

What?

"The clerk gave me the telephone number and I tracked it to Terre Haute, which is, what, only 130 or so miles from here. His home address is the same as a Federal prison there."

A prisoner with a credit card?

Chapter 75

The Conversion

The Federal penitentiary complex on Terre Haute's out-skirts houses approximately 2,500 male inmates. There's no mistaking the 1,200-acre complex for anything but a peniten-tiary. There is no human activity on the flat, wide and tree-less grounds that completely surround the colorless, but uniformly laid-out, buildings.

The main entrance is a two-lane road that crosses this bar-ren expanse. It ends at two huge doors fronted on each flank by security checkpoints. Of course, you could hardly expect to be greeted by balloons, fountains and statues, considering this prison is where the Federal government carries out most of its executions, the most notable in recent years being Okla-homa City bomber Timothy McVeigh. The current housing in-cludes international terrorists, mass shooters, sex traffickers, serial killers, kidnappers and assorted politicians.

We had no problem getting inside after thorough pat-downs, and the facility has not seen many escapes in its 80-year or so history. Our request to meet Ben Cooper---boosted by a Harrison College trustee with connections---by-passed the usual bureaucratic formalities. The petition went straight through to James Winston, the warden.

"So you never connected with Cooper himself?" asked Newt, as we drove to Terre Haute to keep the appointment. "He does know we're coming, though. Right?"

That's an affirmative, I assured him. The warden himself took care of this.

"Will this be a big surprise for him, then?"

"Shouldn't be. I wasn't there to listen in, but our contact gave Winston an idea of who we were. We'll just have to see how the dialog goes and look for openings."

Making the trip with us were students Kate McDonald and Pete Gray, who, though growing up not far away, was totally oblivious about the federal penitentiary in his hometown's back yard. This figured to be an experience all of us would not forget.

Newt had done more than his share of jailhouse interviews while a reporter on large newspapers. My experience---bailing out fraternity brothers in college for disturbing the peace and similar alcohol-enhanced offenses---was limited.

We would get a half-hour with Cooper, no more, Winston assured us. The warden did have somewhat of an idea about our mission; that we were doing some sort of study project and his inmate might be able to help us with background.

At age 82, and with no chance for parole until he was in his 90s, Ben probably saw talking to a bunch of college kids as a break in the boredom. When he heard we were from Harrison College, he had to be further intrigued if he still had a memory. There had been no mention of Marlene.

The Terre Haute penitentiary had a progressive reputation in criminology and rehabilitation, Winston said. Professional social workers and psychologists came often to get material for case studies. College students working on projects were not as common. He was relieved to know Newt and I would accompany them.

"You could say Coop's kind of a success story for us," said Winston. "Or, I should say the Rev. Cooper?"

"REVEREND?" Damn! Did we have the right Ben Cooper? All our effort for nothing? Our unrehearsed, but uniform, chorus of wonderment almost knocked the warden off his chair.

"Yes, the *Reverend* Cooper," he answered. "Ben's one of our true success stories. Found God a few years back. That's not particularly unusual in a prison, but he took it a few steps more. I thought you knew. I figured that's why you were here. Why are you here?"

Let the tap dancing begin. Winston seemed genuinely confused that we were not here to check out Cooper's religious conversion, if indeed one took place. This was news to us, but, taking charge, my explanation of our motives seemed to work.

As interns for the local newspaper, the *Hoosier-Record,* I explained we were looking at historic, migration patterns in Harrison County. The Butte construction project, responsible for importing workers from south of the border, was a big player. We were trying to pin down their working conditions, such as salaries, benefits, etc. Ben, I said, was one of the key Butte employees we uncovered in our quest.

Well, OK, maybe it was bullshit. Maybe I stretched things. I could always explain to the students later why I wasn't totally straight. On the other hand, it wasn't too far from the truth. You could say Cooper, a foreman, was a logical source for background. So, what if we do ask: Oh, and by the way, did you murder Marlene Scott?

The warden bought it. That's all that counted at this late date. He informed us Ben, or Rev. Cooper, worked closely with the penitentiary's full-time pastor as a volunteer, assisting in mostly clerical duties and, in the process, enjoying liberties extended to few inmates.

Winston was sure to make it known that the terms of his sentence meant it was likely Ben would spend the rest of his life behind bars. He was in prison for bank robbery and kidnapping (Federal offenses), a case in which he stuck up a bank in rural Illinois and held a teller hostage in his escape across the Indiana border. Though he did not harm his captive, there was no leniency whatsoever due to his long, lifetime record of lesser convictions.

Chapter 76

Let the Game Begin

First, there were niceties as we crowded around a table in the prison chapel, an image of a Crucifix tacked to the wall just over Ben's left shoulder. There were introductions, a few attempts at humor that drew polite laughs, and my generic, soft-pedaling of our Harrison College mission that made no reference to Marlene.

None of us had an idea what Ben looked like before this gathering. I am not sure what others expected. A devil with a pitchfork? Tattoo of a Swastika on his skinned head? He did not quite fit what I envisioned.

Cooper looked youthful for someone in his 80s. He had totally gray hair, but it was a butch with a flat top. Maybe 5-9 or 5-10, a little stocky, and he appeared as if he might have been an athlete at one point in life. There was a slight limp. An old football injury? His face, though craggy, was a bit on the pinkish side, almost as if he'd been spending time in the sun.

If there were physical giveaways about his background, they were this: His hands were extremely rough and large, with uneven knuckles and one pinkie bent to the side. His face had several scars, one on the lower half of his chin and a longer one high on his right cheekbone. Also, a tiny portion of his left ear lobe was missing. To me, these were evidence that he had been in more than a few nasty, barroom scraps.

"So, guys, you want to talk about Butte's days in Harrison? That right?" he asked, getting us down to business. "I'm not sure what I can add to whatever it is you want. That was a long, long time ago."

Before we got started, he wanted us to know something and lowered his voice almost to a whisper. We drew a little closer.

"How did I, a convict, become an assistant to the pastor? How did I become an ordained preacher? What am I doing in a prison? I'm sure you're familiar with my criminal record. But you don't know this: Three years ago, I became a born-again Christian, praise the Lord. Seriously. Right here in this chapel, thanks to a blessed man, Rev. Marvin Franklin, the prison chaplain who showed me the light.

"See, it's right there in the Bible, the Book of Chronicles: 'If my people, who are called by my name, will humble themselves and pray and seek my face and turn from their wicked ways, then I will hear from heaven, and I will forgive their sin and will heal their land.' I pray every day, many times."

I could see Kate roll her eyes a bit. Pete's jaw dropped a few inches. Newt kept his head down, scribbling away in his reporter notebook.

Ben went on to explain how he joined Bible classes taught by Rev. Franklin in the Terre Haute facility. Then he was baptized a Baptist, which, with his high school diploma, opened the door to becoming an ordained pastor in the House of The Open Christian Bible Church---pretty much a mail order transaction, best I could tell.

He further explained that, because it was a denomination comprised mainly of convicts behind bars, it was not well-known in mainstream Christianity. I made a mental note to do some digging on this.

"See, it's right there in the Bible, book of Isaiah: 'So do not fear, for I am with you; do not be dismayed, for I am your God. I will strengthen you and help you; I will uphold you with my righteous right hand.'"

Kate rolled her eyes again, a flicker Ben appeared to note. Pete's jaw did not drop this time.

Our opening questions, finally, were perfunctory.

His several references to "greater glory of God" withstanding, there was little indication his demeanor matched his background. There were mostly mellow, diverted references to possible, revealing topics. Influx of Latinos who worked with him ("Some fine Christians among them"), night life ("I am the Lord thy God, thou shalt not have any strange gods before Me."), his brushes with the law ("He that is without sin among you, let him first cast a stone...") and so on.

We were running out of time. There was enough here to include in our series, but we were no closer to solving the No. 1 question: Who killed Marlene Scott? Until Kate popped the question. Ah, youth.

"Rev. Cooper, I have to ask," she said, as we appeared to be near the end of our allotted time. "When you worked in Harrison for Butte, what do you know about who murdered a Marlene Scott? Our research showed you quit that job only two days after she went missing. What do you remember about this?"

A pregnant pause? You could hear a pencil drop? Deer in the headlights? They all seemed to fit. Definitely, you could've heard a clock tick if there'd been a clock in the room. Newt, who held onto his pencil, looked up from the notebook.

An ever-so-slight smile momentarily appeared on the good Rev. Ben Cooper's face. "That's it, right?" he said. "That's why you came here for this interview. That's the real reason you wanted to talk to me. Everything else was crap?"

"Well, it was one of the questions we wanted to ask," said Newt. "We thought you could shed some light, if for no other reason than you were in Harrison at the time. At the very least, you could add something to the picture."

"Who are you people, anyway," he asked, his face turning a deeper shade of pink. "You're obviously not law enforcement. You can't arrest me. If you could, it wouldn't make any difference. I'm not going anywhere. I'm already in the pen."

My turn.

I explained that this was a school project, an around independent study exercise revolving around the local Hoosier-Record newspaper. Their work on Marlene's death was strictly a cold case feature since it's been 50 years. The students were in it strictly for academic credit. The only financial gain might be realized by Newt, but no one would get rich. He simply sought solvency for his newspaper.

Cooper took it all in. Then his smile widened an iota.

"OK, you want a story? I'll give you a story. Why not? I'm already in prison, probably forever.

"Yes, I did it." He paused, apparently to organize thoughts, then continued: "This is something I have carried for many years. It is a great relief to unburden myself before the Lord God Almighty."

Where did we go from here? Did anyone else know?

"I never told anyone until I got here. Rev. Franklin knows, though. When I became born again, I confessed my sins to him. Sort of a Catholic thing. But it's right there in the Bible: 'If we confess our sins, he is faithful and just and will forgive us our sins and purify us from all unrighteousness.'

"The reverend pledged not to tell anyone without my permission. He never asked again. He hears a lot of stuff in Terre Haute, probably worse than me. I had a lot of other bad things to tell him, too. So, it's sort of a preacher-member thing, like a lawyer and client. I figured I had that going for me. Why not get it off my chest? I done a lot of bad things in my life. I know that. This born-again thing just felt right."

"Could you tell us more," asked Newt.

"Well, I was drunk at the time," he said. "So, I can't remember it all. Maybe I never wanted to. Probably just as well. But bits and pieces popped up in my mind over the years. I do sleep a little better since I confessed. I found out her birthday, started sending flowers to her grave. Looked it all up on the Internet. Maybe this'll help you, too. Can't hurt me. I'm not going anywhere."

To the best of what he could recall, Ben replayed the events of that cold Friday night 50 years ago in Harrison.

Not long after she stalked away from the Monarch Café, Ben, in his car after rounds of drinks in a downtown bar, spotted Marlene walking into town in the opposite direction. He hit the brakes, did a quick U-turn, pulled alongside her, and offered her a ride. She accepted and immediately it was obvious she was angry about something.

"I guess today it's hard to believe she'd get in a car with a stranger, but it wasn't that big a deal at the time," he added. "Kids hitchhiked all over the country in those days. I could see she wanted to talk. I just pulled over, became a listener."

Marlene quickly accepted a drink from his backseat stash. Ben, seeing where this could lead, continued to have a very sympathetic ear. The first drink led to more alcohol, fewer inhibitions, and Marlene soon was in a stupor.

By then, Ben had driven to a secluded, rural location. He started undressing Marlene---"I didn't care what shape she was in; just didn't want her puking in my car"---when she suddenly became aware of what was happening, bolting from the car and dashing half-dressed into a farm field.

Ben caught up with her. She resisted his attempt to get her back into the car, things got physical, and escalated. "I think about that a lot," he said. "I know I probably punched her, hard, a few times, God forgive me.

"I stalked off, sat in the car having a few swigs and a smoke. I waited. She never returned, and I figured she just went off in a different direction. To be honest, I never did know what happened to her until I heard they found a body a few months later. I didn't even know her name.

"A year or two later, I drove back to Harrison and checked where her body was found according to a newspaper clip. No doubt about it. It was not far from the spot where we parked. My life was a piece of shit from that day forward.

"Look. You guys do what you want with this. Like I said. I'm not going anywhere. I'm going to die behind bars anyway. Maybe this'll give closure to some people."

Chapter 77

Start the Presses!

For Newt Ames, and just about anyone else in the newspaper business, there's nothing like the adrenalin rush from producing an exclusive, Page 1 story sure to be devoured by readers.

This happened a dozen or so times when he was a star reporter at the *Courier-Journal* in Louisville and, in minor roles earlier as an intern on papers in Des Moines and St. Paul, Minn.

He couldn't imagine what it would've been like in the Watergate era working for the *Washington Post*. Phone ringing off the hook. Calls from the White House. Bloody competition with the *New York Times*. Foreign news outlets jumping on the story. The whole world following each development, and you're in the middle of a storm.

In Louisville, after he broke important, local stories, it meant Newt'd walk into his regular stop for breakfast on his way to the office and see diners glued to his article. Then, he'd get to his desk and be greeted by dozens of messages, mostly reporters from other outlets trying to cadge leftover details for their catch-up pieces.

Newt lived for those adrenalin-fueled scenarios. He pretty much knew they'd become rare after purchasing the Harrison *Hoosier-Record*, but he could always hope. In each of the 12 years of ownership, those hopes began dissipating as he became less a practitioner of journalism and more a bean counter.

That's why on the first morning after the Marlene Scott story appeared in the *Hoosier-Record*, and when he routinely walked into the Dough Girls for coffee and a cinnamon scone, he was startled to see everyone reading his paper.

Several held up their newspaper as a greeting. Almost everyone looked up when he laughed.

"On me," said Dot, handing him the pastry and coffee. "You're our hero."

There was science at his end dealing with the students' work. In addition to editing and rewriting the raw copy, he plotted how it would get played both in print and digitally. This was no small matter.

Newt decided to divide the content into a series of three parts, better to stretch things out a bit for the extended exposure it would bring the *Hoosier-Record*. Also, he would highlight the students with head shots and thumbnail sketches in the kickoff segment.

The introductory article would reveal Ben Cooper as the culprit and give hints of important elements to follow about the fateful night. No need to keep everyone waiting to learn the identity of the guilty person. The town had been through enough suspense. Fifty years of it.

There would be comments from local officials, but remarks from those related to the crime in other ways---Gene Brown, Nicholas Walker, etc.---would be spread across second and third installments. Just spoon feed details.

While the Marlene Scott story was old to many Harrison residents, a review of the basic facts was necessary to establish the overall narrative. There would be many readers new to the crime.

For sure, Newt figured to get bombarded with phone calls, everything from outside media doing their version of the development to whack-o's with their version of events. To handle the crunch, he'd hire part-time help to take calls and help with the paper's regular duties.

For now, he was quite pleased with the first article being devoured by readers in the Dough Girls' bakery. If this was an indicator, the *Hoosier-Record* was in for a record run. Here was the series kickoff:

This is the first Hoosier-Record story in a 3-part series focusing on the mystery surrounding the death 50 years ago of Marlene Scott, a 17-year old high school student. The apparent crime hovered over Harrison like a bad dream. No more.

Thanks to reportorial efforts by four Harrison College students, Craig Conley, Peter Gray, Kate McDonald, and Jingfei Zhang, plus Maria Lopez, and led by instructor Phillip Doyle, the cloud has been lifted. Local law enforcement officials are expected to officially close the books on what had been an open case. This newspaper is proud to display their work.

---Newton Ames, Hoosier-Record publisher

By Craig Conley, Peter Gray, Kate McDonald, Jingfei Zhang and Maria Lopez
(First in a series)

When last seen alive, Harrison teenager Marlene Scott was in the parking lot of the local Monarch Café. She en-

gaged in a raised-voice argument with another youth and then, according to eyewitnesses, angrily left the lot and stalked down Jackson street.

The date was Jan. 11, 1969, and it was approximately 8 p.m. The temperature was a penetratingly cold 17 degrees, and it was dark with the moon entering its final quarter.

Marlene's decomposed body was discovered two months later in a local farm field. For over 50 years, the cause of her disappearance and death remained a mystery---until now.

An exhaustive, recent review of then-gathered evidence by a Harrison College Independent Study class for the Hoosier-Record, plus their gathering of new facts and previously unknown narratives, has uncovered the startling identity of the crime's perpetrator.

"Yes, I did it," said Ben Cooper. "This (Marlene Scott's death) is something I have carried for many years. It is a great relief to unburden myself before the Lord God Almighty."

At the time of Marlene's death, Cooper was a journeyman construction worker employed by Butte Construction Co. working on the Thomas Turkey expansion project near Harrison in 1968-70. He was a foreman and heavy equipment operator.

Cooper confessed to the Hoosier-Record in a recorded interview, which was turned over to the Harrison County district attorney office. The confession was made in the Federal Correctional Institution in Terre Haute, where, at age 82, he has eight years to serve on kidnapping and armed robbery convictions.

Shortly after the latest incarceration four years ago that led to his current status, he became a born-again Christian. A year later he became an ordained pastor in the House of the Open Christian Bible. In this role, he serves as an assistant to the penitentiary's staff chaplain.

"This is an important development with credible information," said Harrison County Sheriff Lester Birnbaum. "My office is not in a position at this point to commit to following up with charges; it's too early. That could change in due time."

Birnbaum has been county sheriff for just over 25 years, a period in which the Marlene Scott death remained an open case. There is no statute of limitations on murder charges in Indiana, he noted. The sheriff added that, though the state has capital punishment, there has not been an execution for more than 15 years.

While Cooper's fate regarding Marlene's death remains a question mark with law enforcement officials, his confession appears to end 50 years of local innuendo, conjecture, and, in some cases, hurtful rumors attached to previous suspects. Though not usable in court, his admission was supported by a lie detector test.

"It's not unusual for inmates to be found guilty of past crimes after they are serving time here," said James Winston, warden of the Federal Correctional Institution in Terre Haute. "These cases get adjudicated in different ways. There is no formula. This crime was especially seri-

ous, from what I've learned, and yet Rev. Cooper has been an exemplary prisoner."

Over 100 persons were interviewed in the Harrison College student efforts for the Hoosier-Record, including a short of list of prime suspects at the time of Marlene's disappearance and who still are living.

This included Gene Brown, Marlene's stepfather, who died shortly after maintaining his innocence. Former Harrison community theatre director Nicholas Walker also was interviewed.

Lawrence Charles, a Harrison College student, and also a prime suspect, was not interviewed. He lives in Petaluma, Calif. However, evidence was introduced in this project that, when confirmed by the sheriff's office, clearly exonerates him.

Florence Scott Brown, Marlene's mother, was deceased as well as Jimmy Bartow, a classmate and boyfriend of Marlene's at Harrison High School. Donald Scott, Marlene's biological father, lives in Texas, where he resided at the time of his daughter's disappearance.

"This is a development that I think everyone in our community can appreciate, no matter their age or how long they've been a resident," said Harrison mayor Lorna Tobin. "We owe a heartfelt thanks to Harrison College for the splendid work its students put into this project."

Harrison College president Jonathan Casey praised the work of the students. He called it a "great example" of what can happen when the school and community work together to solve issues.

The mystery drew national attention. It was the basis for two mini-documentaries on TV networks. Major news organizations, including the Indianapolis News, Chicago Tribune, New York Post, Associated Press and San Francisco Chronicle, sent staff writers to Harrison to pursue the story at various stages.

(Next week: What happened on the night of Jan. 11, 1969?)

The following two stories provided exceptional detail as well as a remorseful, detailed confession from Cooper. His fate remained a question mark. Sheriff Birnbaum gave no definitive answer about formal charges, which, as everyone knew, would result in a conviction.

Cooper, at 82 years old, was destined to spend the rest of his life behind bars. There would be no chance for release unless he reached his 90s. In any case, the truth was he was quite comfortable behind bars. The Department of Corrections, buying into his religious conversion, was deferential in its treatment. He had his own cell with a TV, and spent his days separated from the prison's general population in assisting the chaplain.

He would receive 100s of letters in the weeks after stories were published. Undoubtedly, now he was headed for a higher-than-ever profile with the latest revelation. A book? A film? A documentary? It would be a coin toss. At the very least, his life was about to get interesting behind bars.

Chapter 78

Extra! Extra!

That good run Newt Ames expected for the *Hoosier-Record*? "Through the roof," was the way he described it to former colleagues on metro newspapers, several of whom called to salute his triumph.

Many pals saw the series as a blow for embattled, local journalism, but Newt wasn't too sure of that takeaway. The killer is an incarcerated, born-again pastor admitting a serious crime? Difficult to miss making that into a winner, he answered.

The 24-hour news cycle would chew it up eagerly and move quickly to the next story---a politician's indiscretion, airplane crash, natural disaster, school shooting, whatever. Besides, the reporting and core writing were done by college students who, when it came down to it, were not likely headed for news media careers. Without them and their professor, no Scott stories. The project was not an extension of a journalism class. The college didn't have one, just my writing courses. There was not even a school newspaper.

Nevertheless, the stories were a win-win for the *Hoosier-Record* and Harrison College. They would help build a Town & Gown bridge that Newt and President Casey, quoting

Humphrey Bogart in *"Casablanca,"* both thought could be "the start of a beautiful friendship."

One symbol for a growing bond were *Hoosier-Record* news boxes popping up outside the Milbert Social Center and Grabbe Library on the campus. More important: three, permanent summer internships---one for writing, one for the business side, one for technology in general---would be established between the school and paper.

The Rotary jumped on the wagon, too. Before school let out for summer, club president Fred Jackson quickly scheduled a luncheon program in which the students and Maria would appear for a presentation. This would be their only public appearance before the break and the event had to be moved to the city council chambers to accommodate the crowd.

Interestingly, Flip counted seven faculty members in attendance. This had to be a first of some sort, the college showing interest in a local civic program.

The *Hoosier-Record's* newspaper's circulation saw a spike, adding 250 more subscriptions after the dust settled. That meant it was nearing 3,000 overall in addition to the extra 300 sold over the counter each week during the series' run.

Better yet: A number of mainstream news services picked up the stories, raising the *Hoosier-Record* profile as well as the college's image. The *Chronicle of Higher Education* was among those doing pieces.

The PBS-TV station in Indianapolis sent a crew to start work on a documentary that was likely to get a national run on the network. CBS-TV sent a production person to Harrison to scout feasibility of producing a *"60 Minutes"* segment. Everyone crossed their fingers on that possibility.

Maria might've been nervous to find herself suddenly in the spotlight. She was illegal, after all, and better to keep a low profile. Well, scratch that. She *had* been illegal.

That changed with word her father accepted an offer to teach at DePaul University in Chicago. She had yet to be re-united with her parents and sisters, but that would happen in a month or so in the Windy City. Meanwhile they talked almost daily on the telephone.

The DePaul position came with a family U.S. visa attached. This allowed the entire Lopez crew to also live, work, or attend school together. Not wanting to jeopardize or divert attention from the Independent Study triumph, Dorothy, Flip, and Mary remained mum on Maria's backstory.

Chapter 79

That Toddlin' Town

Officially it was the Chicago Transit Authority's (CTA) No. 11 bus route. Regular commuters in Chicago simply called it "the Lincoln Avenue bus." Maria loved riding it.

Now that the fully united Lopez family had put a tearful reunion behind them and moved to Chicago, they were comfortably housed in a North Side apartment on Berwyn avenue just west of Lincoln.

Since they had no automobile, Chicago's public transportation schedules ruled their lives. The irony was not lost on Ricardo, the father. After a year of his family dangerously trekking from El Salvador to the U.S. on foot, sitting on top of railroad boxcars, crammed into decades-old automobiles, riding in pickup trucks loaded with chickens, via carts pulled by four-legged animals, and, in one frightening experience, crossing the treacherous Rio Fuerte on a homemade raft, now how did they get from Point A to Point B? They simply walked out their front door, went two blocks east, stood at a sheltered stop on Lincoln, and caught the ever-reliable No. 11 bus. If a rider walked a few more blocks, they had the option of taking a quicker CTA train.

Maria preferred the bus. She always allotted plenty of extra time. To her, it was a treat just to absorb everything in the new, urban environment.

The public system of trains and buses would take them anywhere in this giant midwestern metropolis, even airports. The family planned to do much exploring, using public transportation to investigate Chicago's many cultural attractions. And, as Maria pointed out, these travel modes were all air conditioned. This was no small thing when you grew up in a Third World tropical climate.

"Where was the CTA when we really needed it?" Ricardo repeatedly told his family. This was one of many inside jokes the Lopez's kept among themselves.

In just three weeks, Maria had become familiar with several drivers of the Lincoln Avenue bus. One, a friendly, heavyset African American named Gus, loved to chat with riders. She always tried to get a seat close to him.

Like a tour conductor, he would note points of interest to riders on his rounds---parks, statues, libraries, restaurants, historical sites, bakeries, theatres---as they motored up and down Lincoln Avenue.

Maria would jot a few in a notebook she kept, and later Googled them on library computers. Her favorite was Oz Park, dedicated to the Wizard of Oz, a childhood favorite first written by Frank Baum when he lived in the neighborhood. She was determined to learn all she could about this city called Chicago.

The No. 11 bus was efficient, too. From the city's northernmost limit, and down its NW-to-SE diagonal path, it cut straight to within a block of DePaul University, where Ricardo landed a summer course to teach before starting his full-time position---with benefits---when regular classes began in September.

With Father Tony pulling some Vincentian Order strings from distant Phoenix, the Lopez family realized a soft landing in Chicago. In addition to helping them find an apartment and furnishings, Ricardo was given advances on a generous---by Salvadoran standards---salary. If things worked well, his expertise and standing could help the university attract grants.

Topping it off: There was a grocery superstore within walking distance of their apartment, a much-appreciated source of wonderment for the Lopez's. Better yet, it had a "south of the border" section with many offerings familiar to its Spanish-speaking customers.

The two, younger siblings, Daniela and Sara, already were enrolled for summer classes in a Chicago magnet school for international studies. Combining their own backgrounds with what they learned in the detention center, this was an easy segue for them.

Their school was adjacent to the DePaul campus, meaning they could take the No. 11 bus to-and-from classes with Ricardo. Occasionally with Maria, too, who had a part-time summer job in the university law library. She planned to keep working there and take a class in the fall. As an employee, she qualified for a healthy tuition discount.

For Maria, parting from Harrison and Dorothy had been sad. There was a strong bond built among the Independent Study's Gang of Four students. Tracking down a murderer together will do that.

There was a farewell party for her hosted by Dorothy and, while Mary, Flip, and the Harrison students could be confident they would see more of each other, Maria was leaving for Chicago. She was presented with a commemorative t-shirt showing a group picture---the "Gang of Four + One"---with the added inscription: "Maria: Nuestra Heroina."

There was much to celebrate at the event. The *Hoosier-Record* series was a triumph.

President Casey, who made an appearance, could hardly contain his enthusiasm over the Independent Study project--- and hinted of expanding the school's offerings in writing courses, possibly starting a Master of Fine Arts writing program. That could only be good news for Flip.

Also, Mary was given the green light to develop new courses focusing on local Latino developments and possibly adding a faculty spot. Already she knew of at least three good candidates within her Arizona State crew. Furthermore, there always would be an opening for Dorothy in some capacity.

Clearly the overall initiative was a huge success, and everyone knew Maria played an important part. It had been her suggestion that led to Ben Cooper. Her Harrison friends, except for Mary, Flip, and Dorothy, then knew nothing about the perils she and her family overcame for her to contribute.

Could the worst finally be behind her, she wondered as the No. 11 made its way up Lincoln Avenue and homeward bound on this beautiful late June afternoon? Her goal now was to put as many positive accomplishments as she could between her past and present.

Keep moving forward, like Father Tony said, and not backward. Like this bus.

She would like to save enough money and enroll full-time in college. There were many opportunities in a city like Chicago.

No question Pete Gray, their mutual affection steadily growing, would pay a visit to Chicago to visit Maria. Though the Windy City was not that far from Harrison in southern Indiana, he had never been there. That trip would come later in the summer.

Pete told her that he always wanted to see the Cubs play in Wrigley Field. That better not be the main reason for the visit, she joked. Maria looked forward to having him meet her family, which knew nothing of this, ahem, friendship.

Gus's latest round of calling out Lincoln Avenue sites on this day's run for his passengers---Wells Park, Lincoln Square, former German-American Club, Western Avenue---ended the daydreaming, alerting her that Berwyn was only a few more stops. She gathered up her books and prepared for an exit.

The day was so perfect, 75 degrees and low humidity, Maria was tempted to keep walking past her apartment building, maybe go sit in the park a few more blocks down the street. Good thing she didn't.

Maria opened the door to her new home with this jolt: There to greet her were Mary and Flip, two of the most important persons in her life outside her family, standing in the background.

Just as a chorus of "Surprise!" could ring out, Mary quickly stuck out her hand with an envelope bearing a Harrison College logo. "Here, Maria," she said. "Take it and read it. We wanted to deliver this personally."

Maria, trembling, opened the envelope. She read one sheet, then a smaller note attached to it. Her parents looked on expectantly. Ricardo took it from her hand and read everything---twice. Then, he hugged Maria and they hugged and cried---a quiet sniffling into each other's shoulder—before breaking loose.

"This is an application to Harrison College, a blank one, for Maria to fill out," said Ricardo. "The other is a note from the school president, a Mr. Casey, that welcomes her to the school. He invites her to fill out the application. His note is to be considered a guarantee she will be accepted, he says."

The note said:

"Dear Maria,

"Please fill out this application. I will pass it to the admissions department to be processed in time for the start of

the new school year in August. I look forward to seeing you on the campus. We have many exciting develop-ments taking place. You will be a valuable addition to our student body."

Best regards,

Jonathan Casey

Harrison College, President

Then Mary added the frosting: Harrison would take care of paperwork that provided Maria with an international student visa, meaning she could use her Salvadoran citizenship. No more masquerading. Room and board? There always was Dorothy, but it would not be necessary.

Her exchange student status, in turn, qualified her for fat grants and scholarships open exclusively to foreign students. While everything added up to a full ride, she was informed, there was one substantial scholarship in the mix that already was in the bank---the Harrison Rotary Club's annual $10,000 stipend, an easy sell for Flip to his committee.

About the Author

Mike Conklin is a storyteller. He's written professionally for audiences since high school, when his media career started on a small-town weekly. He graduated to local and regional dailies, and, following a cup of coffee in TV & Radio broadcasting, made a long stop at The Chicago Tribune. There, he was a beat reporter, daily columnist, and feature writer with work nationally syndicated.

Mike's also written for the New York Times, a variety of magazines, reviewed books, and, after leaving The Tribune, taught communications and writing full-time at Chicago's DePaul University, where he took leaves to teach at other universities and colleges in the U.S. and China. His previous novels are "Goal Fever!" and "Transfer U."

Acknowledgements

Many people were helpful in crafting *Class Dismissed*, directly or indirectly. No one was more important than Diane, my wife, an avid reader and member of three book clubs. Her edits, suggestions and encouragement were invaluable. A special thanks to Jim Elsener, former Chicago Tribune colleague turned novelist whose counsel has been invaluable. Also, thanks to Virginia Miehe who showed me a world I never knew existed and it was in my own backyard. And, of course, a shout out to Fort Raphael Publishing Co. for coordinating the moving parts.